About the author

D.M. Jones gained a BA (Honours) in Home and Community Studies. After gaining a PGCE in further education, she went on to study Counselling and Psychotherapy. She had a variety of jobs which all involved people, in the social sector and in the private sector, along with running a successful private practice in counselling and psychotherapy. Once you have met her you will never forget her. Positive attitude, storytelling and an ability to make you laugh make her a natural comedienne whose observations on life cannot fail to amuse.

CHASING RAINBOWS

Memories, life and love
are all in the games
we play!

Best Wishes

Dani Jones.

D.M. Jones

CHASING RAINBOWS

Vanguard Press

VANGUARD PAPERBACK

© Copyright 2020
D.M. Jones

A CIP catalogue record for this title is
available from the British Library.

ISBN 978 1 78465 753 6

*Vanguard Press is an imprint of
Pegasus Elliot MacKenzie Publishers Ltd.*
www.pegasuspublishers.com

First Published in 2020

**Vanguard Press
Sheraton House Castle Park
Cambridge England**

Printed & Bound in Great Britain

Dedication

I dedicate this work to Caroline Anne Fawcett, affectionately known as 'Posh', and Kathryn E. Bartle.

Whatever life throws at us, we always chase the rainbows and keep on keeping on.

Acknowledgements

It was my intention to write a book about relationships. I was very surprised when someone said they found it very funny and one person said it was like *Fifty Shades* with class!

Whatever it gives to the individual reader, it would not have come into being without the support of others.

Jane Greenwood, you were always at the end of the phone at three in the morning. I thought I was disturbing you, until you told me you were an insomniac.

Sally Moon, when we met in Skiathos you gave me encouragement to not leave my scribbling under the bed, but to have confidence and faith in myself.

Kathryn E. Bartle, we laughed at our memories and you just kept on pushing me when I was losing faith in myself.

Bev Nicholls Bower, you just kept asking for more and more, which inspired me.

Simon Golding you have been instrumental in giving me advice and for that I thank you.

Philip Goodhand Tait, your song came to me from the universe and your kindness is memorable.

Finally, to all of you who gave positive comments and took the time to read the book in the first instance, I give a massive thank you. Too many to mention, but you know who you are.

This is not just my book.
I could not have done it alone.

I walk along your street
And I try to meet
The folks that live close by you
Maybe they know why you had to go away

Baby if I knew
I could face the truth
But they just say, "I'm sorry,
Really shouldn't worry, there'll be another day"

But a day without love
Is a view with emptiness
And your love brings me happiness
I can't stand a day without love

At night I lie awake
Try in vain to take
My mind off this confusion; was our love just an illusion
I really never know

There's no way to find
What's been going through your mind
There is something warm about you (warm about you)
Seems so sad without you, did you have to go?

Phillip Goodhand Tait

CHAPTER ONE

The man looked down at Adam and asked to get by. They smiled at each other and Adam moved out of his seat to let him pass. The man settled by the window. Adam wasn't too keen on sitting by the window. He much preferred to sit in the aisle, or the middle. He could get a better look at the hostess as she walked by. A tall, slender hostess, wearing just a bit too much make-up, walked by and smiled at him. Her eyes looked admiringly at his face.

Adam noticed that his neighbour was bald; quite fashionable these days. Adam ran his hand over his head. He was glad he still had thick black wavy hair. It was now speckled with streaks of silver, making him more distinguished-looking and appealing to women. Adam's love of women had never diminished, and he was a fine figure of a man for his sixty-four years. He couldn't help himself, and women who were attracted to him were always welcome to spend some time with him.

Adam settled down to read the in-flight magazine whilst waiting for take-off. They were always the same: glossy pages, sales pitches for the discerning traveller, selling products and holidays — how boring! As he flicked through the pages, a picture caught his eye and he went back to the page to take a look. It was an article about a woman who had won the Desmond Elliott prize, a prize for new novelists. He began to read. The bald man interrupted him, as he needed to get something from the overhead locker. Adam replaced the magazine in the pocket in front of him before he moved. "Sorry, mate, I forgot something." Another smile passed between the men and they began to chat.

The hostess who smiled at Adam arrived and he ordered a gin and tonic. The man, whose name was a mystery, asked for a vodka and tonic. Adam learned that the man was head of sales for a small airline and was going to New York to do a deal with the aviation authority. They were hoping to begin internal flights across America in the New Year. Adam took a sip of his drink and made himself comfortable.

Remembering the page in the magazine, he took it out and turned his attention to it, studying the picture of the woman. He was sure he knew her, but where from? The hair was different, the look was different, and no way would he have ever known someone who could write a book. Adam liked intelligent women: they fed his ego; but, more often than not, he got a stupid one who was brainless, looked good on his arm and was easy in bed, and not always that good in bed. The picture he was looking at troubled him. Where did he know her from? He studied the features and the clothes and scanned the face for some kind of recognition. Then he remembered. It was the eyes. How could he have forgotten those eyes that would open wide like caverns of profound mystery and were always laughing? It couldn't be her, could it?

Another sip of the smooth gin and he closed his eyes, resting his head on the back of the seat. Adam went back in time to a year that was filled with love and laughter. He hadn't forgotten the time he spent with her and it began to awaken an age-old longing in his loins. His memory of her was precious and held more regrets than any man should have to carry through his lifetime. Adam took another long drink from the glass and slid down in his seat. As the cool liquid hit the back of his throat, he sailed on a sea of dreams locked away for far too long. Sometimes, memories bring promises of what might have been or can reawaken demons best left sleeping.

Adam needed a woman in his bed (just as much as he needed air to breathe and food to nourish him), but could never decide whether he loved them or hated them. He loved the fascination of women and had never quite worked them out or understood them. He knew what women wanted. They wanted the words. They wanted to hear how beautiful and sexy they were. Sometimes they expected presents, too. Experience gave him a repertoire that Casanova would have envied, and it worked well for him. Adam had always tried not to get involved with women but he needed to feed his ego. The chase was good and the bed was, at times. Then it was time to move on to the next and the next and then the next. They were like rainbows and didn't last too long. Sometimes he equated his behaviours with love and he couldn't stand a day without love.

Back in the day when Adam was very married, he also kept a mistress. The mistress was a relationship he had fallen into by accident, which became long term, very long term. Adam always tried to avoid involvement, but somehow failed with Gerry (short for Geraldine). After eight years she had become a habit and provided an escape from the mundane duties of family. She was still waiting for him to leave his wife.

Life was too easy for Adam and his relationships were never enough. He always wanted more. He was always in search of perfection. Adam could never work out what that actually meant, but he knew he wanted it. What he didn't realise was that through his catalogue of women he was searching; searching for the one to surpass all others.

Now he saw her on the pages of an in-flight magazine. She was the one who had surpassed all others. Even though the hair was different, the eyes and the smile had not changed. That smile was still big and inviting. The woman he let slip through his fingers all those years ago had a way of lighting up the room with her smile. Her face would break out into a beam that could warm the darkest corner. Her light could blind. Her charisma could entrap the strongest of men.

It was such a long time ago that she was lost in the archives of his mind. She was somewhere underneath the heaps of other women he'd been through since. 'Been through' was an apt way of looking at Adam's dalliances with women. He loved the intrigue, and when he had been through his 'class act' and set the scene, he left the woman to believe that she was the one.

Adam fooled himself, he fooled them all, and though not meaning to cause upset in their lives, he would begin to cause upset with his opening lines. His chat-up lines were magic, his voice like soft dark chocolate that no one could resist. His body was a temple where he wanted women to worship. There had never been another woman to equal her and he often wondered what happened to her. Now he knew, as he read the story of her success.

As he took another long drink, Adam allowed himself the pleasure of an intense feeling that came with each breath and reached his groin with a shiver which slowly drifted into a series of reminders. Events that happened so long ago made his memories almost seem like dreams.

~

Carol was on the phone. Adam wasn't really paying attention as her shrill voice screamed at him through the loudspeaker. He was more interested in the pile of papers on his desk. "So, can you do it?" she squawked.

"Do what?" he snapped. Carol really annoyed him at times. "You expect me to do something for nothing?" Carol was beginning to get on his nerves. "No, she is willing to give you a small remuneration, of about a hundred pounds. It is for a charity, after all! I told her you would not do it for free."

Adam said he would call Carol back and asked that she email him the details. He sighed. Why did Carol volunteer him for jobs before asking him? She was an organising, manipulating bitch. He sat back in his chair and stared out of the window, across town hall square.

Adam didn't sleep with all the women he met. He believed that he still had scruples. Carol was one of the unlucky ones. Why should he sleep with everybody, when sometimes a few kisses and a grope sufficed? Her wrinkled face and cigarette-stained breath was enough to deter the strongest of constitutions. He remembered meeting her at a karaoke evening where he was running an event for a company in Leeds. Carol's husband was the company's insurer. Adam liked Donald Johnson. He was a typical Yorkshire man who liked a laugh and football. He pandered to his wife's every need and was also a 'yes' man.

Adam rarely entertained single women as they became clingy. Married women were easy. They were safe and easy to get rid of. Most of the women just wanted words and those caresses that their husbands forgot about after the wedding night. Adam was choosy, though, and women like Carol would never have the pleasure of him. Adam's longest relationships were his marriage to Mary and the years he had with Gerry. He once was with someone for three months and could not even remember her name. He couldn't remember a lot of the names of the women he had been with. There were many one night stands long forgotten.

Adam hadn't forgotten the karaoke evening in Leeds. It was a success and he could see Carol now in the stunning dress of sequins wrapped round the skinny figure that was marred by the nastiness in her face. Her expensive hair was piled high, with wisps framing the diamond earrings that caught the light with every turn of her head. As his eyes travelled down to her legs, he found the most amazing stilettos ever. There was something he adored about stilettos: they carried sex on legs, but not in Carol's case. Not this time!

Adam was repulsed by the skinny, shapeless sticks covered in fake tan. He couldn't remember how he ended up in the back room at the venue, but he did remember graciously accepting the pass Carol made at him, as he was too drunk to do anything else. She was pulling his clothes off as though the three-minute warning had sounded and the world was about to end. Just as her hand began to find its way into his boxer shorts, the moonlight caught her profile and she took on the appearance of a depraved, orange tanned zombie about to initiate the next victim. His eyes widened as he stared into a face ravaged by the overuse of cosmetics and too much smoking — this was leading him to disaster.

Adam drew back, choking out the words, "No, no, Carol, this is not a good idea." He pushed her off and she fell over. Helping her off the dirty floor, he continued to speak. "It's the drink, and I will never be able to look Donald in the face again." Adam took a deep breath and raised himself to full height, before falling over a box that he failed to see. "Please, let's not ruin a good friendship?" he pleaded, as he hit the floor. He sat there for a minute, his head spinning. An incredible guilt swept over him. Perhaps he shouldn't have been nice to her over dinner. Too late. Guilt always followed what he did and yet he continued to pursue the impossible dream, always the slave to the lust in his loins. Adam saw the look on her face and decided the floor was a safe place to be.

Carol, who was now absolutely furious, began to pull on her black, silk, expensive but cheap-looking knickers. Adam had not seen her take them off and decided that he must stop drinking so much at corporate events. Perhaps she never had them on and had taken them off earlier, in anticipation. He had been with women who did that. They would go to the toilet and remove their knickers, allowing him easy access to that which he yearned.

Adam prided himself on his choice of women and he was not going to add an 'ugly skinny' to his list. She was not pleasing to the eye, not in any other way either. He also knew that if he were to start something with her, it might get complicated and she could upset his apple cart. The whole room shook as she stormed out without a backward glance, without a word, slamming the door with such force it nearly came off its hinges.

The fuzz of the drink was now beginning to wear off and, head in hands, Adam sat in contemplation. "Why do I do it?" he spoke loudly to himself. Deep inside, a tiny voice spoke to him. This was a voice he had heard many times before, but chose to ignore. The voice whispered, "You do it because you are always looking for her. You are always chasing rainbows. Why can't you stand a day without love?"

After that night Adam did not hear from Carol again until she called him to ask if he would do the choreography for the opening of her new dress agency. He ripped her off, charging far too much for his services. Carol knew and paid anyway. She loved having him around and always felt the only reason the karaoke night failed was due to Adam being far too drunk. She could wait for her moment to come round again and then she would have him. Carol was totally deluded. She never stopped talking about Adam to her friends. Here she was again, offering him some work, for her own selfish reasons, so that she could spend some time with him.

The ping of Adam's email brought him round from his memory. With the horror of his encounter with Carol lurking in his thoughts, he quickly glanced at the email that ended with, "I will be in touch when I have finalised details with her."

Before the end of the day, another email arrived. It was very clear. "She will meet you in the West End Bar at lunchtime tomorrow at about one. That had better be OK for you?"

After making a note in his diary, Adam sent a reply: "I might be late, so you can start without me." God! That awful woman sounded like a jealous wife sometimes. He knew that he could never like Carol at all, but she was good for business. Stroking his chin, he smiled to himself: life was not so bad.

The next day was fraught with meetings. His demanding advertising job kept him busy. Adam was in two minds whether to go to lunch and meet the unknown woman, or not. It was not going to be worth his while, so why bother? He wanted to cancel, but his curiosity got the better of him. He did not know the woman's name and he couldn't find Carol's mobile number.

The meeting with new clients was about drumming up more business in the food trade, so perhaps a visit to the West End Bar would not be in vain, as they served food throughout the day. As he waited for his colleagues to settle down, he began to wonder what the woman would be like. She was probably one of Carol's old wrinkly cronies that would be propping up the bar in the most popular place in town. Two young men from Liverpool owned the West End Bar and the Satin Club that was upstairs in the same building. Anybody who was anybody drank there and the club was a great success. Adam had taken Gerry there for a meal a few times. A waste of money, as they always seemed to end up arguing. He would drop Gerry off at her flat and return to his loveless bed with the snoring Mary.

After a frustrating morning with idiots who really did not know what they were doing and didn't have any brains between them, Adam decided that lunch was just the pick-me-up he needed. As he went down the steps into the room, he was surprised to see that it was quite empty. He walked over to the bar and ordered half a lager. Adam always felt comfortable in the West End Bar. It was in the middle of town and yet had a country feel to it. A long bar of polished mahogany stretched endlessly before him. Brass pumps reflected in the sparkling glass that covered the walls holding bottles, glasses and the sort of accessories that cluttered swanky bars.

This type of bar would not be out of place in an old western. Lights reflected back into a room dimly lit, casting shadows into deep corners, making it easy for lovers to touch each other in intimate places without fear of being seen. Touching each other in public was abandoning oneself to heady pleasure, at times a recklessness brought on by too much alcohol, too much love or pure lust. Bars such as this were ideal for men such as Adam. He could hide in corners without fear of discovery, using his hands to make the most reluctant of partners moan. He could drink his drink and feel the woman, her moan blending in with the suave tones of the crooners locked in the juke box, singing about everlasting love. Love to Adam was like an orgasm. Amazing working up to it, then it was over, just another memory which could get messy. Groping in pubs was for teenagers. Adam had never grown up!

As Adam ordered another lager, he began scanning the room for a familiar face, someone to chat to while he waited for Godzilla (his pet name for Carol). A young couple were having an intense conversation in the corner. She looked upset. He looked anxious and fed up. There was no doubt they were discussing wedding plans. The magazine on the table gave it away. He wanted to go over and say, "Don't do it mate." But he didn't. He smiled to himself. He didn't miss much.

Adam gave a nod to the barman as he began to remember twenty-one years ago. Why on earth did he marry Mary? What did he do it for? Mary smothered him, she mothered him. He didn't doubt that she loved him. Maybe she loved him too much and eventually it turned into something else. It became more of a mother's love than anything else. There was not much sex, although Mary would probably want more. She had a total dependency and a need for him twenty-four/seven. She made demands he could not meet, did not want to meet; when she spoke his name, 'Adam,' he would wince.

Adam resented Mary: she reminded him of his mother and sisters. He convinced himself that she was the reason for his cheating. She had broken all the promises she made to him and her description of their married life together was just fantasy. There was not the fun they talked about and when the children came along, he took second place. Mary stopped being a wife and became a scrupulous mother. So, he made it his life's work to lure her friends into his arms and he got much satisfaction from it. It wasn't that he set out to deliberately go for Mary's friends; they were just close and convenient. He found much amusement in listening to Mary telling his latest conquest what a good, caring and faithful husband he was. How loving he was! She was as good a liar as he.

They hadn't been married six months when Adam first cheated on Mary. It was with the woman next-door. She was newly married and they had just moved in. He found her crying in the garden one evening when Mary was away. "Are you all right?" he said as he stretched to look over the fence. The sobbing stopped and a red face turned towards him. She was a little thing with red hair and red eyes. Everything about her was red. She was even wearing a red dress. "Would you like a drink?" The red face nodded and soon they were sitting in her kitchen, drinking a cold bottle of chardonnay.

"I don't often drink." The young neighbour gave him a shy smile. "Sorry I don't know your name."

"Adam."

Before long, the neighbour was telling Adam all about her disappointing sex life. Well, it wasn't disappointing her, but her husband Geoff was disappointed. She had saved herself till her wedding night and no one warned her what to expect. "You see, Adam, I thought you just opened your legs and let the man get on with it, and I think there should be more that I need to do. I even bought a book." Red was rather pretty in a plain sort of way and she continued, "It was OK for a few weeks, but then he brought home some handcuffs and a whip. There are some things I won't do, and I won't do that."

It wasn't long before Red was his student and he taught her everything she needed to know about pleasing a man. Eventually, Red and Geoff moved, as they were about to have their fifth child and the house was not big enough. Adam was obviously a good teacher!

Adam prided himself on always being in control of his relationships, and yet he easily fell into the trap that he felt Gerry set for him. She was very different to Mary. Gerry was younger, very cool and aloof, she was not clingy but rather intense at times, especially when it came to their relationship. She was needy in her own way, but they weren't the same needs as Mary's.

At the far end of the bar was a woman chatting away happily to the waiter. She seemed pleasant enough. Adam couldn't just work out her age. As he watched, he found himself caught up in the daily musings of his life. What was it all about? Why could he not be as happy as the girl at the end of the bar? She looked happy. She was extremely animated and her hand spoke together with her words. She was busy gesticulating when she knocked her glass over, spilling the liquid all down the barman. He didn't seem to mind, and after wiping the mess, he handed the woman another drink. It seemed that he was mesmerised by her.

The door banged loudly behind him as Godzilla made a superb entrance. She always did. Gold bomber jacket topped a pair of skin-tight mock-leather jeans — designer, of course! Did Carol not realise how ridiculous she looked, mutton dressed as lamb, crossed with a tart on legs? Pity there was no audience for her this time, as the bar still had not begun to fill up with the usual lunchtime diners.

"Hi, Tony, mine's a vodka on the rocks," Carol screeched at the barman, who obviously knew her. She carried on walking past Adam without acknowledging him. Carol stopped when she arrived at the end of the bar. She spoke to the girl, the one he was watching. They exchanged greetings and Carol pulled the girl down the bar towards him as she began the introductions. Adam took a long hard look at the woman standing before him. She seemed a bit nervous and shy. She hadn't looked shy, chattering away in the distance to the waiter. She wore a pair of old denims with rips in them, exposing the brown of her legs, and an old pair of pumps peeped out from under frayed hems. A bright pink baggy sweater hid the rest of her body.

"Does she have breasts?" Adam wondered. "What might they be like?" He could imagine her sitting and knitting the sweater that was far too big for her.

The sweater gave the woman an air of innocent cuteness, added to by the blonde hair that was scraped back into a ponytail. He could tell that this was hair that did what it wanted, wild and untamed. Adam wondered if she was like her hair. Was she wild and untamed? A long fringe played curtains to the most amazing pair of brown eyes he had ever seen. They were like two great pools of enigmatic love that someone could drown in as they peered into the soul. One of the things Adam prided himself on was being able to read a woman very quickly. He had a system of categorising them and their eligibility, for him to spend some of his precious time on them. He would give marks out of ten and be able to calculate how long it would be before he had them hooked and they had fallen for him. This one was very different: she confused his arrogance and he could not think straight as he tried to pull himself out of those eyes peering up at him.

"Adam, Olivia, Olivia, Adam." Carol could be so arrogantly dismissive. Adam cocked his head to the side. Nice name, he thought, as she held out a small hand, nails of pink co-ordinating with her sweater.

He felt her energy as their fingers met, electricity ran through his veins and hit his vulnerable part.

As she turned to leave the bar, Carol chirped, "Right, my loves, I'm off." With a twirl of her skinny body, she was gone. Adam kept smiling and was pleased that he had made an extra effort with his appearance that morning. He always made an effort. For some reason, today he was even more vigilant as to how he looked when he was preening himself in the bathroom mirror.

At six foot and one inch, he stood out in a crowd, with his thick black hair combed back from his temples. His brown eyes never left the face of the woman he was talking to at the time, listening to the rubbish that came from her lips. He found that being a good listener was one way of captivating them. Look them straight in the eye, bend a little towards them and tilt the head, it worked every time. Now standing before this girl, this woman, Adam knew he looked good. The camel coat that covered his muscular body gave him an air of authority and wealth. Adam never looked any different. He was a man that looked good in casuals, overalls, just as he did in a mohair suit of the finest quality. Adam smiled. So, Carol did not see this little thing in front of him as a threat? If she had, she would have stayed to the death. Today she left very quickly without a backward glance. Sometimes Carol made him feel like he was her handbag, exclusively hers. He made a mental note to do something about it, soon. Carol did not own him. He did not belong to her; even though at times her behaviour said differently, he just couldn't be bothered to put her right.

"Have you eaten?" a chirpy voice full of life, asked. They made their way to a table in the corner and each took a menu. Adam studied Olivia as those amazing brown eyes skated backwards and forwards across the card. She seemed almost oblivious to him. She was obviously hungry. They ordered. As they waited for their food, Olivia explained the event she was organising and how Carol had intimated that she and Adam were very close and that he would do anything for her if she asked him. Adam scowled. Blast that woman! Olivia said that Carol agreed the nominal fee and she hoped he did not expect more. As this was for charity, he could take it or leave it, as it was in a good cause and she had little money to spare. There were obviously no flies on this woman and she knew what she wanted. She talked about her charity with a passion that he had not seen in a long time. It was close to her heart and it seemed that her mission was to save the whole world.

During the meal Adam realised that he had never seen anyone who could talk as much and eat so much at the same time. This woman did not stop for breath. As he watched her, Adam pondered whether to leave this job alone, as the money was low and not really worth it. His time was money and he would rather do nothing than be insulted by the fee. He was gifted and was a master at choreography — no one could touch him and he was worth more than a hundred pounds for the amount of time and effort that he would need to put in with the models, who were not models at all, but Olivia's friends and volunteers. It was signposted 'amateur and disaster' already.

Olivia stopped talking, finishing her food as she watched Adam to see the reaction to her plans. She touched his compassion with her innocence and he knew that little money would be made, but he was up for the experience and the fun. The fun he felt he might have with this woman, or maybe some of her friends, may be worth the effort? She was like a little child, a thoughtful lady and a total out-of-control teenager. She was a mixed bag of everything, which made her a mystery to unravel. Olivia was safe and he could not see himself getting involved with her. She wasn't for him. Not his type at all, but interesting, nevertheless.

As the meal progressed, something happened that shook him to the core. It was a spontaneity that he became aware of far too late. Adam opened up and told this stranger all about himself, his life, his loves and his family. He laid himself bare and told the child in the woman's body what a mess his life was. He was being honest, open and sincere; no chat-up lines, no leading body language. Olivia listened intently, her eyes never leaving his face. She never asked a question nor carried the conversation on; she just listened to him.

As they were leaving, Olivia looked up at him and their eyes met. "Life can be so sad! We do get ourselves into messes sometimes, don't we? We are always chasing rainbows. Life is a big school with many lessons to learn. I'll call you."

Then she was gone, leaving him to stand alone on the pavement, wondering what had just happened. How could someone just disappear, leaving such a profound statement behind? Adam thought back over the lunchtime. Had he ever met anyone like that before? The answer was, No! Surely, he would have remembered. He felt very strange. Olivia never said a word about herself, as she was so engrossed in the charity she was working for. She spoke of the cause as though her life depended on it. Perhaps he should make a play for her? She would certainly be a challenge, a breath of springtime. He heard the voice in his head as it said, "Be careful with this one, she might be the one — and then what will you do?"

Back in the office, as soon as the phone rang Adam forgot lunchtime and returned to his high-flying, executive job, adopting the persona of a true professional. At break-time, he caught himself staring across the road at the newspaper office where Olivia worked. He searched the windows for her, hoping to catch a glimpse of a homemade pink sweater and blonde hair. He had not forgotten those eyes. Her name and smile were imprinted on his brain.

Two weeks later, Adam answered his phone. He knew that voice, it was so distinct. "Hello, is that you, Adam? Can we arrange a rehearsal then?" Olivia chirped. She carried on talking and Adam was not listening to her.

He was busy, preoccupied with his latest challenge, Marlene. He'd been seeing Marlene on and off for about six weeks. He now needed to get rid of her and was running through tonight's dialogue. Adam was surprised that he kept Marlene on for so long. A month was about the average. Marlene was crass, screaming like a banshee when she had an orgasm. He liked his women to moan and speak his name, not scream as though they were giving birth. There was no dignity in the way Marlene threw herself round the bed. It made her look cheap and common; there was no unison, no love-making, just sex. The way Marlene made love was not to his liking and he was now becoming repulsed by her; finding it harder to become aroused. Everything about her irritated him: the way she stuck her disgusting tongue in his mouth, the way she scratched his back and wrapped her legs around him. The most upsetting thing about Marlene was, when he was nearly at his peak and ready for orgasm, she would break wind. It was disgusting! Marlene once told him that she had never been the same after a serious operation up her back passage. She had suffered for years with piles and now she was left with chronic wind, especially when making love. He did not like returning home with scratch marks on his skin, either. Mary might be daft, but she was not stupid.

Coming out of his daydream, Adam spoke rather harshly. "Who is this?"

She sounded almost disappointed as she answered, "Olivia!"

Of course! It was the chatterbox from the charity; how could he have forgotten 'Pink Sweater'? After spending a week looking for her across the road and never seeing her, she was dismissed from his mind.

"OK, when?"

Olivia began to speak quickly, not stopping for breath. "Well, it was the only time I could get. Warren says it will be filthy, but we will have it to ourselves as the cleaners do not come in till Monday morning. Sunday morning was the only time available." What an inconvenience! Adam kept his Sundays free to play the ever-loving family man. However, the prospect of seeing Olivia again might not be so bad, and now he had the perfect excuse to end it with Marlene. "Right, I will be there about eleven." He rudely put the phone down before Olivia could reply.

Adam had forgotten all about the fashion show and now he had two days in which to work out six sets. He rummaged through his briefcase, looking for the brown envelope that had appeared on his desk the week after their meeting. He took out the red notebook. On the first page it gave the venue. He wondered how she managed to secure the Satin Club in the first place. He smiled as he thought of the whirlwind that was her and how unstoppable she was. He bet no one could say no to her. Very neatly written inside were details of clothes and models, leaving spaces for him to fill in. Adam was impressed: she was efficient and organised. Not what he imagined at all — he expected an envelope full of chaos. Olivia presented like a child with enthusiasm, ideas and thoughts all over the place, with no discipline. This little book was full of information and discipline. How wrong he was about her. This was not a bought book from a shop, either. It was homemade and pretty, like her sweater.

Adam spent the following two days in his shed, listening to his music, reliving old memories and looking forward to a job where once again he would be the star and would shine. His professionalism would work to his advantage and his gift would be appreciated by all. Adam's knowledge of music and what worked came naturally to him. He had his favourite pieces, and after an afternoon in the shed the spaces in the little red book were filled and a pile of vinyl was on the table. He had picked some good songs and was now going through dance moves in his head. He could see the models moving across the floor to 'Rhythm of the Night' by De Barge and 'You Don't Have to Take Your Clothes Off' by Jermaine Stewart. Adam had a good feeling and was a little melancholy as he began to play 'Elusive Butterfly' by Bob Lind. As he listened to the beautiful words, he looked out of the window. There, in the clear blue sky, he saw a fading rainbow, and, as a white butterfly settled on the window sill, a tear crossed his eye and he shook it away. Adam was rarely emotional, and this was a weak moment, something he seldom allowed himself to have.

Adam hoped — no, *expected* — at least two assignments from this job, maybe some disc jockey jobs at a birthday or wedding. Perhaps there would be someone at the venue who could take Marlene's place. After all, he was used to running three women at a time. There would be lots of women at this fashion show needing his kind of loving. Adam prided himself on his lovemaking — after years of practice, he knew exactly what to say to a woman, where to touch her and for how long. He felt a rush of blood down below as he thought of the warm mound between a woman's legs that would swell at his touch. He did not waste the opportunity to feel good and he emptied his throbbing sacs. The rule was never to disturb Adam when he was in his shed.

On Sunday morning, Adam rose early and went down to the West End Bar. Today it was bursting at the seams, as the lunchtime lounge lizards tucked into roast beef and Yorkshire pudding. Adam looked round at the ageing men with their little chatty, brainless dollies, who were probably wanting to get as much out of a lonely man's wallet as possible. They were always on the make. Adam was no different: he believed that everyone had an agenda and was on some kind of scam or other. There were also the old married couples who had been together for years. It was easy to tell who they were, as they stared in front and never

27

spoke or looked at each other. You could tell the couples who had children, too, as they were usually arguing.

A woman came up to him. "You must be Adam. Come on, we are all waiting upstairs for you."

"And you are?" Adam did not like being spoken down to and that is just what the tone of the voice did.

The woman laughed. "Me? I am Posh, Olivia's best friend. Well, that is what people call me. My name is Anne." Anne turned and walked off, expecting Adam to follow her. He followed the perfume. He couldn't quite place it, which was annoying, as he was good on perfumes. If a man could identify the perfume a woman was wearing, she would be impressed, and he was one step closer to her cherry.

Whatever Anne was wearing, he knew it was expensive. She looked as though she might be expensive, too. Anne's buttocks paraded in tight leather pants. They were straining to escape and succeeded in keeping his attention. As his eyes travelled up her back, they rested on an animal-print top that left little to the imagination and much to be desired. Anne's breasts looked ever ready for some tantalising and touching. Her thick hair was hanging loose, sleek and controlled. She looked in control. He began to wonder what she might be like in bed: probably totally out of control and excitingly wild. It was obvious that she dressed to attract men. There was nothing about her that wasn't obvious. There was no mystery.

They made their way upstairs to the Satin Club and Adam could see that this person must be someone close to Olivia, as she, too, never stopped for breath. This one wasn't for him — she appeared rather loquacious. . She was probably really nice, but she was not going to make his list of 'must haves'. He wondered if she was a woman who could keep secrets and secrets were something that he needed. Adam took pleasure in sleeping with friends who knew each other, conspiratorially keeping secrets from each other, believing that they were special and his one and only. It made him feel powerful, and even when the relationship ended, he prided himself on all the secrets.

Adam kept his eye on the buttocks that were now having a strange effect on him and Posh was still talking. He had no clue as to what she was saying, as his mind had wandered to his expectations of the future.

Adam peered through the half-light into the club. What a mess! Where was he going? The smell of stale yeast offended his sensitive nose, permeating from empty and half-filled glasses of beer and spirits that covered nearly every surface. There were plates of half-eaten food strewn across disgusting sticky tables that were awash with over-spilling ashtrays and spent cigarette butts. It was a long time since he went to a club on a Saturday night and now, here he was, lost in the aftermath of dancing and pleasure. He picked his way through the confusion, dirt and chaos left by others.

In the distance, on the dance floor, Adam saw a group of women. As Posh picked her way gingerly through the mess, he watched her legs that were held high on stilettos. Adam winced as he felt a stirring deep down inside, that rumbling of excitement just before an erection began. Thank goodness it was so dark no one would notice the bulge appearing in his jeans. He wondered if he could make a hasty retreat into the gents and avail himself of some pleasure. As he followed the chatty woman across the floor, Adam mused whether he should make a move on her after all? Luckily, his embarrassing moment began to deflate and he sighed with relief.

As they moved into the light of the dance floor, Adam saw before him a bevy of women. Wow! It was just like Christmas. A lot of presents covered in different wrappings. There were all shapes and sizes, some young and some old. Adam spoke to himself, "You are going to like this job, forget the money. This looks like it's going to be lots of fun."

Adam did not notice Olivia as he turned his talents to the task in hand. He got down to work immediately and soon became involved with the others. It wasn't going to be easy trying to mould them into dancing, flowing, sexy angels covered in chiffon, organza and sequins. Adam gave the girls a pep talk, and then began to play the music as he explained the sets to Olivia's friends, who were to be the models. Occasionally, he would hear sounds of laughter over the music somewhere in the corners of the room. Olivia had a very distinct laugh. It was loud and clear, with a small giggle wrapped inside. It could take a man to the heights of bliss just listening to it and he began to dream of spending a day with Olivia on his boat. She was so full of life and a total conundrum. A day away from all of this and he could get to know her better. He found that he now wanted to get to know all about her. What she loved, what she hated and what made her happy. Right now, he needed some of what Olivia had. He needed some happy.

Adam called the others to order, ran through one of the sets again before calling it a day, until the next time they would meet. As he turned to walk off the dance floor, he caught sight of Olivia and wondered who she was talking to in the shadows. She was wearing the same oversized denim jacket and peeping from under it was the pink sweater, obviously her favourite. He smiled to himself, wondering if she had any other sweaters. Her hair was scraped back, held in a big black bow, which served no purpose, as most of her hair was escaping all over the place. It was an untidy mess that just added to her beauty.

The weeks began to pass quickly and the rehearsals went well. Adam became aware of how much he was looking forward to the days he was at the club. Olivia would stop at times to speak with him and stand at the edge of the dance floor, moving in time to the music and clapping at her 'girls' when they completed a set. Adam had to admit some of the girls were very good. Unfortunately, some of the older women had no rhythm and moved across the dance floor as though they had wet themselves. Not a pretty sight.

Adam enjoyed women; he got a thrill from their bitchiness, and some of these appeared to be class 'A' bitches. They were office workers and housewives who believed that being a model in one fashion show would take them to the heights of fame. One of the younger girls, Susan, fell for him and began to follow him around. She was rather pretty, with legs that went on and on. Susan was eighteen and Adam found her irresistible. She flirted outrageously with him. She fed his ego, and why not, why not have a go at her? There was nothing stopping him. She would hang on to his every word and he wondered what she wanted? Maybe she wanted the experience of the older man and all that he could teach her. A lesson with Susan might be just what Adam needed. She looked as though she had been around the houses more than once, so it was questionable as to who would teach who, what!

Adam met Susan one lunch time for a drink, and as she began to talk the usual rubbish young women talked about, he tried to see behind the thick layer of foundation and make-up that hid who she really was. She had nice hair, which nearly made up for her stupidity. He soon found there was no decent conversation to be had with Susan. Adam ignored her and asked himself the question as to whether he should take her to bed or just parade her around for a few weeks in order to feed his ever-hungry ego. He did have scruples, but at forty, an eighteen-year-old on one's arm was surely a bonus to a man heading for middle age? He also asked himself what on earth was he doing and why?

Adam knew young girls were harder to dump than older women. They were like unexploded bombs and could wreak havoc in a man's life by telling the wife or stalking him for months. This one was perhaps to be avoided. He once had a two-week fling with one of the daughters of an associate. He was horrified when one of his neighbours told him a young girl had been on the street asking about him. He could never have that happen again. The relationship with Susan would be a non-starter, and it stopped at a drink.

When it got back to Olivia that Adam had taken Susan for a drink, she was very angry. There she was, standing in front of him, tight-lipped, with one hand on her hip, asking to have a private word with him. They went into the back office at the Satin Club for privacy and she began stomping around the floor, calling him a pervert and asking him what on earth he thought he was doing. "It is my duty to protect these girls from themselves and dirty old men like you. You are old enough to be her father."

"Excuse me," he broke into her mid-sentence. "You are beginning to sound like a jealous wife. What I do is none of your business." What was Olivia so angry about? Why had it upset her so? Adam began to feel rather guilty, not because of Susan and taking her for a drink, but more because he had upset Olivia so much. She looked beautiful when her eyes flashed. He wanted to kiss her there and then. He wanted to pull her to him and rest his face against her wild, wild hair which always smelled so sweet. Adam didn't dare, as he knew she might hit him with the first moveable object she could find to hand. He smiled now. "I'm sorry. Do you know how beautiful you look when you are angry?" That silenced Olivia, and with a surprised look on her face, she turned on her heel and left the room. It looked like his telling-off was over.

During some of the rehearsals, Godzilla would put in an appearance. She chose her moments well and would hang around Adam like some bluebottle waiting to chomp on his meat when he least expected it. Carol was cramping his style, but being the gentleman, he was, he put up with her and also the friend that was now in the show. Olivia was manipulated into taking the woman on, as Carol threatened to take all her dresses out if her friend did not get a major role in some of the sets. It was too late to turn back now. The woman joined the group. Adam tried to keep the woman out, but when Carol was in residence, she insisted her friend did more dancing.

Brenda was not young. She was thin-lipped and scraggy, a bit like Carol. A withered sun bed queen who thought she was at least twenty years younger than her age. She was thinning on top, a shining brown scalp showed through strands of lank hair. She had skin that a handbag-maker would die for. Brenda did not fit in with the group, being haughty and lording it over the rest of them because she was Carol's friend. She soon got a nickname: 'Leather Lips'. It was rather sad that a woman of her age had no dignity and took great pleasure in parading around like a balding peacock. There were many women like Brenda, and this type of woman could never see how ridiculous they were.

Adam developed a casual friendship with Olivia; she was extremely professional and her organisational talents were amazing. She made things happen. As the fashion show came closer, he found himself admiring her talents more and more. This little thing with the incredibly loud voice, that no doubt could raise the dead, amazed him as he got to know her better. That voice, which had such a range — from loud, to soft, to sweet — began to enchant him. He did not care if she was screaming or whispering, as long as he could be in the same space as her. Adam found himself feeling content. Olivia reminded him of a bossy little girl. She was rather a control freak, but she was achieving amazing things. She had no real help, and singly (apart from himself, of course), she was staging a massive show in the best club in town practically on her own.

Olivia had the owners of the club at her feet, saying, "Yes, Olivia. No, Olivia". What she wanted, she got. Adam wasn't sure how she managed this, but the personality he was catching glimpses of was her greatest asset. This woman had 'soul'. Yes, she was a soul diva. Olivia did an extraordinary amount of flirting with Warren and Bob, the young owners of the club. They were in their mid-twenties, and when she was fooling around with them and laughing, she seemed ageless. Adam would feel pangs of jealousy. Why couldn't she flirt with him like she did with them?

Adam tried to imagine, many times, what the night of the show would be like. Would she end up with Warren or Bob? He was sure that one of them would get lucky. The way they were all behaving led him to believe that she might have a choice. He took a bet with himself that it would be Warren, as she spent more time with him, drinking coffee and whispering, than with Bob. What did they laugh about? Why did she always look so happy? Maybe she was happy or maybe not? If she was acting, then she was a very good actress.

CHAPTER TWO

"Excuse me, sir!"

Adam stirred from his memories, opened his eyes and saw the hostess looking down at him. He wondered what she would look like first thing in the morning without her make-up. He had often come unstuck with one-night stands that had beautiful faces in a half — sometimes drunken — light, only to wake up the next morning to find Biollante, Godzilla's sister looking at him.

"Would you like another drink?"

Adam couldn't remember having had the first one. He couldn't refuse such a polite request from one so pretty. It was going to be a long night, as his memories were now coming back to haunt him, so why not? "Yes, please, love, can you make that a double." The gin loosened his mind and he was quite surprised by the pictures now surfacing with such intense reality. It could have all happened yesterday.

~

Adam never took Mary on his jobs: he felt that wives got in the way and held a man back. The playboy image Adam created for himself did not include a wife; just as some pop stars never mention theirs, he never mentioned his. It was bad for business. Mary was overweight and too fussy. She was not good for his credibility. She was very disappointed that he would not take her to the fashion show and sulked. Adam was used to the sulking and explained that he would be very busy and that she would not know anybody there. Gerry also wanted to go, and on the same night that Mary sulked, so did Gerry.

Sometimes he would take Gerry with him if it was far enough away from home. She would sit in the background and seemed to understand his behaviours. He was not going to take her to the fashion show, even though she begged him. Gerry only once gave Adam grief, when he disappeared for an hour one night at a working men's club in Barnsley when he was the DJ. The dance floor was full and Gerry was in the ladies' room. As Adam came off the stage, after doing a set of 70's numbers, a woman came up to him. "Can I have your autograph, please?"

Adam was surprised. No one had ever asked for his autograph before. He was a little more tipsy than usual and offered no resistance when the woman grabbed his hand and took him outside the building, which was more of an oversized shed than a purpose-built social club.

Adam couldn't really see the woman in the car park light, but knew something was about to happen and he was up for it. The woman took a marker pen from her bag and before he could blink, she had pulled down her bright pink top to expose two pearly globes that sprung out like ripe melons. "Right there," she said, pointing at the top of her right breast. "You may write your name there, after!"

A cold wind blew across Adam's face which served to bring him round from the fog he seemed to be wandering in. Rather bemused, he wondered what she meant. He tried to focus. "After?"

"After this!" The woman grabbed Adam's head and pushed it down onto her breast. Adam's mouth found the nipple and he had no choice but to suck. The woman smelled of stale tobacco and it was less than a pleasure.

"Oh my God, what is happening?" Adam asked himself. This was a nightmare and the woman pushed her body into Adam's with such force that they both fell over. It was enough to sober the most drunken man and Adam swiftly jumped up and began to run across the car park to the back door of the club.

Adam found Gerry by the bar. She was livid. "Where the fuck, have you been? You left me here with these morons and you were nowhere to be found."

His quick thinking helped, as he explained that he had purchased some vinyl from the owner of the club and they were cutting the deal. Adam had a range of excuses to suit every occasion. It was all part of his act. "Well, I'm here now, aren't I? So, what would you like to drink?" Adam was a fool to make promises to Gerry he had no intention of keeping, and she was a fool for believing him. At one time he was madly in love with her. Gerry thought she was the one. She thought Adam would one day leave Mary and come to her.

Gerry lived in flat-land in a seedy part of town. She lived there alone, for eight years, just waiting for Adam to leave his wife — and in the meantime she had to fit in with his busy life of family, football, boats and work. Adam always had an excuse for not leaving, and she chose to ignore the signs that told her Adam was perhaps not committed to her in the same way she was to him. She would not acknowledge that Adam was losing interest and she could not see any way out of eight years of waiting.

People delude themselves into believing lies in order to make their lives better. Illusions are illusions and usually disappear with the mists of time, sometimes to create another illusion or to reveal a reality that requires action. At times, Adam felt that Gerry used him to get away from her husband. She was married to a man older than herself. He was a wealthy man and she realised that money wasn't everything, so she began an affair with Adam which ended her marriage. She thought that she would get a tidy settlement, but eventually she came away with nothing. Adam thought she might get a tidy settlement, too. To say he was disappointed was an understatement.

Gerry and Adam worked in the same office and he picked her up every morning, dropping her off at night after a peck on the cheek. Their affair began with a harmless conversation. She lied to Adam about the state of her marriage and said that her husband of three years was a heavy drinker and gambler. She made out that her situation was much worse than it was. She knew what she was doing. She would tell Adam all about it in their coffee breaks.

He wasn't sure how the affair began, but before long they were entwined in a passion that took their breath away and then Gerry left her husband, without any thought, to wait for Adam to leave his wife and move in with her. In the first instance, Adam had every intention of doing so, but he did not want to leave his children, especially his eldest son, whom he adored. It wasn't long before Adam was cheating on Gerry as well as Mary. He had no conscience, as he believed everyone was responsible for their own destiny and behaviours.

At one point he began to read a book about sex addiction. There was a test in the back. He did not tick all the boxes, but identified with some of the symptoms. He lied to cover up behaviours. He seemed to have an inability to control or stop his behaviours. He did experience personal and professional consequences, but not often. When he read the whole book, he realised that he was not a sex addict but a serial adulterer. He was a full-blooded Yorkshire male who loved women and there was no mental deficiency in that.

On Tuesdays, when Adam took Gerry home, he stayed for tea and bed games. These were now becoming boring and unsatisfying. There was no spontaneity to their lives, as his life seemed to be ruled by the clock and Gerry became less exciting as she took on the persona of wife number two. The love-making was becoming shorter and shorter, and Adam no longer kept his promises and at times was unable to perform in bed with Gerry. He didn't seem to have that problem with others. He barely touched Gerry: why bother if he couldn't follow through? She would take his limp penis into her hand and her mouth, at times to no avail. Adam didn't feel the need to explain his flaccid penis to Gerry. He didn't want to hurt her. He was becoming a man of double standards and hypocrisy and was beginning to hate Gerry as much as he hated Mary. They had both become an inconvenience in his life. Sometimes, Gerry cried and Adam would leave. He really could not do with women's tears. He felt that women used them to get what they wanted. Tears weren't always honest and were brilliant weapons to use at will.

Choices are available to everyone, aren't they? The ultimate responsibility for what happens to the individual is down to that individual. Tears serve no purpose. Adam cried only once in his life. That was when his mother died. Little did he realise it was a rehearsal for the future. It is not wise to bottle up emotions and keep tears inside. They always come out in the end.

Adam would never leave Mary, he knew that. He sometimes felt conflicted by his own rampant sexuality and his needs for the peaceful life. He was a man of contradictions. Running after women and finding peace were not synonymous with each other. Adam tried to keep everybody happy, whilst sacrificing himself and fooling himself into believing he was living the life he wanted. His arrogance was his worst enemy and he couldn't see that. As a Libran, Adam was charming, gorgeous, quick-witted and entertaining when he wanted to be, but when a relationship began to stagnate, he would get bored. For Adam, a relationship was like a living organism. It needed feeding and nurturing in order to grow and develop. If this doesn't happen, then a man like Adam will run for the hills. His worst nightmare was the routine of relationships. He was living his nightmare with Gerry and Mary. That was a good enough reason for his philandering. Adam was tiring of it and sacrificing the self on a downward spiral of superficial relationships. He slept with women he hardly knew and he wanted to get off the treadmill to find his peace. He was still looking for the one to give him that peace. He was always chasing rainbows.

Adam was day-dreaming and happily singing away in the shower as he prepared for the night of the fashion show. He couldn't sing, but he didn't care, and the soap squirmed with his rendition of 'I Want You' by Marvin Gaye. He turned the tap to cold and returned to the real world. As he slapped on the 'Jazz', it stung, making him feel young and alive. The teenager in him emerged and he felt an excitement that had been lost to him for a very long time. Adam looked superb and immaculate in his very expensive dinner suit, with a snowy white shirt and black silk bow-tie. He looked younger than his years. There was no doubt that Adam was a professional and believed that good dressing was the key to success. Image was everything to him. People judged a person on how they presented themselves and, as women loved romance, there was nothing more romantic than a man smelling good, in a dinner suit.

A feverish shiver ran down his spine as he began to imagine what the evening would bring. His thoughts wandered to Olivia. Would she be wearing the pink sweater and jeans? He was beginning to think they were the only clothes she had. Thoughts of Olivia began to fade as Adam began to run through his lists of models and routines. The music selected was the best yet. Work them up and then slow them down, leaving the love songs till last.

The fashion was only part of the evening, as Olivia had hired a woman singer from Scotland who sang lounge lizard love songs and a George Michael look- and sound-alike. There was also a raffle, and when the show was over, a disco at which Adam was going to enjoy himself.

Two hours of hard work and then a night-time of play. His anticipation got the better of him as he felt a twinge in his manhood that would very soon turn into an embarrassing bulge. He waited till his erection was complete and then lost himself in a dream while doing what came naturally.

Adam left his car at home and ran the two streets to Chris's house. Chris was his friend, who kept all the equipment in the back of his van. They would be late if he did not get a move on, but needs had to be satisfied, and perhaps he should not have appeased his manhood. Chris and Adam did many gigs and had worked together a long time. There wasn't much that Chris didn't know about Adam. He rescued Adam many times from women who could not resist his charms. As they pulled out of his drive, Chris began to ask questions. He was not able to attend any of the rehearsals, as he was painting his mum's front room. His girlfriend of seven years had just dumped him and he was not really in the mood for doing anything but painting. It was good therapy. Chris always helped his friend, and it was time to get back out there in the party place. "What's the talent like, then?"

Adam hated it when Chris spoke about women like that. Adam fooled himself into thinking that he respected them. He replied in a flippant way, "Depends what you are after tonight, Chris." Adam turned away and looked out of the window, trying to keep his mind off 'brown eyes and pink sweater'.

Just before they entered the town centre, Chris broke the silence. "I am dying to meet this Olivia. You have not stopped talking about her for weeks."

Adam was surprised: he did not realise that he had spoken so often about someone that he struggled to chase out of his mind. This was the woman who never stopped talking, was rather bossy and he wasn't interested in. "Yes, I suppose you are right. I have talked about her, but she's not my type; she's a bit of a mystery and I can't read her at all. She's not for me."

Adam thought that Olivia was remarkable and had a bit of a hippy philosophy, being rather laid back and perhaps a bit too loud for him. He wasn't prepared to discuss Olivia with Chris. Adam enjoyed a challenge, but he didn't fancy her. Why should he? There were some gorgeous leggy blondes on the team and they were much more to his liking; his usual type for a dalliance. Perhaps he might ask one of them to have a drink with him later? Adam needed a Barbie on his arm and not a Yorkshire country bumpkin. That is what Olivia reminded him of. Just now he did not need a challenge. He did not need complications — he needed an easy lay.

They arrived at the club at six and after unloading Chris and Adam had a few drinks before beginning to set the stage. Most of the girls were coming straight from work. Warren and Bob provided a meal for them all, accompanied by wine. A lot of wine! Adam could hear the girls laughing in the restaurant as he ran upstairs. He felt this was definitely going to be a good night. The dance floor shone, the girls were getting excited and he was ready for the success coming his way.

He entered the room quietly and surveyed the scene. One side was a full glass wall so that diners could watch the people on the dance floor below. The walls were a moody midnight blue and fitted high chrome lights gave a chic designer look. Next to the restaurant was a private sitting area for those intimate moments during love songs. The deep burgundy and gold decor gave it a feeling of a bordello. This could have been Paris, France not the centre of Bradford, West Yorkshire. A man could begin to make his dreams come true in the dimness. He could make his passion flower bloom. Warren and Bob had certainly provided many intimate love corners in their establishment and Adam wondered if he might just get into one on this night?

Adam coughed loudly and there was a hush as the girls all turned to look at him. He knew he had made an impact by the momentary silence that fell and by the widening of certain eyes. Adam knew all about body language. He was a master at it — hence the fact that he had few disappointments when it came to women. He settled himself into a corner for a few quiet moments and was surprised to find himself scanning the place for Olivia. She was nowhere to be seen. As he took a long sip of his gin and tonic, he decided that she must be somewhere else in the building, doing what she did best, organising and bossing people about in her loud 'hear me now' voice.

The girls began to leave the room and make their way to the dressing rooms. Some of them appeared not to be sober and a frown crossed

Adam's face as he allowed himself a moment of worry. He rose and went to the glass wall, looking down on the empty silence below. Left alone with his thoughts, he wondered where on earth Olivia was: it was nearly time for the doors to open and people were already queuing round the block. Anne entered and walked over to a table awash with empty wine bottles. She picked up two that were still unopened and as she turned to leave, Adam asked about Olivia. "I didn't see her when I came in. I could really do with a word before the show starts."

"She was here earlier, but left to go home and get changed. I think she was going to the hairdresser's, too."

So! Olivia would not be sporting the scraped-back ponytail look this evening. He wondered what she might look like without the pink sweater.

A screech woke him as Godzilla walked into the room. "There you are! I have been looking all over for you. Don't you think you should be downstairs on stage? The doors will be opening soon."

Adam turned to face Carol, his eyes slowly travelling up her body. They started at her feet and scanned quickly as they rose to meet her badly made-up eyes, mascara bleeding underneath, in the humidity of the room. She stood very close to him and he could smell her 'fag-ash' breath. "Couldn't she at least chew gum or suck mints?" Old veins on her feet were adorned by gold sandals, the straps wrapped around anorexic ankles. Legs that would have made a chicken feel beautiful. Poor old boiler, Carol! The black dress with silver straps that crossed orange-coloured bony shoulders was far too small for her. The mask of her make-up would have graced any clown's face.

Carol said she had spent the afternoon at the hairdressers. Adam smiled: she shouldn't have bothered. She had wasted her money. The style did not suit her: as usual, too young for her years. It was obvious by the way she was presenting that Carol thought that she looked really good tonight. Perhaps she thought that tonight was the night to try once again with Adam. He hoped not. She was going to be unlucky and his annoyance hit Carol in the face. "Carol, I was taking five; it is going to be a long night and I just like to meditate a while before I go on stage. I shall be down in good time and when I am ready."

"You don't strike me as a man who meditates. Don't you mean, you just want to run through who might be your next seedy affair?" She carried on squawking back at him.

Adam had to laugh. "You don't know me as well as you think you do. Come on now, you know that I don't do that. Is it my fault that women are naturally attracted to me? I would much rather just do my job and go home," he lied, as he looked at Carol with appealing eyes.

She was not finished yet. "Sure, well, I heard all about you and that Susan."

Adam readied himself for more bitching as he moved away from her. "OK, so if she wanted to take things further, who am I to stop her? Susan is a very nice young lady. Carol, I don't have to answer to you, so mind your own business." She had really annoyed him and he had really annoyed her. Carol turned, tossed her head and stormed out. Adam's laughter followed her down the stairs. He loved the movements of a jealous woman, especially one who hungered after him, the way Carol did.

Half an hour later, the club began to fill up, people finding seats and friends greeting each other. It appeared that there were lots of people here who were good friends and related to each other. One of the bar staff brought Adam a message. They would not be starting as planned as there were still people waiting round the block. It was unbelievable, the amount of people turning up for the show.

"Where were they all coming from? How did she do it?" (Olivia explained to him later that the printer had printed too many tickets and not numbered them. She sold them all.) Adam was wondering where Olivia found all these people. Surely, she couldn't know them all! How did she always get exactly what she wanted? She obviously had the golden touch. Adam's eye caught the door as it began to open. An amazing sight stepped into the room. A blonde entered the room, hair piled high on her head. A tight, red, figure-hugging dress that was more like a second skin than a dress, moved slowly through the crowd. He could not see the face, but the breasts must have been the most beautifully shaped pair that he had ever seen. Whoever she was, she looked interesting. He watched her as her head bent forward to listen to someone talking to her. His eyes fell to her hips. They were hips to grasp, to pull close and hold tight. There was no doubt in his mind: whoever she was, he had to have her. Adam felt the stirring deep inside and his penis began to slowly tickle, speaking to him that it would be ready when he was. He would definitely seek her out before the night was through! The dress moved as the woman moved. The low neck and back revealed a glowing tan of beige brown.

Bringing himself back to the moment, Adam was beginning to get annoyed: where was Olivia? She should be here. This was her show. Chris began to play the opening score and Adam's attention soon returned to the record decks. A tap on Adam's shoulder startled him. He turned in the small box that was the DJ's stand.

"Hi, sorry I'm late, but I needed some space and had to get away for a while. I have been here all day. Needs must, you know."

Never in his life had Adam been lost for words, but he was now. He couldn't speak as his eyes met a face that was engraved on his memory. Olivia stood before him in her red second skin. He took a deep breath and swallowed hard. Never had he seen such a transformation. This woman was like a chameleon and could change to suit whichever situation she was in. "Do you like it?" She grinned up at him, with an almost embarrassed look and a flushing of the cheeks.

Adam was too dazed to say anything much. "What?"

"The dress, do you like the dress? Carol lent it to me. I think she wanted to wear it; she said it wouldn't suit me when I chose it off the rail and everyone said it would. I don't think she is very happy." Olivia did a twirl and grinned up at him. "I think it's great — don't you?"

Adam stood before her. Not only was he dazzled by her, but also quite speechless. The only way he knew this was Olivia, was the chirping and the fact that she did not stop for breath. How can someone talk and smile at the same time? Olivia did not wait for his answer. She was gone, running across the dance floor to greet her mum and other friends.

Suddenly, Adam began to sweat and was finding it hard to concentrate. After checking in with Chris, he left the stage and took himself across to the bar for a drink. As the iced alcohol hit the back of his throat, he coughed and began to laugh. The little minx! She had hidden herself under that pink sweater for all those weeks and tonight she came out in all her glory. He liked a challenge. She would be a challenge. He was ready for the chase. "OK, madam!" Adam looked across at her, before returning to the stage. "I am ready when you are."

The evening went very well. The only glitch was when Carol began to introduce her fashions. She was terrible. Her voice droned on and on. It was embarrassing and Adam could not get the microphone off her. Eventually, he managed to pull it out of her hand. "Thank you, Carol. That was good." Adam addressed the audience, giving details of Carol's shop and telling them that they could purchase the fashions at the end of the show. He could see that she was not happy, so he told her that there was some pink champagne behind the bar with her name on it. Carol couldn't resist pink champagne. He needed to get her away from the stage. It got rid of her for a while.

The girls were a hit, and when Susan stumbled and nearly fell, Adam raised his eyes in disgust, knowing that Susan had drunk too much wine. He was a little annoyed at Warren and Bob for supplying so much free alcohol. The singers were brilliant, especially the George Michael look-alike. He sang like George. He looked like George. It was very hard to believe that he was not George.

Olivia was having the time of her life, flirting with Warren and Bob. Adam spotted her talking very intently to Warren in a corner. Warren was laughing and could not take his eyes off her. Adam felt a pang of jealousy. He was really confused. Why would he be jealous when there was no way he would be doing anything with 'brown eyes, pink sweater'! One moment he felt Olivia was not for him and then the next he was thinking about her. Olivia talked too much. He preferred quieter women. So why had he married a chatterbox? Mary! Mary was boring. Olivia was fascinating. She was intelligent and could talk till the cows came home. Adam made his mind up. He was determined that he would get a dance with Olivia, if only to put his arms round that gorgeous body.

The show ended and Adam's job was done. He handed the stage over to the regular DJ for the disco and left Chris to load up the van. The club was beginning to empty a little, as some of the older people had only come to see the fashions. Mums and aunties were leaving for a cup of tea and the warmth of bed. They would soon be side by side with snoring husbands who had lost their passion down the years, the stirring in an old man's loins long gone. The erection of youth only a distant memory to the man who was now only interested in his newspaper, the snooker, his belly, his prostate and television game shows. Adam felt sorry for older women.

Adam could never imagine himself not looking at a woman without desire. Apart from the certain few, Carol being one of them. With Mary, he performed a duty. That was when he could get an erection. He serviced her as an obligation when he had to, the image of another woman floating in his mind. This enabled him to keep Mary happy for at least two weeks. To Adam, age was just a number and he was aware that he was getting older; mid-life was the pivot to a downhill slide into old age. He would be forty-one next year. He hoped that he might die an old man without developing a prostate problem and still having the ability to get the erection of a young stud.

He knew a lot of older men found it hard to get erections, and when they did, they found it hard to maintain them. His friends at the golf club would often talk about their problems whilst in the sauna. One man brought in a vibrating cock ring and they laughed at him. Adam was rather disgusted, as he would never use anything like that or any toys. His hands, mouth and tongue were all he needed. He was a very plain man but by no means simple. Adam would sit and listen. He would never talk about sex or other personal matters. These men were always in competition, and it reminded him of school, when the boys would size each other up in the latrines. Why did there need to be a competition? He was determined to stay virile until he was a very old man, but felt no need to talk about it. The physical side of a relationship was very important to him; but more important was the compatibility, the companionship and the laughter. This was something now lacking in his relationships with both Mary and Gerry.

The evening was very successful for Carol, who sold all her fashions backstage, making a huge profit. She promptly left after counting up the money as Adam could not help but wind her up and made it quite clear to her that he would be busy with either Susan or Red Dress later. Adam scouted the room for the red dress; where was she now? He walked over to Anne at the bar. "Hi." He slipped his arm around Anne's waist. He just could not control himself at times. He was a very tactile man who had to touch the woman if she was near enough. He couldn't just look, he had to feel. It never occurred to him that he was invading personal space, and if it had, he would have done it anyway.

"Hi, Adam. Hasn't it been a good night? Do you want a drink?"

"No, let me, please." Adam reached for his wallet as Anne asked for pink champagne and Adam reminded himself not to ask her again. He should have known she was not a 'half a pint of lager' girl. In a not-interested kind of way, as though it was just an enquiry in passing, Adam asked Anne where Olivia was, as he had not seen her in a while.

"Carol wanted the red dress back. She made Olivia take it off. Carol is a right cow! You would have thought she would let her wear it for the night, wouldn't you?"

"Oh, dear! Oh no, what happened?"

"She took it off and gave it back to her."

Adam knew why Olivia had to give the dress back. Anne was right. Carol was a 'right cow'.

Adam scoured the room and saw a blonde head bent down, listening to Chris. Whatever it was he was saying to her was keeping her interested. Adam continued to make polite conversation with Anne and began to ask personal questions about Olivia. Eventually, he bade a hasty retreat and, after visiting the toilets, he made his way towards Chris and Olivia.

She was now wearing a loud green and purple trouser suit. No one could have got away with that fashion statement except Olivia. It summed her up precisely. Adam wondered what Chris talked about, as he had this habit of warning the women off. Chris had scuppered Adam's plans so many times before. Adam knew Chris liked Mary and meant well, but wished that he would mind his own business. Chris did not like the way Adam picked women up and then dropped them. Sometimes at venues, Chris was left to do a mop up operation of Adam's misdemeanours. Adam's disloyalty to his marriage and his mistress was always on display.

Adam gave Chris a knowing look. "Olivia, have you been avoiding me, and is it not time for that dance?"

Olivia smiled up at him. She should not have done that, as it sent a shiver down his spine and he knew he would have to have her, however long it took. "Look, Adam, half my village are here and it would not be

46

the right thing to do, to be seen dancing with you. You know how people can get the wrong idea and tongues will wag. Sorry, but I won't be dancing with you tonight."

Disappointment showed in his face. "Come on, we have worked hard for weeks, and what harm can one dance do?"

His question was followed by a silence that seemed to last forever as Olivia began to wistfully look around. He began to feel uncomfortable and wondered if perhaps he had made a mistake. "What the hell!" A mischievous grin lit up her face and Olivia grabbed Adam's hand and pulled him onto the dance floor.

Adam sighed with relief, feeling as though he was dead and in heaven now. This woman could dance. Not only could she move her body in disturbing ways, but she could talk at the same time. He asked himself, "Does she ever stop talking?" Without warning, the music slowed and as the words from 'We've Got Tonight', by Bob Seger, wafted towards them, Adam impulsively drew Olivia to him. She stiffened for a moment and stopped talking. He wasn't listening to her anyway. This moment of first bodily contact would stay with him forever. Adam held Olivia tightly, but not too tightly as to scare her off. His fingers spread across the small of her back, pulling her pelvis towards him. He could feel her breathing gently into his neck. He could smell the heady aroma of her perfume as she began to get warmer and relax. Lost in time and music, Adam felt Olivia's breasts firm against his chest, gently rising as she moved in time to the beat, allowing his body to lead her. There were no words to describe the feeling now crushing his maleness, only a satisfaction accompanied by a "Wow!", which wasn't really a word but more of a sound.

"Can I see you some time?"

Adam was not expecting the sharp retort that followed. "No."

Stung by such a small word, Adam pulled Olivia closer and as they continued to dance, he became more and more hooked into the rhythm that was her body, her sensuality. He began to feel something unknown. He was not sure what it was. One thing he was sure about, he was living in the moment. She was that moment.

Olivia made it clear by the sharp 'No'. There would be no other moments. As 'Love Is Love', by Culture Club, ended, Adam thanked

Olivia for the dance and walked her to the bar, where he ordered some drinks. He wondered if a few drinks might break her resistance. Adam remembered that she was driving, so probably this was not the best idea he ever had.

A few moments later, Olivia excused herself as there was an incident at the main door and she was needed. Olivia returned. She appeared shaken and distressed. Seemingly, an admirer of hers was trying to get into the club. The man was inappropriately dressed for the occasion and the bouncers were not letting him in. Olivia took a drink. "I don't know what to do. It's Simon Arthur, someone from the charity that has sort of been in love with me for a while. He has driven up from Sheffield and will not go away. I have had terrible problems and my family think it is really funny. He calls me at home and sings Bob Dylan songs down the phone to me. He even gave me a record, 'Unchain My Heart' by Joe Cocker." Adam couldn't help but laugh. "It isn't funny. My family think it is, too, and wind me up. I don't like it." She went on to tell Adam more. "Well, actually it was me who helped him, and now he seems to have some sort of fixation on me." Olivia took another sip of her drink and went on to explain that Simon was once suicidal and she went to his home after a call from his girlfriend. It seemed that, as his life was coming back on line again, he wanted to show his appreciation.

Adam smiled again. He could see why men might fall in love with Olivia. He thought back to the rehearsals in the previous weeks and the capable woman who was present at them, even though she looked like a demented teenager most of that time. Earlier that night, Adam saw a sexy woman in stilettos wearing a second skin which did nothing to hide her womanly figure and perfect breasts. Now he was looking down at a frightened little girl who did not know what to do. "What are you going to do?"

She shrugged her shoulders and looked around the room. "No idea, to be honest. What if he tries to follow me home?"

Adam felt he might have the solution and secretly thanked Simon Arthur for turning up. This could be to his advantage, and what he was about to say next might just work. He looked at Olivia sympathetically. "I might be able to help you there. Chris went home ages ago and I was thinking of calling a cab or asking for a lift from anyone going my way.

I live in the opposite direction to you, and if this guy sees you leaving with a man, he might just go home. If you wouldn't mind giving me a lift home, then perhaps if he does follow, we could lose him together?"

The look on Olivia's face told him to back off. She began to whisper, "I don't know. It is very late and maybe it is not a good idea taking you home." In the next moment, a wide grin lit her face up. She agreed the idea was not so bad after all and, yes, perhaps that should happen. Adam saw another side to Olivia via the sparkle in her eye. He was beginning to know this woman and she had a reckless streak. She was a very complex person and perhaps he should set himself the goal of unravelling that complexity?

Half an hour later, Olivia and Adam were sitting in her car down the road from his house. They were talking and laughing, as if they had known each other forever. She looked beautiful as she chatted away about the show, her hopes and dreams. Her eyes were catching the lamplight that shone through into the car. Olivia suddenly went quiet and serious, looking as though she was going to make an announcement. Adam couldn't help himself and leaned towards her. She stopped and looked at his face; she studied it and he watched her as he saw in her eyes that she was questioning herself, trying to make her mind up. What to do next? He saw a shyness in her that he had not seen before. When he moved closer, he noticed a slight movement in Olivia's mouth, as her lips began to quiver in anticipation. He pulled her closer to him and he felt the flowery scent of her hair; felt the softness as he ran his fingers up the nape of her neck, pulling her closer and closer until their lips met and he became lost in the sweetness of her breath.

The first kiss is always so special. Adam's lips brushed lightly against Olivia's as they said, 'Hello.' He pulled her nearer as he opened his mouth, moving the tip of his tongue gently into the moist cave he was about to explore. The tips of their tongues met in a greeting that led to an intensity of feeling that shook his body, the beauty of their breath moulding into one. The wetness of their mouths spilling into each other spoke volumes that required no words, but created a need for more kisses. Adam wanted more and knew he wanted to be with her forever. It was a message in that first kiss. The knowledge that this woman might be the one he had looked for all his life awoke in his brain.

Adam felt Olivia's body against his and the hardness against his chest that were nipples. Nipples that were excited by the flow of energy that ran through them. He lost all sense of time and did not know how long they kissed for. All he knew was that he could not remember a kiss such as this. Olivia knew how to kiss, and their lips fused perfectly in an embrace that he would not forget. Adam wondered what else she could do, and if the rest would be as good as the kissing. He knew he would have to stop soon as he felt a hardening that shocked him by its magnitude. This woman was dangerous. She might just get in the way of his life. He heard the voice in his head as it asked, "Is she the one?"

Olivia pushed Adam away. "I'd better go. I don't know what happened just then." She looked surprised and answered his question about meeting for dinner. "I am married and I do not get dressed up to go out at night with men. I don't know why I kissed you."

The frosty tone in her voice made him rethink. "OK, Olivia, there is no harm in us having lunch, is there?" Adam sounded hopeful. She bent her head and shook it as she told him that in the morning, she was going on holiday for two weeks to Mauritius.

With ego deflated, Adam said his goodbyes and got out of the car. He watched Olivia as she drove off. He felt sadness at the thought he might never see her again. It was beyond belief that she had turned him down. Had his kiss and the way he held her had no effect on her? He did not know. Olivia was like a closed book. As Adam opened his front door, he let out a long sigh. This woman reached right into the core of his being and he needed to let her go. As he closed the door behind him, he spoke out loud, "Oh well, some you win and some you lose."

CHAPTER THREE

A new account was in progress and the commission was phenomenal. Adam was working flat out to meet deadlines. He used this as a reason to get rid of Marlene and decided to put extra women on hold for a while and concentrate on a career that had been neglected of late. Marlene didn't take the news too well. He told her after a rather fraught battle in bed. Surely, he would have a bruise on his back from the way her legs battered him in those torrid moments of orgasm. Perhaps he should have thought the ending out a bit better. "Marlene, I don't think we should see each other anymore. I am going to be pretty busy in the next few months."

Marlene was so predictable. After ranting and raving, the tears began. She threatened to tell Mary, who was one of her best friends. Adam shook his head. "Now then, what good would that do? Do you want to lose your best friend, too? You knew we would not last forever." Marlene rang Adam a few times and then she disappeared from his life.

Thoughts of the fashion show, one of his most successful, became a dull memory as ideas for his new client crowded his head. Only once did Adam allow himself a thought of Olivia, and he wondered if she was enjoying Mauritius. He knew she needed a rest, as she worked incredibly hard on her last project. An incredible amount of money went into the charities' coffers.

One morning, after a particularly nasty argument with Mary and a moody car ride to work with a sullen Gerry, Adam entered his office and found a postcard at the bottom of his pile of mail. It showed a glorious white beach surrounded by a turquoise sea. He recognised the perfectly formed, neat handwriting. It was from her. Olivia was thanking him for his contribution to her project. He took a sip of his hot coffee and sat down. Well, she'd thought of him in Mauritius. He smiled. Adam let his mind wander to that last kiss, which was the first kiss. The feeling in it did not lie. Her lips did respond to him there no doubt about that. He was so shocked when she said 'No' to him, and yet she found the time to send him a postcard? Why had she done that?

Adam's pulse upped a beat. What was he to do now? He began to think of Olivia and realised how much he missed her, her quirkiness and those big brown eyes. He made a decision. There was nothing to lose. He knew when she would be back in the country and decided he would call her at the hospital where she did voluntary work. He was missing her so much and just wanted to hear her voice once more.

On the morning of Olivia's return to the hospital, Adam rang the office and spoke to the social worker. The social worker confirmed that Olivia was due in at eleven and asked if he would care to leave a message, as this was the third time he had called. "Yes, please; will you ask Olivia not to call me tomorrow as I am having a late lunch and will be out for the rest of the afternoon?" He replaced the receiver and knew if all went well, he would hear from Olivia, soon. A bit of reverse psychology never did any harm. Adam was not wrong. The next day he answered his phone.

"Why did you do that? I didn't know I was calling you. Have we arranged something? Have I forgotten? Oh my, that's dreadful; I don't forget." Olivia didn't stop for breath, she never did. Adam smiled. He remembered that the two words Olivia used the most were 'dreadful' and 'wonderful'. Yes, he missed her. Now he so wanted to see her. "Adam, are you there?"

"I wondered if you enjoyed your holiday and if perhaps you changed your mind about that lunch?" He could hear Olivia breathing down the phone. He could almost hear her thinking. He heard a big sigh.

"Thank you again. We did have a brilliant time. It was wonderful. I couldn't have done the fashion show without you. It is still 'No', and I think you were a bit cheeky ringing me like that." Olivia lowered her voice. "I really am sorry, but I cannot meet you; there is no reason to do so. I wish you all the best for the future. Goodbye, Adam." The line cleared and she was gone.

Adam looked at the receiver for a long time before putting the phone down. "Well, that was short and sweet." He scowled, feeling that he had been put in his place once more by the brown-eyed, ever-smiling Olivia.

A month passed and the new account was doing well. Adam was meeting all his deadlines. Soon, all the contracts were to be signed and

Adam was busy thinking about taking some time off work. He had put all thoughts of Olivia out of his mind, until one day when he was tired and looking at his mail. Adam switched on his answer machine. He was not really listening to it as he was busy sifting through the envelopes in front of him. First, he heard Carol — he switched her off and the next message pinged. A memory stirred as he heard the end of a sentence, and thought, "I know who that is." He rewound the tape.

"I couldn't believe it when I got the call. What do you think? She said she wants us both. I can't do it without you. I know you are probably too busy, so I could tell her no. It would mean more money for the charity. I know I said that I would never have lunch with you, but this is different. This is business. Shall we meet for lunch? Call me, you have my number."

Adam rewound the tape, listened again and then went on to the next message. "Oh yes, sorry, I forgot. There is another event before that if you are interested?" Adam switched the machine off. Stroking his chin, he wondered what on earth Olivia was on about. It made no sense. He turned his chair to the window and wondered if he should ring her back. Olivia made it quite clear the last time they spoke that she was not interested in him. There was no pot of gold at the end of that rainbow. Was he going to chase another rainbow? This one always faded in front of him.

The resistance to Olivia's request lasted one week. Adam picked up the phone and dialled her number. It was the only way he was going to get her out of his mind. Olivia explained to him that a woman from a night club in Leeds called her to say that she was at the fashion show. She was very impressed and wondered if they would like to do one in her club. Olivia went on to say they would not be able to use Carol again and she had found another fashion house. She had not heard from Carol after the argument about the dress on the night of the show. Carol was jealous that night, not just because of the way Olivia looked, but because of all the attention she received. "That's why she made me take the dress off before the evening ended. It all got very silly. I wouldn't use her if she was the last dress agency on earth." Olivia really felt that Carol would not be good for the big club in Leeds.

Olivia was not concerned by Carol's bitchy behaviour, something Adam admired Olivia for. She just got on with things and didn't let anything stop her. She was focused and just a bit obsessive. Luckily, that night she had a change of clothes with her: the loud purple and green trouser suit. "What do you think? She would like us both to go over and have a meal and get a feel for the place."

Adam listened to the chirpy 'non-breath' dialogue. He asked Olivia about dates and she told him it was up to them to decide what day they would like to visit the club. Olivia went on to tell Adam about the young Chinese designer and his African partner she had in mind to do the show. "They approached me, so it was easy. I am going down to see them tomorrow. It seems weird, but they are cousins. Changpu, the Chinese one, who I think is the boss, does lots of patterns using turtles; isn't that exciting?"

"Turtles?" Adam could not stop himself laughing.

"Yes, they symbolise patience, wisdom, endurance and good luck. Anyway, they want us to do a show on Saturday afternoon on a catwalk outside their new shop. The lord mayor is opening it and the newspapers will be writing an article, so perhaps we could get the Leeds show advertised? What do you think, Adam?"

Adam thought for a moment. Did he really want to do this? He did want to see Olivia, so perhaps he should. "Do you know, Olivia, I think you should slow down and stop to breathe now and again." Adam and Olivia arranged to meet the next day to pay Changpu a visit.

Not being able to concentrate, Adam left work early the next day and had a few beers in the pub down the road before he was to meet Olivia. Now he was nervous, his mind racing and his heart beating to a rhythm that was far from healthy. As he waited for her on the corner of the street, he wondered if she might have changed in the past few months.

Olivia ran round the corner and straight into him. Adam noticed her hair was longer and blonder, probably the Mauritian sun. She had the most beautiful tan which enhanced those gorgeous eyes that suddenly crinkled as Olivia laughed. "Oh, goodness me, I am so sorry. How wonderful to see you!"

Adam's eyes ran down her face to the glossy lips that looked big and kissable. He so wanted to pull her to him and kiss them, standing there on the street. Instead, he gave her a big hug. They went inside the shop and Olivia introduced Adam to Changpu and Chacha.

"Call me Cha and he is Cha. Thank you for gracing our presence. I hear you are a good dancing organiser."

Adam looked at Olivia. Chang, Cha and Olivia began to laugh. "Sorry, man, I just can't help myself. Call me Chang" Chang's accent had a soothing effect on the situation and Adam shook his hand firmly.

"I can see we shall have good times and laughs working with you two."

Chang and Cha went off to sort the dresses they were to show Adam and Olivia. Adam leaned across to Olivia. He noticed she was wearing a different perfume. "Are they for real with names like that? Nice perfume." He didn't realise that Olivia was on her high horse.

Olivia decided that Adam was perhaps not that intelligent and decided to blind him with her knowledge. "They are good boys and come from an old background with more history than you and I put together. Their names were chosen for their meanings. Changpu means forever simple. Not in the way you would think, but the way life should be. No complications!"

He listened as she went on. "Chacha means strong man, not only physical but in character." Adam looked at the business card in front of him. He was becoming more confused. The card read MacKenzie brothers trading as Changcha Fashion House. Olivia saw the bemused look run across his face. "Two Scottish brothers toured two different continents and came back with wives." Where did she get all this information? Adam wondered if she knew the colour of their underpants, too! Then he remembered how he had told her things on their first meeting, things he had never told anyone before. Olivia had a way with her that made people open up, and she was a mine of information.

The two boys returned with a tray of tropical juice laced with gin. They all drank together and as they discussed the two future events, became firm friends. Adam looked at the fashions, which were outstanding and original, and he decided that he loved turtles. Olivia removed a small red notebook from her bag. Adam knew what would be in it: a list of models, clothes and spaces for him to add his notes. After a productive afternoon, all parties were happy and agreements and dates made for the future. Just as they were settling down to chat some more, Olivia looked at her watch and jumped up — she had to leave for an urgent dental appointment. She ran out of the door and disappeared up the road to her car like a whirlwind.

It was very hot that Saturday afternoon when the team gathered outside 'Changcha' Fashion house, to give another great performance of music and dance. The girls were pleased to see Adam and they all agreed that they would like to do the fashion show in Leeds. Another success! Adam was rather taken aback by the attention he received from Olivia that day. She appeared anxious and nervous; seemed out of her comfort zone, hardly leaving his side. This was very unlike the night she had people queuing round the block. "Are you all right, Olivia? Is everything OK?"

"Yes, all's fine." Brown eyes looked into his and contradicted her words. Olivia did not look fine, and once she realised that he had noticed her discomfort, he saw the cheeky grin sneak across her face and a shadow cross her eyes. Olivia looked him straight in the eye. He wished she wouldn't do that, as the last few times they met, that gaze ignited something deep inside his belly. "Adam, I am fine. I am just a little tired, that is all. I have to go."

"Are you still OK for next Thursday, the meal in Leeds?"

"Yes, of course. I am looking forward to it."

Olivia informed Adam that her husband might join them. Adam wondered why she did that; no way would he be inviting Mary or Gerry. He looked forward to the two of them getting to know each other better, but it now looked as though that wasn't to be. A husband in tow was not what Adam really wanted as he hoped to reignite the kiss.

"I think it is time you and he got to know each other, seeing as you and I shall be working together again. I don't want him to think there is anything going on between us." The words slipped out of Olivia's mouth as she got up and kissed Adam on the forehead, before disappearing. She was so maddening. That kiss lingered like a punch to the heart.

Later in the week, Adam received an email from Olivia telling him that it would be just the two of them after all. Her husband was busy with work. Adam stared at the computer screen, his mind running wild with thoughts of what might be. Another kiss or more, perhaps! Rationality stepped in and told him to grow up; had she not made it quite clear they would only have a professional relationship? One of his favourite songs ran through his head. "Who's making love to your old lady, while you were out making love?" by Johnny Taylor. Mary crossed his mind. She had joined a Yoga class and never stopped talking about the instructor, Jim. He realised that she wasn't mothering him as much these days and had changed her hairstyle. No, she wouldn't, would she? She'd better not be.

With Olivia there was a firm boundary in place and Olivia would not be stepping over it. She made that quite clear on more than one occasion. The night they went to Leeds, Adam made even more of an effort with his appearance. He was about to have a free meal in the best club in town, that was attended by footballers, film stars and pop singers. He would be with a woman who he found stimulating and challenging, who kept saying 'No' to him.

He met Olivia at the corner of his street. She arrived on time, in her little blue car, and they drove into the city centre. Olivia chatted all the way as she wound in and out of the traffic. She was already thinking of the logistics and how they might produce an even better show than before. They pulled up outside a brightly lit building. Olivia got out of the car and handed her keys to the parking boy. Adam was bowled over as she turned to face him. "Are you ready then?"

"Yes. I am always ready. By the way, you look absolutely stunning. Your husband is a very lucky man."

Olivia was dressed in black. The dress was quite long, to just above her ankles, and the neckline high at the front, running down to a V at the back. There were buttons running down the back, ending in a fishtail of lace panels. She wore black tights — or could they be stockings? — above red stilettos that complemented the red earrings dangling at each side of her smiling face. Adam felt so proud to have her on his arm that evening; he wined and dined her and they danced the night away.

Towards the end of the night the lady, who originally contacted Olivia joined them and asked how their night had been and what they thought of the club. Would they be able to put on a fashion show? Of course, they would! The date was set and a bottle of champagne sealed the deal.

On the way home, Adam and Olivia were euphoric. They sang along with the songs on the car's tape system. They sang along with Marvin Gaye and Tammi Terrell. As they sang 'Ain't no mountain high enough', they looked at each other and smiled. Happy and carefree, Adam suddenly came out with a statement. "Now then, I hope you aren't going to drive down a deserted lane and have your wicked way with me?" He was startled by Olivia's reply.

"I don't know the area very well or you might have been in luck, Mr!" Without warning, Olivia veered off the road and turned down a dark lane, drove past a big school and came to a halt beneath some trees. She turned to look at Adam. She laughed. "Actually, I think this lane leads to nowhere, or it might be leading somewhere. Neither of us has a curfew, so perhaps we can begin our adventure now?"

What on earth was she talking about? Adam was lost for words: this was not the Olivia he knew — perhaps this was her twin sister? It was very dark under the tall trees. The moon twinkled between the bare branches, its light dancing like diamantes on the bonnet of the car. Olivia turned the volume down, making a bizarre statement about cows not liking soul music, only liking classical. They sat staring out of the window, not looking at each other, as they discussed the events at the club. An air of embarrassment was settling in for some unknown reason. In a rash moment, Adam turned to look at Olivia and told her how beautiful she looked. "It's not just the way you look tonight, it is everything about you. I have never met a woman like you before and I have met more than a few."

Olivia thought, "I bet you have!" She looked at Adam. There it was on her face, that wicked grin.

Olivia leaned across and kissed him on the cheek, thanking him for the marvellous time and the compliment. She sat back in her seat and their eyes met, and, as their lips slowly parted, they came together. At last the longed-for second kiss. Her lips were so soft and moist. Their lips moved in unison, and when Adam gently probed Olivia's mouth with his tongue, the response was overwhelming. Their tongues danced together as he pulled her into his arms and held her close. He could feel her large breasts pushing against him. He felt a welcome tingling start between his legs. As the kissing continued, the tension left Olivia and before long they were climbing into the back seat. No words were spoken: the kisses were sending messages loud and clear. Adam did not want to scare her off, so worked his magic very slowly. He held her head in his hands. He stroked her hair, her face. Adam could feel the mounting passion stirring in his loins. He tested the water by slowly bringing his hand up to cup Olivia's left breast. Half expecting to be pushed away, he was pleasantly surprised by the response to his touch. He felt the nipple stand to attention, almost screaming at him to be touched, nibbled and squeezed. This was some sexy woman!

In a moment of madness, they stopped and got out of the car to empty their bladders. There was no awkwardness, just the familiarity of friendship that allowed such a personal act to take place. Adam was waiting in the car when Olivia jumped in beside him. There was that wicked grin again. It ran across her eyes and she kissed him quickly, before nibbling his ear. Out of the blue, unexpected words bounced onto his ear drums. "Would you like to make love?" Olivia held a pair of red lacy knickers up, playfully swinging them on the end of her finger. "We know where this was all leading to and you could have spent the next half hour trying to get them off, so I saved you the time and the trouble."

Adam was lost for words, completely stunned by the woman in the back of the car with him. Surely this was a wind-up? This was Olivia's twin, and for the first time in his life Adam was baffled by the change in the woman and was not sure what to expect. Adam became unaware of how his body contorted to fit into the small space between the seats of the little car. All he felt was Olivia beneath him, his manhood deep inside her. Her legs were wide apart, feet firmly placed on the car window as she pushed herself up to meet his thrusting spear, slipping in and out to the rhythm of his breathing. One last deep thrust and he felt like a million birds took flight. Adam's mind was swept away on the tide of orgasm. He lay on top of Olivia, exhausted and empty, her body moulding perfectly into his. The only thing between them was the embarrassing silence and the black dress which was up around Olivia's waist.

The moonlight caught her tanned belly and buttocks as she slid from beneath him. Adam sat slumped across the back seat, not believing what had just happened. Olivia quickly wiped herself and pulled her dress down. Looking composed and so beautiful in the aftermath of such lust, Olivia became very matter-of-fact. "We'd better go now. It is very late."

They drove along with their thoughts and their silence, until it was broken by a remark that was to set the scene for the forthcoming tomorrows. Olivia's eyes never left the road as she sped on. A sombre voice trickled through the car. "What has just happened changes everything. There is no going back!"

Adam did not want to go back; he wanted to go forward to tomorrow and the day after and the day after that. Before Adam got out of the car, Olivia turned and took his hand, looking up at him, and he saw the sadness pouring out of those large brown eyes that held his for more than a moment. She leant forward and kissed him hard. "Goodbye, Adam, it was a brilliant evening. Thank you." She was thanking him? Should he not have been thanking her?

As Adam watched the little blue love machine disappear round the corner, he tried to make sense of what had just happened. He couldn't. How do you make sense of an enigma? Olivia was a mystery of complexity, dropping clues as to who she was in such a way as to confound all reasoning, which kept him wondering and wanting more.

A sleepless night was spent in reliving the moment. Adam was remembering that moment when he touched Olivia's warm welcoming mound, when his eager finger shocked her and gently pushed its way inside to feel the moist welcome, she gave him. He could feel her still, her legs wrapped around his back, pulling him deeper inside until he exploded. Languishing in the feeling of the tide crashing against the rocks, Adam felt the warm trickle of his love juice as he realised his explosion was real and not in his dream. Nothing seemed to make sense anymore; it was all unreal. The reality was, he had to get out of bed before Mary woke and smelt the ammonia that was creeping between the sheets.

Adam didn't have any contact with Olivia again until the day she picked him up to go to the first rehearsal in Leeds. It felt like a reunion, and all the girls were excited to be doing another show. It was a hard afternoon as they were on a tight schedule, and when it was over, Adam asked Olivia if she would like to go for something to eat before they went home. He took her to a discreet Italian restaurant in the centre of Leeds. They chatted about superficial things as they walked down the sunny street, no mention being made of the night down the lane. Adam was desperate to discuss what happened that night. Was it a one-off? Were they to embark on a relationship? Olivia behaved as she always did. It was as though nothing had happened at all. Adam, always the gentleman, held the door open, and they chose a table near the window. They ordered garlic mushrooms for starters and a pizza to share.

Adam ordered the wine and they settled down to their accustomed banter. His eyes never left Olivia's face as she chattered away, talking about anything and everything. It was something he enjoyed about her. Olivia was so clever and could talk about most things. She was an observer of life and very funny, a natural comedienne, making everything interesting. Adam *was* interested. There was no doubt about that. After taking a sip of his wine, Adam looked out of the window, watching an old couple holding hands, walking up the street. He could not think when he last felt so comfortable and happy. He really liked being with Olivia. He loved the way she was, so natural and honest. What you saw was what you got. Her animated face showed such expression. She wore no masks. As Adam watched the cars go by and listened to her, he thought he could sit there forever. It was almost perfect.

Another bottle of wine was ordered. It was a hot day and they were drinking fast. Adam took a sip after the waiter uncorked the bottle and he nodded. He studied the glass and took another drink. He was trying to work out why he felt like he did. What was going on inside of him as his heart beat faster than ever. What was he thinking? Was he thinking, is this the one? What was she really thinking? In a moment of reckless abandonment, Adam said something he hadn't said for many a year. "I love you." Olivia carried on talking. Had she heard him? Was she ignoring him? "I love you."

This time she stopped and looked at him. "Adam, what did you just say?" She waited for his reply.

"I love you. In fact, I don't think I have ever really felt like this before." He looked down at the crisp white napkin draped across his knees. He felt embarrassment take a grip.

Total silence descended like a thick grey fog. Adam didn't know where he was. He dared not look up. He dared not look at her. Right now, he was wishing that the ground would open up and swallow him. There was an uncomfortable stillness all around them. Adam twisted the corner of the napkin, feeling Olivia's eyes piercing his skull, burning through, sending shocks down to his heart. This just wasn't like him — what was happening?

He heard the clink of glass; she must be pouring herself another drink. Why, oh why had he said that to her? Speaking to his knees now, he said it again. "I love you." What seemed to last an hour was a moment in time that stood still!

Olivia gave a big sigh, which signalled him to look up and across at her. She was looking at him intently and began to laugh, her cheeks rosy with embarrassment at his sudden declaration. She asked him if he knew what he had just said to her. Of course he knew. It was not something he said much in his life, but when he did, it was meant. Olivia frowned. "You have been drinking and don't know what you are saying. These words are serious stuff."

Adam held his tears back. He couldn't do anything about his embarrassment. "I know, and I could not have said it without the wine, but it is not the wine speaking, it is me. I'm not sure where it came from, but it is the truth, Olivia. I love you. I have never felt like this before. I think about you all the time. I want to call you a dozen times a day. I look out of the office window, hoping to catch a glimpse of you at work."

Olivia sat back in her chair to compose herself. Adam was coming to her office more often than before and they would discuss the rehearsals. Sometimes there was nothing to discuss and Adam would say he popped in for a coffee in passing. Some days he seemed reluctant to leave and would chat to Anthony, her boss. Now things were beginning to fall into place. How stupid could she be not to have realised what was going on? Adam looked at her with pleading puppy-dog eyes, asking her to forget it. "I should not have said it. I am sorry."

Olivia looked everywhere but at Adam. She shook her head, paused for a moment, before rising and coming round the table to him. She sat in the chair next to him and pulled it closer. Turning and studying his face, Olivia took his hand between hers. "Well, you see, Adam..." Negative thoughts got the better of him and he knew what was coming next.

She cleared her throat. "Well, it's like this." Olivia stopped, reached for her glass and took a long drink of the cool wine. The torment was now becoming too much for him. Why could she not just get on with it? He could begin to nurse his wounded pride, kick himself and vow never to open up his feelings again. Adam realised just how difficult he had made things for her, for them. It was too late to take back what was said. Could he? Could he tell her it wasn't true, that he didn't love her? That would have been a lie. Adam was sick of lying. He continually did this to others and to himself. For maybe the first time in his life, Adam was being honest, and now feeling rather silly. He felt his stomach clench, sending waves of nausea mixed with anticipation through his body. Olivia kept hold of his hand, squeezing it tighter with every passing moment. Adam studied her face. She was giving nothing away. There was an expressionless veil covering her thoughts. He wanted the fog to lift — he wanted to see what was happening. Olivia began to speak slowly, as though she were choosing her words very carefully. She was tripping through vocabulary as though walking on thin ice, which might break at any time. "Adam, I thank you for what you have said. We have known each other quite a few months now. Our children have become friends and I know your wife, Mary. You have, by your words, now made things very complicated indeed."

Adam thought his heart was going to burst. He poured another glass of wine and decided that he would get very drunk tonight when he was at home. It might drown his sorrow and numb the rejection that was on its way. He felt so angry with himself now. Everything spoilt by a rash, impulsive statement. Why could he not have kept his mouth shut? Why had he declared his feelings for Olivia? He could have kept them secret. They sat in silence for a while. This was going to be difficult, as he was expecting a long goodbye. Adam would never see her again. This time she would be gone for good. Olivia stayed beside him until the sweet was served and she returned to her side of the table. They ate in an uncomfortable silence.

As she finished eating, Olivia put her spoon down and stared across the table at Adam. "The reason that this has now become more complicated is that, I love you, too."

Adam sat there absolutely stunned. He could not believe it. This was the last thing he expected. He was expecting the big brush off, not this. He smiled. He forgot about everything, his wife, his mistress, everything, and looked at Olivia, who was now smiling back at him. They both said it together: "I love you." He dared to ask her if this meant that they might meet sometimes — would she come out with him? Olivia nodded.

Over coffee, they now discussed what happened down the lane in her car. They both laughed and Olivia looked even lovelier now that she was relaxed and he was enjoying her company more and more. Walking hand in hand back to the car park, they talked about their feelings for each other and what had been said in the restaurant earlier. They never gave a thought that someone who knew them might see them. They were oblivious to their surroundings. Once in the car, they kissed passionately and Olivia abandoned herself to Adam's touch. She surprised him further when her hand slid down to his crotch and rubbed him gently. The erection that followed put a strain on the buttons of his jeans. All of a sudden, Olivia stopped what she was doing. "What time is it?" Looking at her watch, a look of panic crossed her face. "Oh my God, it is late! We really have to go right now." Olivia started the car and Adam wondered how long it would take for the bulge in his pants to disappear. His uninvited erections were fast becoming a problem to him and he really did not know what to do about them.

CHAPTER FOUR

Olivia agreed to meet Adam the following day and have lunch with him. Things needed discussing, such as how often she could get away and when and where they would meet. Olivia said there would be plenty of time for them and they had to prioritise. Their first priority must be the show. After that, they would have the whole summer. They would have forever.

Quite soon it became apparent to all that there was something going on between Adam and Olivia. During rehearsals he watched her. His eyes never left her. The feelings in his eyes could not be masked. She would smile and look away very quickly; too quickly. The girls would come across them huddled together in corners, whispering. Adam felt that he was having the time of his life, until one night in the club when he really did have the time of his life.

Adam left Chris in charge whilst they were going through the routines as the girls were practising to 'One Night in Bangkok' by Murray Head. Olivia and Adam left the dance floor and ran upstairs to the drinks lounge. The drinks lounge was a small room at the back of the club, overlooking the dance floor. Tables in dimly lit alcoves were cluttered with dirty glasses. Lights of blue and purple shone down the walls, giving the room a mystical feel. Olivia and Adam came together, their lips meeting in frenzy. They did not have long, as they might be needed downstairs and anybody could walk in on them. As always when they were together, they forgot where they were and abandoned themselves to be in the moment.

Adam was quick to find his way round Olivia and into her clothes. His hand deftly moved inside her bra, gently squeezing her left breast, rolling her nipple between his fingers. Olivia moaned as an acknowledgement of the pleasure she felt at his touch. Slowly, his other hand crept across her belly and down into her knickers; the soft hairs under his fingers between her legs were enticing and he worried that he might explode too soon. Adam found her clitoris, the flower of a woman's being. He began to stroke its petals gently. He felt the blood rush as it began to swell beneath his fingers. Adam removed his hands and took hold of Olivia's shoulders, his eyes never leaving her face as he pushed her slowly down onto the table behind them. They were oblivious to the crashing glasses as they fell off the table, making room for what was to happen next. Olivia's legs opened, allowing Adam free access to the inviting gap which widened at his touch.

The warmth of her vagina surrounded his fingers as he gently pushed two inside her, lubricating the place where he hoped he would soon be placing his boy. Olivia undid the buttons on Adam's jeans and quickly pulled them down. His erection burst forth as though mounted on a spring. Adam loved the way her hand slid down his shaft to play with his testicles. The two globes were like putty in her hands, sacks of fluid that danced about between her fingers.

Olivia moved closer to the edge of the table while Adam slid her knickers off and put them in his pocket. They looked at each other for a moment. A moment that seemed like forever. Olivia's eyes were like shining stars in a dark sky, her face covered by yearning and passion. There was little time to be had and they moved quickly. Adam entered Olivia with such force that she nearly fell off the table. He held her ankles and legs high in the air as he began his sex dance. She gasped. He quickly built up a rhythm, pushing deeper and deeper to the tune of his passion. He knew she was enjoying it, as she, too, was playing the same tune, moving in a synchronicity which the most ardent of lovers would envy. As Olivia raised her hips to meet him, her dampness turned to a river of wet and he felt a slow trickle as she moaned for more. This was pure 'I love it' juice.

Adam pulled out and rolled Olivia over onto her belly. With her legs supporting her on the floor, Adam swiftly took her from behind. He pushed and pushed. He held her by her shoulders and rode her with a fervour so strong that all sense and reason were left behind as he felt the tingling that signalled the onset of his orgasm. There was one almighty thrust that nearly sent Olivia across the table and prompted an, "Oh my goodness!" from her. This was the beginning of the end, the ferocity of the storm surprised them. This was not making love. This was primal sex of the best kind. Unadulterated lust! Adam straightened himself up and handed Olivia her knickers. She stumbled as she tried to put them on in the darkness. Soon, they were both laughing at their naughtiness. Like small misbehaving children, they returned to the rehearsal. It appeared that no one missed them. They thought they were safe.

Adam and Olivia spent the rest of the evening winking at each other. Another memory made to take to their future together. They were both ecstatic in the aftermath of passion. Yes, that was truly a night to remember. They christened a posh club in Leeds by having sex on a table, frontwards and backwards, and the residue of their moans would forever echo in that room.

CHAPTER FIVE

Adam turned to look at the man sitting beside him. The man looked about the same age. He might have been a few years older. They were both travelling to New York and Adam wondered what the man would be doing there. Usually, Adam would strike up a conversation with fellow travellers, but not today. The short chat they had earlier was enough, as Adam was too preoccupied with his past. He closed his eyes and took a deep breath. Today was filled with trepidation. There was a very unsettling feeling in the air that Adam couldn't quite put his finger on. On days like today, things happened that were beyond his control. Adam looked at the man again. Did he know him from somewhere? No, he didn't think so. There was that strange feeling that one gets sometimes of having known someone before.

The man was tapping his fingers on his knees as he listened to music, headphones crowning his baldness. Perhaps they did have something in common. Adam loved people, but his passion was music. He wondered what the man was listening to. Music and songs were milestones in Adam's life. Music is the key to memories, as it makes the soul dance and the spirit leap. He had quite a few 'Olivia' tunes on a tape somewhere lost in one of his boxes. A certain song would bring her to mind and the pictures of their yesteryear. In the years gone by, Olivia dwindled to a small figurine on the horizon of his past. A memory tune would set off questions about where she was and what she might be doing now. Adam looked out of the window, over the clouds towards the bright sunlight, bringing to mind the songs of his history that were stored in archives that held his secrets. He closed his eyes and saw a river and heard 'Music of Goodbye' by Al Jarreau in the distance.

~

The fashion show in Leeds was a success. Adam and Olivia shone and business was good. They made such a good team. Olivia was dressed immaculately. She was a master of change, as one minute she was like a little girl, in baggy clothes, and the next a sexy siren in a tight dress, fishnets and sling-back sandals. Her hair framed her face, giving her a confusing sexy, innocent look. It did not matter what colour lipstick she wore: Olivia's lips always looked inviting. Adam now knew what was under the dress and it took great willpower to resist the curves that were her body. How he managed to keep his hands off her all night was down to great willpower. Adam looked across the floor just before the girls came on to do their first set. His brown eyes met Olivia's orbs of soul and the room disappeared, as Human League began to drown out the chatter with 'Together in Electric Dreams'. Adam felt the words. He knew that he and Olivia would always be together when that song played. As he stared at the vision that he knew he would be holding in his arms later that night, the familiar stir down below began. He was looking at Olivia, who was wearing a gold sequinned dress, standing in a beam of light that was shining down on her. Never was there a moment that was as perfect as this, and they gazed at one another, smiling the knowing smile of secrets and love. They were together in electric dreams.

Adam got more than a little bit drunk that night as his ego rode on a giant wave of yet another success. On the way home, he didn't take much notice of where Olivia was driving. He was too busy talking about whatever came into his head. He was full of the entertaining ramblings of a drunk that cannot always be understood. Adam knew it was very late and neither of them cared. As long as they were together, that was all that mattered; they would think up lies to tell when they reached home.

Since the affair began, Olivia became more adventurous and less cautious. She believed that you had to live for today; the rest did not exist. She could not always see the chaos that she was creating as she swam through a sea of hedonism. Yesterday was gone. It was a history that cannot be changed. Tomorrow was forever coming, but never quite arriving. It was a chameleon as it changed into today! The only important moment was the now. They were living under a brightly coloured rainbow that would not last forever. They could not last a day without love.

When Olivia stopped the car, Adam stopped his drunken chatter and saw that they were in a wood. He knew they were near home, as they had driven for a while. Olivia pushed her seat forward and got into the back. Adam followed her rather clumsily, bumping his head on the roof. He wished that he was not so drunk now as he knew that what they were about to do next would be a blur in the morning, if even remembered. Most of tonight was already a blur. Then it began. Olivia and Adam were at each other like sumo wrestlers, pushing and pulling to get to the delights hidden beneath their clothes. It didn't quite work out as it should have, as Adam suddenly felt his salivary glands begin to work overtime. He opened the car door and got out quickly. If he was going to be sick, best to do it out of the car. He forgot that his trousers were round his ankles. His legs would not move and he took off, sprawling onto the muddy ground before him.

Olivia did not see what happened as she was getting out of her side of the car. She missed the show. As she tentatively picked her way round the back of the car, she saw Adam flat on his face in a mound of dirt and dead leaves, his dignity and sexual appeal now in tatters. Olivia bent down to help him up, and as Adam began to rise from the floor, so did the contents in his stomach. They were better out than in and spewed forth like a pyloric missile. Olivia could not stop herself laughing. "This is dreadful. Are you OK?"

Adam looked at her, his dark eyebrows meeting in the middle of a frown. "I don't know." He looked like a little boy who lost a shilling and found a penny. He could not have looked more ridiculous. There were twigs sticking out of his hair and his white legs, shining in the moonlight, were covered in mud. His mohair trousers rested on the tops of his now very dirty shoes. Never in all his life had he been in such a demeaning position. His failure to complete a love moment left Adam feeling very down.

Olivia turned away. Adam knew she was laughing: her shoulders gave it away. He quickly tidied himself and looked at his watch. It was four in the morning and they really had to go home. As they got into the car, Olivia began to giggle; she could not help herself, and she laughed out loud. "If this wasn't true, it would make a good book!" What a thing for her to say when he felt so crap! He soon forgot what had transpired in the woods as a song came on the radio that was the finale of the night. It was 'Together in Electric Dreams'. Tonight, they had been together in the mud, also.

Olivia and Adam soon settled into a routine. They snatched moments, afternoons and evenings, when they could get away from their other commitments. When she went to work, Olivia always parked her car in front of the hotel behind Adam's office. Some mornings he would see her as he walked into work with Gerry. He would catch Olivia watching them as she put her money into the ticket machine. Thank goodness this did not happen every day, but when it did, he would panic. Adam was afraid that Olivia would come across and speak to him. He would then have to explain to Gerry who she was. One thing he knew for sure was that Gerry and Olivia must never meet. Olivia was rather unpredictable and rash. One thing Adam was learning about Olivia was that she liked to live dangerously. Her spontaneity meant that she threw caution to the wind and he could never be sure what she might do or say next.

When Olivia left work in the afternoon, he would sneak ten minutes with her in the car park. They found it hard to be civilised and not give in to their passionate urges. These urges ran rampant through their veins, as they made small-talk in such a public place, telling each other what they were doing, discussing their families and when they would next meet. They would sheepishly grin at each other as Adam would watch Olivia drive away.

Olivia had a friend, Josie, who began to lend them her cottage on Wednesdays. That's what friends are for: not to judge, but to be of help, to be there, without saying a word when things go wrong. Josie was such a good friend and it was wonderful for Adam and Olivia to be able to sit on a sofa together, to make love in a bed with clean sheets instead of the back seat of the cramped blue love machine. The more they met, the more they learnt about each other. Love blossomed and time passed quickly. Adam and Olivia would snuggle up on Josie's sofa and listen to records. They would play their favourites to each other and sometimes sing together. One time, Olivia was quite surprised when Adam became very sentimental over a song. He turned to look at her as the needle dropped on 'A Day Without Love' by Love Affair. He sang the chorus. "A day

71

without love is a year with emptiness and your love brings me happiness. I can't stand a day without love." Adam sat down beside her and held her in his arms. Adam pulled Olivia close and rested his face in her freshly washed hair, rinsed in lavender. He knew this would be one of the moments never to be forgotten. It was that moment when two souls became one. It didn't always have to be carnal when they met, but most of the time it was. Togetherness came in many ways. Togetherness was very much like self-actualising. It was beholding a beautiful sunset, words of a song touching the soul, moments of ecstasy forever in the heart.

Those Wednesday nights were their little piece of heaven, their escape from frantic lives, when the only two people in the world were Adam and Olivia. Olivia always brought food with her: she loved to feed him. Their music nights at Josie's were full of bliss, and after clearing away the cups and tidying the kitchen, they would lock the door and leave the key for Josie to find on her return. One night, Adam pleaded with Olivia. "Can we have just one more song, please?" Olivia could not resist those brown eyes. She never said no to Adam. "It's important and we can be a bit late tonight, can't we?" Adam never wanted to leave. Tonight, the love-making had been extra special and went on and on.

Adam went across to the player and found the record he wanted. He looked across at Olivia as Sad Cafe began to sing 'Every Day Hurts'. Their gaze held as the messages of love, sadness and pain passed between them, the words of the song touching their hearts. Without speaking, Adam and Olivia acknowledged that one day this would all come to an end. There would be no future for them. For the time being it was their escape from things that were difficult in their lives, as they were both meeting a deep need that neither could understand.

That night they left Josie's on a sombre note. When it was Josie's birthday, Olivia and Adam bought her a book to thank her for supporting them. It was *Jonathan Livingston Seagull* by Richard Bach, and Olivia thought that everyone should have a copy on their bookshelf. Olivia was on a journey of self-discovery and she was learning more and more about the way she seemed to barge through life without thinking things out properly. Adam was amazed at the way she could talk for hours about philosophy, people and the world. He knew she was very clever, but never realised how intelligent she really was. But was her behaviour intelligent? What she was doing was not very intelligent at all. It was almost a contradiction of everything she stood for. Olivia and Adam spent many nights in the love cottage on the edge of the moors. Those times were the most important and the most memorable.

One Sunday afternoon on the way to a rehearsal in Leeds, they stopped and called in at a garden party. It wasn't one of Olivia's sanest moments. She failed to tell Adam that her mother and step-mother-in-law would be attending. Josie's friend was holding the event for the charity that Olivia ran. Josie was the treasurer and they made a good team. It was a glorious sunny day and Adam looked immaculate as ever, sporting beige slacks, pale blue shirt and navy blazer. Olivia looked like a little girl in her pink and yellow sundress. She wore Marilyn Monroe sunglasses and her hair was scraped back into a fifties, ponytail. "I hope you don't mind, but I do need to just drop in." Olivia smiled at Adam. "You can stay here if you want, but I don't know how long I shall be."

As they came through the gate of the garden, Olivia grabbed Adam's hand and dragged him to the tea tent. They sat down at a small wooden table with tea and scones when two ladies joined them. Olivia introduced Adam to her mother, who looked him up and down. "Hello, I saw you at the last fashion show. It was very good. I hear you are doing another one together. Doesn't your wife mind?" Olivia's mother did not wait for an answer. "My daughter is good at what she does, don't you think? She has always been wilful. I don't know how she does it. She gets people to do all sorts for her. Do you know her husband? He works so hard for the family." What was her mother doing? Could she be intimating at something? Or maybe she was just as chatty as her daughter. Adam smiled a very uncomfortable smile.

Little did he know, it was about to get much worse, as the stepmother-in-law began to ask prying questions. Adam wondered if Doris was a news reporter in her spare time. She was like a dog with a bone and she was not going to give up with her questions. She certainly put him on the spot with her observations. "You two do seem to spend a lot of time together. Olivia is hardly ever home these days." Doris began to send Adam on a massive guilt trip.

Olivia laughed and saved Adam replying by chirping in. "You know how much this charity means to me and the amount of people it helps. There is so much to do and I do it. Adam has kindly come onboard and is a great asset to all of us."

Doris eyed them both suspiciously. "Yes, of course he is. You, Olivia, just seem to have run a bit wild these days, you are never at home when I call and you need to think about what you are doing."

Adam hoped that they would be leaving for the rehearsal soon. The four continued to make small-talk until eventually the two women rose and said their goodbyes. Olivia's mother kissed Adam on the cheek, which meant she liked him. She liked everybody. Doris gave a pert "Goodbye", followed by a look that told Adam that she knew what they were up to.

When they sat in the car, Adam asked Olivia why they had gone there. He wasn't best pleased and did not look at her. Why on earth had she taken them there? Olivia looked at him with that wicked cynical grin that would light up her face. "It was time for you to meet them." She turned the ignition and drove away. Did Olivia know what a dangerous game she was playing?

A few weeks later, Olivia mentioned the garden party to Adam. She said her mother never said a word, but Doris had plenty to say. Doris rang Olivia a few days later and told her that she knew what was going on. It was obvious, and probably other people saw the connection between them in the garden. She said they could perhaps have been more discreet and not parade about like two juvenile peacocks. Adam asked Olivia what she said to that. Olivia opened her eyes wide, that well-known grin spreading across her face. "I lied, of course."

Adam didn't often daydream, but one day while he was having some 'me' time at his boat, he began to think about his relationship with Olivia, and as one thought led to another, he found himself thinking about the meaning of love. He had always been interested in the word 'love'. He looked for it, chased it, read about it and researched it. He never believed that he felt it. That was until he met Olivia. He was now experiencing feelings and emotions that were awakening in his soul, deeper than ever before. There were countless films and books written about it. There are all kinds of love: sexual love and love of family. There is love for pets, love of money, love of material things, and spiritual love. Many times, had he heard and read, "I am not in love with you, but I do love you." What does that mean, being 'in' love and just loving?

Loving is for the material, possessions and pets, family, work, what a person does. You cannot be 'in love' with those. Does that mean that 'being in love' is about romance and passion for someone with whom you had a sexual bond and relationship? With that type of love there is a downside. There can be jealousy, obsession, infatuation and ownership. Adam was fascinated by the love of two people and all that it entailed. He read books and listened to music about it. This was a secret romantic side of him that most of the time remained hidden. If there was an exam on love, Adam would surely pass it. He knew so much about it, but wasn't sure if he could do it.

Love is a law unto itself and cannot be owned. It comes and goes of its own accord. It can be colourful and brilliant like a rainbow, and then it might begin to fade and nothing can stop that. Love can be blind, unconditional and without reason. People say things they think explain the way they feel. "I don't know why I love her, but I do." Love cannot be controlled. The physical side of love, perhaps, is controlled by oestrogen and testosterone levels in the body, to a point. There can be instant attraction, with love and attachment growing over a period of time. At times, attraction can be inexplicable, with no reason. Attachment can be a bonding at different levels. It can be superficial or go very deep.

Love needs commitment, without which it can be termed infatuation or even lust. The love that is obsession can destroy the purity of what is and lead into disturbing behaviours and the person wanting to own the other, strangling their right to personal space. Infatuation does not last, but obsession can go on forever if not dealt with. Obsession can be destructive and grow like a poison, in the name of love.

As Adam stopped polishing the boat, his eyes rested on a passing bird, and he felt a rush of feeling rising from his toes through to the top of his head as he thought of Olivia. She loved birds. In fact, she loved all animals. The nearest Adam believed he had ever been to love was now. He loved 'Brown Eyes'. Those eyes were the most beautiful he had ever looked into. They were pools of desire that spoke to him: "I want you."

In his musings, Adam came to understand why he never loved Mary and why for a time he thought he loved Gerry. That was before it began to fade and go sour. It was about the needs met by the other person. Mary mothered him: therefore, she was a mother-figure. Gerry never said much at all unless it was to moan: so she was more of a habit and didn't really figure at all, as she was no longer meeting any of Adam's needs.

Defining love is difficult and a very personal experience. Falling in love might be easy, but staying in love was hard. On many occasions, Adam felt that he was falling in love, but it began to fade after the woman said something or did something that changed his feelings very quickly. He found that love did not conquer all. It disappeared as a rainbow fades in the sky, until the next one appears. It was the rainbow that he was always chasing but never catching. Love did not make allowances for flaws, did it? Did a person have to tick all the boxes of perfection, or was it reasonable to make compromises just for the sake of having someone in your life?

People search for love, yearn for it, compromise to get it. They put up with things in order to have what they think is love. You cannot have love, you cannot own it. Love comes and goes as it pleases. It is free.

Adam felt that Olivia ticked all his boxes. His question was: for how long? As Adam finished off the polishing, he wondered: "How do I know that I love you, Brown Eyes?" Not because he said it in the Italian restaurant. Not because they had the best sex ever. Not because he felt a stirring in his loins every time, he thought of her; and not because Olivia said she loved him. Adam's feelings were fluid. They ebbed and flowed like some tidal river. He felt that love was marked by happenings and occasions of great feeling, leaving footprints and memories on the heart, with sighs and smiles and longing for more. Love at its best is unconditional; it comes as a gift. It is that 'in the moment' feeling people hope will stay forever, and sometimes it does.

During the summer months, Adam and Olivia continued to see each other when they could. On days that they did not go to Josie's cottage, Adam would leave his car parked behind the George and Dragon near the canal. Olivia would drive them to his boat on the river. They spent quality time there, doing what lovers do. One particular Wednesday, Adam played truant from work and they spent the whole afternoon and evening on the river. Olivia picked him up in her new car, a white one. The little blue love machine was no more. There was more room in the back of this one and the back seat had been christened on more than one occasion, as physical need for each other would overwhelm them. This would lead to moments of passion that left them both tired and spent.

That day was one of the hottest days of the summer. Olivia had her hair clipped back off her face, the blonde curls hanging down her back, just waiting for Adam to run his fingers through them. Her blue cropped vest complemented the magnificent cleavage of her breasts that were straining to burst out of a perfectly fitting bra. Olivia always wore beautiful undergarments. They were co-ordinated and complemented her delightful figure. She wore boxer knickers that contradicted the phrase 'less is more'. In this case, it was reversed to 'more is less'.

Adam thought about Mary and the way she let herself go after having the children. Now she wore old granny knickers for comfort and was in her element playing mother to everybody she could play mother to. Mary had no further use for Adam, apart from his role as provider and taxi driver. Mary was very different to Gerry in the underwear department. Gerry wore thongs. Little straps of colour that left little to the imagination and were stupid. Gerry thought she looked sexy in them. Adam didn't. A lot of men loved those little pieces of material stuck up the bottom. Maybe that was why he was going off Gerry. Maybe it was the thongs? Adam loved the knickers Olivia wore. He also loved it when she took them off and he loved it even more if he took them off for her.

As Adam got into the car, he noticed the hamper on the back seat. He asked Olivia about it.

"It's a late lunch. Not sure what to call a meal between lunch and tea; the other side of twelve it's brunch," she laughed. "I know, let's call it tunch. We will have tunch!" They rolled the windows down. The tape in the car was playing old sixties songs and they sang along to them. They were lost in the happiness of each other and a glorious summer's day. Olivia's brown legs were barely covered by the white shorts, and Adam rested his hand on her thigh as she drove, moving his hand ever closer to her mystery, teasing her. Adam already knew what would happen that afternoon: good food, good music, good woman and good everything!

CHAPTER SIX

As Adam and Olivia came through the gate, they looked at each other and smiled. The boat looked inviting as it bobbed up and down on the river. Adam carried the wicker hamper down into the cabin, while Olivia tied the bottle of champagne to a rope and slowly lowered it into the cool water. As Adam went about his business, unlocking, sorting, readying the boat for the 'off', he hummed to himself. This was a happy moment. He had waited for this moment for so long. His first dream of Olivia was to be on this boat with her.

Olivia chose some music to put on the player. She decided on something demure as she sensed that this would be an afternoon to remember. Being a 'forever' drama queen, Olivia thought everything out, right down to the smallest detail. Because she gave lots of thought to what she did, her friends called her a control freak. She didn't think she was. She was just extremely organised. It was important to her as she was always making memories. When the perfect music began, Adam shouted down to Olivia, asking what it was.

"Have you not heard of George Gershwin?" Adam gave a negative reply. "'Rhapsody in Blue' is one of my favourite pieces." A faraway look came into her eyes as she remembered when her husband bought her the record for their second wedding anniversary. That was a different time, and now she was much older but not much wiser. Adam entered the cabin to see a table of splendour. It was covered in food to nibble on: pâté, salmon, strawberries, cheese, salad and sliced tiger bread with fresh butter. During 'tunch', Adam and Olivia laughed and joked, feeding each other titbits from their plates. They quickly cleared the table and washed up in order to clear a space in the small cabin. After the sumptuous meal, Olivia poured the champagne and they sat together at the back of the boat. The sun warmed them, smiling down on them as they chatted about nothing in particular.

This was a perfect picture of two people in love, a perfect afternoon, a perfect time in their lives. Lost in her thoughts, she sipped the champagne as the bubbles tickled her nose. The music brought thoughts of the past. Olivia thought her marriage to her childhood sweetheart would be forever. Then he went and had an affair, which killed her dreams and ruined her idea of how things should be. Olivia crawled her way through the battle with the 'bunny boiler' and saved the marriage in order to give her boys the good life that they had grown used to. Had she let her husband go, then their lives would have changed, and she loved her husband even after he did what he did to her. Olivia did not like what she was doing now, but she knew she must not feel the guilt as it would ruin the pleasure of the moment. She was perhaps foolish to live in the moment, but it was part of her that she could do nothing about. This was not revenge for what had happened previously, as the horror of what her husband did was many years gone by, and whilst forgiven, it was not forgotten. There would always be three people in her marriage. It was as it was! This was a diversion from the hard time at home and, once set in motion, the ball would not stop rolling.

Sometimes, Olivia felt like Scarlett O'Hara from *Gone with the Wind*, who also didn't give a thought to the consequences of her actions and only lived in the moment. Olivia liked all kinds of music, and Adam found he was learning a lot from her — and not just about music. He was learning the true meaning of feelings and love. One of the things that he loved about Olivia was that she was a very industrious person. She was always scribbling into a notebook that she kept in her bag. Adam knew that if he were to remember anything about Olivia in the future, it would be her writing. That would remain with him throughout his life. It would become a fond memory. For now, it was a reality, his reality.

Now and again Olivia would read some of her poetry and stories to him. Adam liked what he heard, but was no judge. He was not much of a reader and had nothing to compare it to. His eyes would never leave that beautiful, expressive face. He would watch the animated emotions run across her features and he would sigh. He realised that she had missed her way. She could have been an actress. Adam had a contentment that he had not felt in years.

It was very hot in the small cabin as they lay in each other's arms. They were stuck together by a layer of sweat. The result of their love exertions left them complete and satiated. Adam stroked Olivia's hair, thinking that if there ever was a perfect moment, then this was it. He wanted it to never end, to go on and on and on.

CHAPTER SEVEN

Adam heard a voice. "Sir, would you like another drink or anything from duty free? We will be coming around again before we land."

Adam opened his eyes and looked around, and a feeling of disappointment met him as he realised that he wasn't in the nightclub or on his boat. He was on a plane, miles away from Leeds, the memory of a nearly forgotten past still brightly shining in his mind. Adam politely asked for another gin and tonic. At this rate, he would not be sober when he reached his destination. He was determined to make this his last drink. He stared at the photograph on the page before him. Of course, he remembered Olivia. He had never forgotten her; just hidden her behind his more recent memories.

She did not look much older. Age had treated her well. There was the same twinkle in her eyes topping the cynical smile that, without warning, would turn into a cheeky grin. Something was different, though, and he studied the face that he had kissed a thousand times in another life. Then he saw it. Behind the smile, in the eyes, there was a sadness that startled him. Adam wondered if he was part of the sadness. There it was again, his arrogance, his ego. She probably wouldn't even remember him. He felt a lost yearning. Feelings long gone now began to return with a vengeance. If only things could have been different. Adam carried many a regret that could not be rectified. He had come to realise that dwelling on the past was an utter waste of time. The only way to survive was to never look back and to always look forward.

Adam washed the feelings away with a drink of the cool alcohol before him. He looked out at the clouds, a bed of fluffy cotton wool beneath the giant metal bird winging its way across the skies to a new life and new experiences. His thoughts began to wander back to his time with Olivia.

~

Adam and Olivia spent many happy hours on that little boat on the river. Driving down the A64 towards York was always a pleasure. Olivia would always drive, which left him free to watch those beautiful brown legs as they moved up and down, controlling the clutch and the gas. Adam would gently stroke Olivia's inner thigh and she would concentrate on the road, trying to ignore his hand working its way up into her knickers as they were waiting for red to turn to green at traffic lights. His fingers would probe and poke as a small gasp would break through the rhythm of her breathing and a feeling of warmth would flood his active hand. As they sped along, Adam would fantasise about taking her at the side of the road. He abandoned himself to his primal desires for her. He loved to feel the wetness of her passion. When he wasn't touching Olivia, he spent a lot of time thinking about touching her.

In Olivia's company, Adam saw no one but 'She'. Olivia was she, with the amazing body; she, with the beautiful brown eyes; she, with the long blonde hair. She was all to him and he lived for the moments that they could be together, however long or short the time might be. They would escape into their private world of love and sex. The safe havens on the boat and Josie's cottage somehow made right the wrong that they were doing. Gone were the days of climbing into the back seat of the little love machine, and contorting in a steamy, enclosed space of love juice and sweat. Having a bed to lie on and some private space brought some seriousness to what they were doing together. It made something right that wasn't right at all.

They fooled each other into thinking that they were not hurting anyone. They fooled each other into thinking they were doing no wrong and there was no guilt attached to their clandestine meetings. How wrong they both were. The lies and cheating on their spouses, was bad. They both ignored the fact that it would only hurt others if their secret became public. How could two adults be so naïve? Adam was hurting four people — his wife, his mistress and his children, — with his constant lies, and he was lying to Olivia, too. Olivia was hurting her husband and her children by her behaviour. She was not being true to them. She was not meeting her obligations. Both Adam and Olivia became hedonists overnight and they did not seem to care. Olivia was the spirit of love that brightened Adam's day when they spoke on the phone. Adam was the nemesis that Olivia was unaware of. They talked for hours. Talking of dreams of what their children would have been like, where they would have lived and how happy they would always be. Adam wanted Olivia so much, and as his thoughts wandered further into the past, he felt a rush of blood to the part of him that longed for her most; which was not his heart.

~

A pulse began to throb between Adam's legs and he discreetly moved the magazine. He thought it might hide his rising bump. He took a drink, hoping his embarrassment would soon subside without eruption. It was time to rise and stretch his legs, amongst other things. He moved out into the aisle and made his way to the front of the plane. As he waited his turn for the lavatory, Adam surveyed the aircraft. It was full, and he could not make the faces out of the travellers. He made a mental note to get his eyes tested. Ten minutes later, Adam was back in his seat, feeling gratified and ready to enjoy the next drink.

~

Adam had never ever been with a woman who was so positive, so passionate. Olivia taught him the meaning of joy and love. He felt more alive than he ever had before. This would be a day to remember — he could feel it in his bones. As Adam navigated the boat upriver, he held Olivia close. She always smelled so nice, the same perfume, the heady scent of 'Opium', and one he knew he would never forget. It played with his senses and made him want her again and again. Once more Olivia put some music on the tape that he did not know.

"It is *Out of Africa*. Have you not seen the film?"

"No."

She went on to tell him the story of Karen Blixen and her life in British East Africa and her love affair with Denys Finch Hatton. Olivia told him that Meryl Streep and Robert Redford were well cast and the film won seven Oscars out of eleven nominations. Her favourite song was 'The Music of Goodbye' sung by Al Jarreau and Melissa

Manchester, which was not actually sung in the film. Only the tune was played. As Adam and Olivia cruised up the river, they listened to the words, which were a reflection of their affair and the love they had. As the song ended, Adam pulled Olivia closer, never wanting this moment to end. Olivia waved at a cruise boat going by. It was filled with smiling tourists. "It's a true story and they didn't get together as, in the end, he died and she went back to Denmark." Olivia was not stopping for breath, again! "I remember the first line. Meryl Streep was so good. She began with, 'I had a farm in Africa'." Olivia put her head back and laughed as she ended with, "I had a man on his boat."

Fifteen minutes later, they moored up near a bridge and walked into the town, hand in hand. Stopping at an ice cream parlour, they bantered about which flavours to get. The assistant waited with a big smile on her face and a certain look in her eye. "I can tell you two are in love."

Olivia and Adam looked at each other and smiled a knowing smile. They window-shopped and discussed which ornaments they would buy for their pretend house and which toys they would buy for their pretend children. The afternoon was moving quickly into the evening and Olivia became quiet and thoughtful. In a concerned tone, Adam asked her what was wrong. Olivia looked up at him with tears in her eyes. "One day I shall tell my grandchildren, I was so happy once with a man in York."

Adam felt his heart melting under those words as a rush of love hit him, like never before. He became lost in the moment and floated into his imagination, leaving his thoughts in the privacy of his mind. He didn't know what to say.

CHAPTER EIGHT

As Adam was flying to New York, he was remembering his time with Olivia in every detail. He could smell the river. He could smell Olivia's perfume. He could almost reach out and touch her as though she was standing before him. What he wouldn't give now, just to see her once more! He shook his head: what a fool he was to have let her go. He should have thought more. That was his problem, sometimes Adam didn't think. He took a large drink, nearly missing the table as he put the glass back down. The man beside him looked at him. "Are you all right?"

Adam looked at the picture on his lap, then at the man. "Yes, I am fine. Must be tired." He put his head back and closed his eyes. He did not want to talk just now. He could not stop the memories that were crashing into his mind. Adam silently screamed, "Please stop. This is really hurting me." The memories laughed and kept on.

~

Summer turned into a glorious autumn. Olivia and Adam continued their affair. They met when they could, but found it difficult to work around children, school runs and the demands of being married to other people. They never missed their time at the boat. Wednesdays were so special, and one afternoon by the river, as Adam stepped back into the cabin he gave no thought to the time, as earlier he told his PA, Hilary, that he would be tied up all afternoon in Leeds with clients and would not be returning to the office that day. He told her if Mary rang to pass the message on that he might be late home. He really did not want to speak to Mary today as he knew he would be interrogated by her and she would just go on and on. It reminded him of when he was a young boy and his mother would always be asking questions that had no answers.

That day, the drive across to York was again filled with music and laughter. Olivia made him feel like a twenty-year-old. She brought him happiness and joy. The boat looked inviting as they came through the locked gate that kept things safe. Olivia went down into the cabin, while Adam busied himself. A fisherman walking along the footpath caught his eye. Lost in a moment, Adam realised that time was precious and he rushed his jobs, as he wanted to spend as much time as he could with his colourful rainbow. He thought of Olivia as a rainbow: she was always dressed in bright colours. Olivia had so many colourful sides to her personality. She was amazing. He heard the music that was coming from the cabin. It was calling him to stop what he was doing.

As he came down the steps, Adam saw Olivia laid on the bunk with a white sheet pulled up to her chin, knowing that underneath was a body perfectly formed, that fit him so well. He knew it was waiting for his lips and his caresses. Big brown eyes were peering up at him above a grin that lit up the room. Olivia held her arm up and beckoned him to join her. She did not have to ask twice. Adam undid his belt and slid out of his trousers, his eyes never leaving hers. His manhood was standing to attention in anticipation of a lustful adventure in the bowel of his boat. That afternoon the passion was like no other. It was perfection, as they slowly swayed to the motion of a lust that was born of fervour for each other. This kind of lust only surfaced in illicit relationships as time flew by unattended.

Adam worked his magic on Olivia's body. He gently stroked her and, kissing her lips, began to slowly move down the skin that had a faint aroma of lavender. He lingered at her nipples. He dipped his finger into the juice that was on the bedside table. He watched the drops slowly drip onto areola that were screaming for attention. He placed his mouth over the area, licking and sucking the sweet blackcurrant that was now running down onto breasts that were free and inviting. The way Olivia responded to his fingers, his tongue, his mouth, was awesome. They were moments in time that he would savour and remember, until he would be kissing those glorious breasts once more. They made love slowly and with grace, until one final thrust confirmed his passion and he spilled out into her with a deep-throat moan. He slowly pulled back to look down as he was about to leave the warmth of her love bucket.

They lay together, spent and happy. Two people could never be as close as when they are curled up together in the aftermath of loving.

Love-making brings an intimacy that exceeds friendship. It binds people together in an everlasting promise of more to come. Adam began to wipe up the juices that were created in a moment of wanton neediness. He took a wet wipe and put his hands between Olivia's legs. He slowly wiped the passion water that sprung forth from his loins and mixed with her waterfall of lust.

Olivia rose from the bunk and put on Adam's shirt, her modesty returning. They put the bunks up and replaced the table top. The bed disappeared. Order and function restored to the small cabin. Neither spoke as they dressed in silence, knowing that soon they would have to return to the real world. They would have to return to their respective families, to their other lives, and this would be just another memory. Before they returned home, they sailed up the river, singing "At night I lie awake and try in vain to take, my mind off this confusion; was our love just an illusion, I'll never really know." This song, 'A day without Love' by Philip Goodhand-Tait was fast becoming their song. The aroma of Olivia's perfume, slowly penetrated the heat of a dying summer afternoon. They were truly in the moment. Nothing else existed, only each other wrapped up in a dream.

Driving back to Leeds, they dwelt in sombre moments as they knew they would soon have to part. Olivia appeared to be fine, if not a little quiet. Stopping at a pub on the ring road, Adam went to buy Olivia her usual gin and tonic. As he carried it and his pint of beer back to the table, he smiled wistfully. They always stopped at this pub for the last drink to leave their time together behind them. It was always so sad for them. Returning from the ladies' room, Olivia was again wearing that wicked grin that Adam had come to love so much. She was always laughing. It was part of who she was. Olivia did not have a bad bone in her body. She never criticised and never spoke ill of anyone.

Olivia loved, she played and she cried. At times, when his conscience got the better of him, Adam would tell her they must stop meeting. Olivia would turn to look at him and her big brown eyes would cry. The fear that overcame that beautiful face at the thought of losing him would make him feel worse than he already did. Olivia was an innocent who loved him for who he was: she had no agendas. The problem was that Adam did have an agenda. He always had an agenda.

On the rare occasion that guilt got the better of him, Adam would remember that he was married and he could never escape that fact. At times, Adam wondered if he could perhaps leave the marriage to be with Olivia forever. It wasn't the first time that Adam had dreams of being released from his sad, superficial life. He spent most of his time pretending that it was what he wanted. He would tell himself that he was happy. Adam was not happy. Truth be known, he would never leave his wife and he would never be happy. Married men seldom took that leap of faith into a life with the woman they really loved. Most of the time they were just replacing the sex that was lacking as the familiarity of a marriage could kill passion. They sought to find the thrill elsewhere. There would always be a lonely woman in a loveless marriage always chasing a rainbow and living more than a day without love.

Adam continued to think that all he wanted was to leave everything behind and start a new life with Olivia. Change can be so difficult. One day Adam would have to make some sort of decision and someone would spend some time hurting. He would make sure it was not to be him. He was tortured by his lust for Olivia and his love of her. His addiction to her always got the better of him. It always outran his guilt, and he would quickly forget the vows and promises he made to Mary all those years ago. He would also forget the promises he made to Gerry.

Olivia was obsessed with Adam. Maybe more than she was obsessed with music. There was always a tune in the car and now it was Dillard and Johnson's 'Here We Go Loving Again.' They drove back to end the day with a sad parting kiss, they said goodbye. The final kiss of their clandestine meeting would linger on Adam's lips as he always watched Olivia drive away before he returned to his lie of a life with his motherly wife and his sullen, troubled mistress.

Adam realised that whilst Olivia was one, in a long line of women, he had affairs with, he loved her with a passion he had never felt before. She reeled his heart in so tightly in the chaos that was his life. She brought a wildness of spirit that was a contradiction of the peace that came, as she ran barefoot through his soul. Olivia taught Adam how to live in the moment, for that is all they had. Those stolen moments in time that would remain forever in their history. Experiences that played a part in moulding the people they were to become.

Olivia taught Adam the true meaning of what love is, and there were no words to describe it. Love just *is*. It is not words. It is doing. It is action that confirms words that can be meaningless and empty when coming from the wrong person.

CHAPTER NINE

August of that year was one of the hottest. Adam was on his own, as the rest of the family were abroad at a family wedding. He didn't want to go. He could not stand the thought of sitting with Mary's noisy relatives and having to tell her that she looked lovely in the hideous orange silk dress that she had bought to take with her. It actually made her look like an over-ripe peach. Mary bought the dress at Carol's dress agency, and he just hadn't the heart to tell her it did not suit her. He was not that callous. She believed she looked wonderful. Adam could not tell her she looked like a burst Satsuma. He did not want to burst her bubble.

It wasn't that easy to get out of his obligation to go with his wife. Adam used the excuse that he had a large account to close, so he had to stay. He told Mary he would try and make it, catch another flight if he got his job done. It was another lie to add to his long list of lies. Adam felt that it would give him some time to spend with Gerry, who was becoming fractious and demanding. He knew that he neglected Gerry. It was hard juggling three women. He was beginning to detest Gerry and could not see a way out. He was in such a dilemma. He was scared that she might tell Mary about their long affair if he dumped her. He knew at some stage he would have to let her go; the question was, when? Adam hadn't seen much of Olivia. They had spoken on the phone a few times. She seemed very busy, and it was beginning to annoy him. The last phone call didn't go too well. "We could go to the boat for the day. She won't be back till September."

Olivia was rattled with him. "Oh, well, as long as you got rid of your family, I suppose that is all right then? What shall I do with mine then? Bring them along?"

Adam concentrated on his work, but it did not stop him looking across the square to catch a glimpse of Olivia at work. After a few weeks when he hadn't seen her, he called in. Michael, her manager, said that she was taking leave and would be back in a few weeks.

Then there came a diversion to his dilemma when one night he got the surprise of his life. 'Brown Eyes' was out with her friends that night, celebrating a birthday, and he was having a quiet night in. Late into the night, when Adam was feeling quite lonely, the phone rang and he heard a drunken whisper. Olivia was whispering to him and he gave her back the words that he knew would melt her resistance, as he needed her so much. As the sex-laden words passed between them, Adam found that his erection was beginning to dictate his thinking. How could he be rational when all he could think of was the brown body on the other end of the telephone? He wanted her so badly. It was the middle of the night.

Olivia lived far from him and she was drunk, very drunk. It did not stop him telling her how much he wanted her. How much he wanted her body. How much he loved to play with those nipples in his mouth. How he loved to suck them hard to the point of pain. This was the pain that began the ecstasy. He talked to her of her Venus mound and the entrance to her ever-demanding love tunnel. The way her muscles would tighten round him and drive him wild. He went on and on. Adam pleaded with Olivia to come over to the house, knowing it would not happen. They played cat and mouse over the network. After much coaxing and many a sexual innuendo, he knew what would be coming next.

"No, I can't come." Olivia put the phone down on him.

Pouring himself a large brandy, Adam smiled and returned to watch the film he had paused earlier.

Half an hour later, there was a large bang at the door. Adam, enthralled in his film, had forgotten about the earlier phone call. The door banged once more. "No, it can't be?" It was! There she stood, barefoot, at his front door. Olivia was wearing a turquoise duster coat that covered her from her neck to her ankles. Tiny painted pink toenails showed beneath. Her feet looked luminous in the moonlight. It was full moon that night, a time for lunatics and madness. The moon cast an eerie shadow over Olivia and his mouth dropped open in a wordless gasp. The coat was way too big for her and he looked at her feet. Where were her shoes? Adam's eyes slowly travelled up to her face. Olivia was wearing a stupid grin as she swayed in the night air. Their eyes met.

"Aren't you going to ask me in, then?" She was slurring. Adam had never seen her so inebriated. She was some crazy lady to have driven across town in such a state. He knew that Olivia worked hard and deserved some fun. He wasn't sure if this was fun or not. Adam liked to play safe, and this was certainly not safe. He took hold of Olivia's hand and led her past the kitchen and into the lounge. He made her a cup of coffee as he chastised her for driving over in such a state. Olivia never said a word, and an awkward silence fell between them. Adam did not like the silence. It made him feel very uncomfortable.

He never ever knew what Olivia was thinking. Sometimes, silence came before she did something rash, and he couldn't tell what that might be. They had done some mad things together and she never failed to surprise him. Adam loved Olivia for her spontaneity. Perhaps it was something to do with her being a Leo. She was the queen, the entertainer who took centre stage in life. She was all that Leos can be and more. She was all he was not. He wondered why he had avoided her in the previous weeks. He had not returned her calls and as the weeks went by, he almost forgot her. Adam was busy and trying to keep Gerry sweet. As Mary was away, Gerry demanded more of his time, and he regained his feelings for her in a way that surprised him. He could not bring himself to end his relationship with Olivia, so he chose to ignore her. He could not ignore her now and was kicking himself for being so lustful on the phone.

Olivia asked Adam to put some music on. He chose George Benson, as it was past midnight and the time called for some mood music. He thought it might calm Olivia down, but was not sure if he wanted her to calm down or not. Adam didn't know what he wanted. 'Loving on Borrowed Time' began, and a cool, deep voice entered the room. Adam sat down beside Olivia and asked her why she had not taken her coat off, as it was a very hot night. He went on and on about her driving whilst drunk, a very stupid thing to do. Very stupid indeed!

Olivia turned her head slowly to the side and looked at him, her thick dark eyelashes framing her brown pools of soul. For a split second he saw the wickedness in those eyes that were now burning into his, accelerating the rising heat in his groin.

"I will take my coat off when I am ready."

Adam wondered what she meant. He knew Olivia well enough to understand that she thrived on the theatrical, so he waited. Adam watched Olivia slowly take the last sip from her cup and put it down on the floor.

She rose from the sofa and began to slowly move in time to the music, turning towards him. Adam sank back deep into the softness of the crimson cushions, savouring the moment.

Olivia ran her fingers through her hair and peered at him from under the lashes that framed those pods of beauty. Oh, wow! Was she going to do a lap dance or just a strip? Olivia's hand reached for the top button of her coat. In a very controlled way, she began to unbutton it, her eyes never leaving Adam's face. She reached for the last button, making sure that the coat never opened, and stood up straight. Without warning, the coat was thrown across the room and there she stood in all her glory, her naked body shining in the lamp light. Adam was aghast and absolutely mesmerised: never had he thought she would be naked under that big coat. Not even when he saw her bare feet at the door. The moment seemed to last forever as his eyes left hers to travel down the magnificent body that had lain with him many times before. Adam felt as though his manhood would explode. Well, he couldn't ignore her now, could he?

Olivia smiled, never losing the wickedness that masked her face. She fell to her knees and slowly ran her hands up the inside of Adam's thighs until she found what she was looking for. The belt on his dressing gown came loose and Adam was now exposed and at her mercy. Olivia's hand reached for his shaft and she leant forward, taking him into her mouth. Adam gasped and let out a loud moan. He felt that if his manhood did not explode, his brain might or his heart might. He loved it when she sucked him hard and milked his manhood in a way that no woman had ever done before. This might have been due to the fact that Adam's feelings for Olivia were real. There had been many women before her, and Adam hoped this would be the last one. He could not go on like he was doing. There had to come a time when he would grow up and stop running around like a teenager who had found a penis between his legs.

Olivia knew what she was good at and performed well. Just as Adam was about to orgasm, Olivia stopped and pulled back and straddled him as she slowly lowered herself down onto his throbbing manhood. Adam went slowly and deeply into her cavern, closing his eyes in pure ecstasy as he searched for her womanhood, the spot that would make her scream. She leant forward, her tummy resting on his, and he began to stroke her breasts gently, as if they might break, were he not careful. Erect nipples stood waiting in anticipation for his mouth. Olivia began to sway backwards and forwards, her hips moving up and down, up and down. All Adam had to do was feast on her breasts, lie back and enjoy. As Olivia began to move faster, he felt her buttocks banging against his legs. Adam felt Olivia's wetness as it began to pour forth, lubricating in order to open her more and more to accommodate his hard, throbbing joy stick. Then the world ended — one almighty thrust and he filled her with his juices and they lay together, his arms around her, never wanting to let go. The floating sensation soon left him as he realised, they were leaking all over the velvet sofa.

Adam ran to the kitchen to get a cloth, as the juices would play havoc with the velvet pile on the sofa and probably leave a stain. He would never be able to explain a stain on Mary's beloved sofa. When he came back from the kitchen, he met Olivia's gaze above the collar of the coat that was now firmly buttoned up again and hiding the love machine that was she. Olivia grinned and winked. "Well, you won't ever be able to sit the same again on there, will you? Now that I have shagged you on it?" She was right: they had christened the sofa. Olivia had marked his space, come into his house and had her way with him.

Olivia stood on tip-toe, kissed him and suddenly she was gone. Adam sat down. He was stunned. Had he just woken up from a dream? Was this real? Was this the rainbow he had chased? It *was* real. He could still smell her perfume. He stared at the large wet mark on the sofa. When Olivia had her orgasm, it was like turning on a tap: she went on and on. The faint odour of sex permeated the room as he lost himself in the foggy meanderings of what had just happened, only to be roused by the phone ringing. Adam knew who it would be and he came back to reality very quickly. "Hello, Mary."

CHAPTER TEN

The cool breeze was blowing through Adam's hair. The heather was in bloom, providing a purple and mauve blanket that shimmered in the sunlight. The harshness of Ilkley Moor and its surroundings were lost under a bright blue sky. The breeze was still holding the warmth of a receding summer. There she was, his Olivia, running towards him in a gathered multi-coloured skirt and white gypsy blouse, her hair flowing freely in the breeze and her face only carrying a hint of mascara and some neutral lip shine. Adam was lost in the moment and his heart skipped a beat. No one was likely to be here on the moor that he knew of. There were only sheep for company and the occasional kestrel searching the moor for its food. They often met by the Celtic cross and would sit for hours, talking and loving. Had Emily Brontë been alive, she might have commented, "There they are! My Catherine and my Heathcliffe." Olivia was like Catherine Earnshaw in *Wuthering Heights*. Catherine was a wild woman full of passion who never stopped to think about the consequences of her actions. She was a manipulator of Heathcliffe, as well as Edgar Linton in order to get what she thought she wanted. Adam knew that Olivia, in time, might get what she wanted. Although he wasn't quite sure what that was. Just now he wanted her badly as she ran towards him. Was she what he really needed? People did not always get what they wanted — they sometimes got what they needed. He wanted and needed her, there was no doubt about that.

Adam and Olivia both manipulated each other. Both had needs that they were able to meet. Both were actors in the stage play that was being written and constantly rewritten to address both wants and needs, with little thought for others in their lives. They often made love amongst the heather. It wasn't always the most comfortable environment, and neither cared who saw them. They abandoned themselves to the elements and the harshness of the moor. The moor left them with scratches on their bottoms and legs. It did not matter. It was a sign of the wild abandon in which they took each other to new heights of passion.

Not long after their day on the moor, Adam met Olivia after work in their usual place. What happened in the ten minutes behind his office was to be a surprise for them both and quite unexpected. Olivia looked so sweet and innocent that day, when he realised it was all getting too much for him. "We can't go on like this." He looked away in sadness. It did not stop what he said next. "It is best we end it now. I am so sorry." The silence was demanding and Adam slowly turned to look at her. As Olivia looked up at him, the little girl innocence on her face changed to one of shock-horror. Her eyes widened and darkened into deep pools of tears that he knew she would not let spill. He was taking away this little girl's lollipop. She sat in silence, staring at him. The silence began to deafen him. He had not expected this. He thought she might beg and plead with him like other women he dumped in the past. Or perhaps she might get angry and hit him. One woman, whose name he couldn't remember, gave him a black eye. He had found it difficult to explain to Mary where his injury came from. Olivia was different. She just continued to stare at him as a solitary tear ran down her cheek.

"I'd better go. I am sorry, Olivia, truly I am." Adam choked on his words. "It has been a wonderful experience, but the longer it goes on the chances that we shall be caught are increasing, and I don't want you to get into trouble."

Olivia turned to look out of the car window. A wave of panic began to rise from deep inside and she felt sick to her stomach. She could not speak, but heard the voice in her head screaming, "Why? Oh, no! This is not happening."

Adam went on to say it was not easy for him and he would never forget her and the time they had together. No one could ever take the memories from them. He stepped out of the car and, without a word, Olivia sped away. That was it, she was gone. Adam slowly walked back to the office, wondering if he had done the right thing. He felt terrible as he began to question his motives for dumping her. There was no answer, and he knew that he would probably regret his spur-of-the-moment decision.

As days turned into weeks, Adam found himself staring across the street to the office where Olivia worked, hoping to catch a glimpse of her. He never did. He never saw her. He would look to see her in the car park after work, but she was never there. Her car was never there. He began to wonder what she was doing now. How she was? He missed the wicked grin. He missed the chatterbox that came out with such wonderful 'one-liners' that he had to laugh. There was never a dull moment in Olivia's company, and he always used to wonder what she might say next.

One rainy afternoon, his curiosity got the better of him. It had been one of those days. A lost contract and some sharp words from his boss sent Adam on a downward spiral. A wedding he was hosting was cancelled and the day got greyer as it progressed. Adam was missing Olivia so much. He never had grey days when she was in his life. She had a knack of putting positive perspectives on everything, no matter how bad it seemed at the time.

He picked up the phone, not knowing the type of reception he was about to get. "Hello, who is this, please?" a tiny, sing-song voice greeted him.

"I miss you." Nothing happened. "Olivia, are you there?"

"Yes."

"I miss you." Nothing happened. This was as unnerving as the day in the restaurant when he confessed his love for her, all those months ago. "Can you forgive me? I made a mistake. Can we meet?" He could hear her breathing and he just wanted her to speak, to say something. He wanted her to tell him he was a bastard for what he did to her, to shout 'go to hell'. He was probably going to hell anyway for the lies and everything else in his life.

"I miss you, too." There was a click of the phone as Olivia disconnected the call.

Adam needed a coffee and as he walked over to the machine, Gerry looked up at him and smiled. It was Thursday, the day he went to tea at Gerry's and bedded her, before he went back home to Mary. Adam didn't return Gerry's smile. He didn't want to be there. He was finding it harder and harder to get an erection with Gerry. He also wanted to keep his options open. Gerry was another mess he couldn't get out of. There was no escape. His life was a minefield just waiting to explode. Adam closed his office door behind him and put the coffee down. He sat at his desk with his head in his hands. Adam did not often feel sorry for himself, but today was an exception. He could not bear to think about the mistake he made and what he had thrown away after such a perfect summer. What a fool he was to have hurt Olivia and tell her it was over.

Well, after the phone call, he knew it definitely was and she would not be forgiving him. She wouldn't even speak to him. He was close to tears, when he was roused from his sombre thoughts by the ringing of the phone. It was the receptionist downstairs. "I am sorry to bother you, but there is someone here to see you and I can't find it in the appointment book."

Adam forgot to ask who it was before he replaced the receiver. Had he forgotten an appointment with a client? He was quite forgetful these days. Things were slipping from his mind. He was too preoccupied by what he did to Olivia, how much he hurt her. In hurting her he also hurt himself and worried that it was all beyond repair. He needed her and he had no idea how he was going to get her back into his life. He had a grief that reminded him daily how much he hurt someone he should have kept close. As he looked in the mirror, Adam put his jacket on. He was still extremely handsome, with no silver in his dark hair showing through.

Adam looked down at the small tie-pin he kept on his desk. It was a small gold anchor that Olivia bought him for his fortieth birthday. The card beside it was written in French. He did not know any French and had to ring her to ask her what it said. The anchor was symbolic, as she called him her 'anchor man' and she was his 'Brown Eyes'. "Oh, well! C'est la vie." Adam knew what that meant, as Olivia used it often. He took a deep breath and left the office, walking past Gerry's desk without a smile. Adam knew he would have to go down and do some grovelling to the forgotten client. He searched his mind to figure out who he might have forgotten. This must never happen again; it wasn't good for business, and he thanked his lucky stars that he was in the office and not out at a meeting.

As he came down the stairs, the receptionist smiled at him and nodded across to the closed door of the interview room. "In there." The receptionist returned to the crossword, hidden out of sight.

Brushing himself down, Adam walked across to the door, thinking, 'Here goes.' As he opened the door, he turned on his charm and fixed a humble smile onto his face. He was oozing executive confidence as he closed the door behind him and turned to greet the client, his speech well-rehearsed. The words never came as Adam was looking at Olivia. Adam's heart bounded over hurdles as he looked at the colourful rainbow before him. Olivia was dressed in a multi-coloured shift dress which did not hide her curves. She was sitting behind the table; she looked up and smiled. The smile turned into a grin. "Hello, Adam, how are you?"

CHAPTER ELEVEN

Felix was running away again. This time he was running away to America. He was never able to escape the demons that were always following him. The biggest demon was his alcoholic wife. He never saw it coming. He never saw the drunk she would become. Even as teenagers, she began to show signs of becoming a lush. Linda never knew when to stop. She always had to have a last drink and Felix always made excuses for her. It got to the point when she began to lie about her drinking, and it was not long after that their social life became non-existent. Linda became a total embarrassment, making a fool of herself in front of their family and friends. It is what some drunks do. There was no social life and there hadn't been a love life for many years. Their physical life ended after the birth of their daughter. It wasn't as though Linda had a hard time at the birth. It was that her mother had brainwashed her into thinking that sex was for making babies and, seeing as she didn't want any more babies, she kept her legs closed and her knickers on. Linda didn't make love to Felix any more. She got drunk a lot and fell over instead. Felix found an early escape from his sad life by finding another way to meet his manly needs. Unfortunately, it involved women, lies and loneliness. To say Linda was frigid was an understatement. He tried to keep the marriage alive. He discussed the future with her, he bought her presents and cooked her nice meals — and what did she do? She scorned him, with her out-of-control words bordering on abuse.

It was so lonely being in a loveless marriage and he was always looking for the one who would take him away from it. Felix just wanted someone to love him and who he could love back. Wasn't that what everybody wanted? He threw himself into his career and became married to the job that brought many perks with it. As Sales Manager of an airline he had power and he used it. Felix found escape routes from his domestic hell. He stole moments of ecstasy and peace with anyone he could. He developed the gifts of a charmer and his position gave him what he needed in order to fulfil his desires. Felix never had to look for women, as there was an abundance of them in his line of business. On his travels he gained much experience and was master of the 'mile high' club. He christened many toilets over many countries in the world with many women.

Felix was now on his way to what he hoped would be a permanent escape from his sad life in England. His organisation was now going global and branching out into the American internal flights market. This was to be his last trip to 'seal the deal', and all being well, he would soon be living in his own apartment not far from Kennedy Airport, where he would stay until his retirement in a few years. Felix knew Linda would not move to America. She wanted to be near her daughter and her grandchildren. Linda's ageing mother lived with them and needed some care. Felix did his bit and shared the care. He couldn't stand the old bat, and this made life difficult as he greeted her with false smiles and made small talk, hating her all the while. He couldn't do it anymore. He wanted his life back.

Linda enjoyed her roles as mother and grandmother. She never was the wife he wanted. She never instigated sex and in the thirty years they were married she never said 'I love you' first. She was not romantically demonstrative and at times totally ignored him. Felix wished that things could have been different. In her younger days, Linda had the beauty of a *Vogue* model. Then she developed psoriasis and her confidence disappeared. She began to let herself go and did not take good care of herself. Now the alcohol was taking its toll and Linda's face was ravaged by drink and bitterness. Over the years, Felix began to think it was never him that Linda wanted but his fertility, his money and his standing in the local community. He gave her the materialistic things that she craved; and, of course, an endless supply of drink to keep her functioning. Felix knew how much she detested him, his good looks, his success. Linda was no longer interested in him. She did not care what he did or where he went; theirs was now a marriage of convenience. Convenience for her, and Felix was the fool by staying when he needed to get a life for himself.

Linda had never seen the barge that Felix kept on the canal, moored several miles from home, at Llangollen. She didn't care about her husband or anything he did. Whilst she never appeared interested in what he did, Linda would call Felix several times a day. She was always checking up on him, accusing him of infidelities, asking him to not forget to bring more wine home. If Felix forgot, as he sometimes did, Linda would scream at him. Sulks would inevitably follow. Tired as he was, Felix would drive to the supermarket to purchase her favourite tipple and then spend the rest of the evening waiting for her to slip into a stupor that at times triggered abuse. Linda would call him terrible names and was known for her hefty slaps. How could a man be so powerful in his work and career and then become a cowering mouse as his spouse whiplashed him with her words? There was no answer to that. Felix just took it and said nothing. Domestic abuse was not always men hitting on women.

Felix began his career as an admin clerk at the airport. Sitting opposite him every day was Eleanor. He liked Eleanor: she was very sweet, with dark auburn hair that fell to her shoulders, and with a homely figure that perhaps could lose a few pounds. Down the years she had kept her looks, unlike the anorexic, thin-lipped Linda. Eleanor had a simple outlook on life and was easily pleased. The affair began by accident at an office party. Her kisses were warm and uninspiring, but they were kisses, and she made no demands on him. It was a perfect contrast to the 'drunk'. Eleanor was a convenient escape from his sad marriage. Doesn't everyone need an escape from sadness? As Felix moved up the career ladder, certain sacrifices were made, in the fact that he had to stay married, a requirement of the organisation where he was moving to greater heights. Felix continued to secretly see Eleanor throughout the years and she was happy and content to be used by him, as and when he was available. This became less and less as he became busier, travelled more and had wider access to women who were meeting his physical needs and voracious sexual appetite.

Felix's career would not stand any scandal, and so he continued to do the best he could to juggle a rather hectic life that also contained many lascivious women. As Felix grew older, he also grew more cowardly and became cruel to women as he vented his feelings on those with whom he would spend one or two nights and who he callously abandoned when done. He was interested only in his lust and how many 'notches' he could etch on the bedpost. Felix did not believe in condoms, like a lot of men his age: he believed he would never catch anything and he chose his subjects carefully.

He was wrong and contracted an STD more than once, infecting both Linda and Eleanor. Linda forgot herself one night and in a last-ditch attempt to have some form of physical contact with his wife, Felix persuaded her to have sex with him. It was very dissatisfying and the last time that it would ever happen. Two weeks later, Linda announced that she had gonorrhoea. She was very angry at the humiliation, knowing that she had to acknowledge something that she had known for many years but chose to ignore. Her husband slept around and took his love elsewhere, which in turn made her drink more to quell her unhappiness. Linda was never lonely with a bottle.

As for Eleanor, she confronted Felix on more than one occasion. Once, she returned from the doctors to tell him that she now had chlamydia. In his arrogance, being the good liar that he was, he managed to convince Eleanor that he had only shared a bed with a stewardess one night in Bangkok when the hotel was full and there was only one room left. The air hostess had come on to him and he was drunk. He told Eleanor things happened without his consent. Eleanor bought the bullshit and nothing more was said. The antibiotics did the rest.

Felix loved his barge. He found the solace he required on the canal and spent more and more time there by himself. This was his sanctuary, where he was true to himself and could put his complicated life to one side. This was one place a woman was not allowed. It was his bolt-hole from the world. An escape from the chaos he created. Felix dreamed of a new life, and now he was on his way to America to make his dream a reality and to reinvent himself. He found that getting older was taking its toll on his ability to maintain an erection, something that was never a problem in his younger days. Sex continued to be of great importance to him and always would be.

America was to be the new life where he would escape the banshees that haunted him. America was to be where his erection returned. Felix knew there would be a few more years of hard work, after which he would retire, buy a boat and go fishing. He thought that he could live off his memories. He no longer felt he needed a woman. The significant women he encountered on his life's journey he would recall as and when he required help to stimulate himself. He had even stopped that on a regular basis, as disappointment followed a semi and his wrist would become weary after his effort to spout forth with the juices that he thought made him a man. There were many and varied memories of one-night stands, weekends in exotic places, long-haul flights and half-hours with complete strangers. Felix was not sure if he ever made love to anyone, as his time was precious and he was far too busy. He just had sex. His sexual encounters were training grounds for perfecting his seduction methods and emptying his throbbing scrotum.

Felix took a drink of his vodka tonic and looked down the aisle of the plane, as his attention went to the film on the screen before him. He smiled to himself as he remembered the goodbyes and tears that he left behind in Lancashire. The years had not been kind to his feelings and he was now hard and ruthless. His behaviours instigated too much heartbreak and too many tears in the women he had sex with. Felix lost his feelings when his marriage drowned in drink and his wife became all-powerful as her abuse of him spiralled out of control.

Felix waited many years to fulfil his plan and he had the last laugh when he put his cases in the taxi. He told Linda, who was crying on the doorstep, that she would be hearing from his solicitor. She screamed at him, "If you stay in America, I will kill myself, and I mean it this time."

Felix had slowly turned to look at her. "Well, my dear, I don't give a flying fuck." Rhett Butler spoke similar words to Scarlett O'Hara. He didn't say 'flying fuck', though. Linda was no Scarlett O'Hara and he was no Rhett Butler. 'Don't give a flying fuck' seemed more apt than 'don't give a damn'. With a wicked smirk on his face, Felix got into the taxi and he was gone.

Felix turned his attention to the man seated next to him. His eyes were closed and he looked asleep. Felix wondered who he might be, where he was going and why. Perhaps they might chat later, after lunch. It was quiet on the plane as the attendants were at the back, chatting, and the aisle was empty. It was the time just before they began to serve lunch, after which they would try and sell duty-free goods to people who had more money than sense.

Felix took a sip of his drink and looked up to see a woman walking towards him. He couldn't see her clearly, but noticed she was elegantly dressed in a business suit and white, crisp blouse. "Now that looks like my kind of woman, one with some class." As she came closer, he noticed that she was beginning to smile, the smile turned into a grin. She was looking straight at him. She must have mistaken him for someone else, or perhaps she was smiling at the man next to him? The woman was stunning. Her big brown eyes twinkled with humour. Felix could see that as she came nearer. It was her smile that drew him to her. She had a wicked look about her. The words from Noel Pointer's 'Classy Lady' began to sing their way through his mind as his eyes could not leave the woman, now so near to him. Just as the vision came to the row in front of him, her head turned towards him, she continued to grin and a glint appeared in her eye. She winked and continued to walk by. Felix was taken aback by the gesture and rather surprised.

He looked to the side as the man next to him stirred and he saw that he, too, was staring at the woman walking by. The man had a shocked expression on his face; he looked stunned. As they looked at each other, Adam wondered, "Do you know her?"

"No! Maybe, I do. Yes, I think I might, but it has been a long time and for some reason I thought she might be winking at you."

"No, I don't know her. My name is Adam, by the way." Adam smiled as he lied. He was in shock as his past had just winked at him. Felix asked him if he was going to New York on business and they began a 'getting to know each other' session. They found that they had similar interests, in that they both loved sailing and each had a vessel that they spent most of their free time on. Both had high-powered jobs and were hoping to stay in America now and perhaps not return to England. They both hoped to build new lives for themselves for the last time, before they retired. Neither mentioned their mistresses or their wives. Felix and Adam liked each other and exchanged business cards, saying they should keep in touch, before they both sat back to wait for lunch.

Felix wondered if he should have asked Adam how he knew the woman and thought perhaps something might come up in conversation later. He began to think about what just happened. The woman was rather beautiful and seemed very confident as she passed him by. As the fog began to lift from his past, Felix began to see the woman amongst the long line of women that danced about in his memory. He could not remember her name, but thought that perhaps somewhere in the clouds of his mind he could hear a voice. It was a small echo in the baggage he carried in his head. Felix stared at the seat in front of him, knowing that it would eventually come. He might remember the story of where he might know her from, if he had ever known her at all. Surely, he would not have forgotten a woman who looked like that? But he had a lot of women and he couldn't be expected to remember them all. Too many one-night stands for that!

CHAPTER TWELVE

After a lunch of salmon and spinach, washed down by a light chardonnay and followed by a large brandy, Felix fell into a deep sleep that became filled with dreams that began to unravel the mystery that was the woman.

~

Frankfurt airport was crowded that sunny day in November. Felix was annoyed that he had not managed to secure direct flights to Munich. Everybody had to change flights. He was not a happy man as they waited for cases that had to be carried across the German airport to the next check-in. As he became more frustrated, Felix became aware of a small person next to him. Was she talking to herself or to him? "Absolutely bloody stupid, this is. Other airports do transfers from plane to plane, no need for this at all. Oh well, they obviously think differently in Germany."

Felix turned to look at the woman, who looked more like a little girl, so it was hard to determine her age. Wild auburn hair curled round her blue woolly hat and she was drowned by a matching royal blue coat. Was she part of his group? If she was, he hadn't noticed her before. He noticed she wore beige leather boots of good quality and although everything looked a bit big on her, he could see she had taste. "Sorry, were you talking to me?" he spoke to the hat.

"Of course, I am talking to you can you see anyone else? You organised this fiasco, didn't you? And if you think I am going to lug my case a mile across this airport, that will not happen. This is so ridiculous." She scowled at him from under the brim and continued to look down the line for her case.

Felix shuddered. Was this one going to be trouble and moan her way round Germany? There was always one! It was only a small minibus and he would not be able to avoid her. Being a natural gentleman, when her case arrived, he took hold of it and, with his own in the other hand, began to stride towards the next check-in desk.

Felix chuckled to himself as she struggled to keep up with him. His long legs marched away and she followed. She ran beside him as he strode across the departure hall, meandering his way through the crowd. At least it stopped her talking for a while. The next time they spoke was in the airport at Munich. The landing had not been the best, as the pilot dropped the plane down to the ground with rather a bang, before putting the engines in reverse. As they waited, once again, for their cases, the 'twitterer' (Felix loved giving nicknames to people; it was the untamed schoolboy in him that he could not resist) carried on twittering. "Do all your pilots land like that? No wonder the carpets on board are brown." Olivia laughed and stared at him, waiting for confrontation.

"What do you mean?" Felix sighed. Well, she wasn't funny at all. He was not used to women who were sarcastic, and he presumed that was what she was being.

Once the group boarded the bus, Felix sat at the back and began to study the people before him. There was Garth, who was eighteen: he seemed pleasant enough. Rebecca, the same age, was sitting next to him and they were giggling. Kevin was driving the bus and chatting to Pablo as they made their way to the autobahn. They were managers at 'Into the Sun,' a small family run business of tour operators. They were going to take turns at driving around Germany. Felix knew them well, as they went on many trips together. He wasn't sure if he liked Kevin and Pablo. Business was business and he played matey, matey with them. It was all part of the job, as these trips were working holidays.

They toured around, looking for new hotels and making themselves known to tourist offices in Europe. Trips like this were a nightmare for Felix, but he did his duty and if he could get laid in the process then perhaps, they weren't so bad after all. Tourism was a growing business and 'Into the Sun' was growing quickly alongside it. It was important that all employees had experienced the countries they were trying to sell to the travel agents. It gave authenticity to the brochures and made the job easier, as advice was first-hand. There would be fewer repercussions due to people being misinformed by ignorant staff.

Felix began to look at the women. None stood out as yet, apart from the 'twitterer,' and she was definitely one to avoid. Felix hoped to have at least one conquest in the next week. He was a very sensual man and needed to have sex regularly. He did not like satisfying himself, not when he could find a woman to do it for him. He did not much care who it was, as long as it was someone pleasing. He saw Paula sitting next to Louise, who was sitting behind Pablo. She was a manager and she scared him with her buck teeth and piercing blue eyes. Paula was definitely out of bounds, and she was twenty years his junior.

Felix knew that Paula wanted him, as there were one or two embarrassing moments on previous trips when Felix had to fight her off, and they never mentioned the incidents again. He couldn't 'poke' that fire as it wasn't even lit, and the mantelpiece left a lot to be desired. When they were touring France, there was an awkward moment when Paula knocked on his bedroom door late at night. "Felix, are you there? I have brought some champagne." Felix began to regret paying Paula a compliment earlier that night. He began to fake a loud snore, hoping she would go away. Paula tapped a few more times and left his door to return to her room to drink the champagne alone.

Felix looked at Louise. Perhaps he would pay some attention to her this trip. She was a divorcee in her fifties. Felix felt that at times she and Paula were in competition for his attention and favours. Well, he couldn't help being so sexy, could he? The problem with Louise was that she was rather timid, and when she did open up, it was always about her failed romances; so boring. She really needed a therapist, and Felix was not a therapist. He thought he was a sex god, or maybe could be a good sex therapist. The problem was that he wanted to do and not to listen. Each trip, Louise became more daring, and Felix knew he would not have to say much to get her into bed with him.

"Yes, I might just do Louise, as she looks the best in such a bad bunch."

"What did you say, mate?" Kevin was looking at him rather funny.

"I was talking to myself."

"That's a bad habit to get into, mate."

Felix turned to look at the last seat occupied by two new members of staff. There she was, doing what she did best. The 'twitterer' was twittering to her friend Heather. They were laughing loudly at something said, and as he watched, she turned to catch his eye and winked, before going back to her conversation. Felix realised that she smiled a lot. He also noticed what a beautiful smile it was.

Felix settled down in his seat, looking out of the window. "Oh well, let's get this party started," he whispered to himself, as they sped off into the depths of Germany. He was not going to enjoy this trip, huddled in a minibus with a group of people he had nothing in common with. This was not his idea of a good time. That was until they arrived in Hamburg.

CHAPTER THIRTEEN

"Excuse me, sir."

Felix woke with a start to see a dark-haired stewardess bent towards him. "Were you having tea or coffee, or another brandy?"

"I think a brandy, don't you?" Felix smiled as he looked her up and down, his eyes resting on her breasts. He saw they were held in place by a Wonderbra: they would probably be like bee stings in natural form. He settled down in his seat as another in-flight film began. It was a documentary about Germany and the building of the autobahns. How boring. Why would anyone want to watch that? Something stirred in his brain. The dream he had after his lunch began to return as he took a drink. The veil began to lift.

~

Oh, God! He did know that woman who winked as she walked down the aisle. Hamburg! That was it. No, surely it couldn't be? Felix quickly turned in his seat to see if he could see her. She was sitting ten rows down to the right of him. He couldn't believe it! It was the 'twitterer' from all those years ago. She was sipping champagne and talking to someone he could not see. How had she changed from a duckling to a beautiful swan? That was an unkind thought, as she wasn't really that bad back then; she just ruffled his feathers and they got off on the wrong foot. Felix turned back to the screen. The film about the autobahns turned into a German thriller about a building contractor. He rang for the stewardess to order another drink, a double brandy. He needed it.

~

For the first three days of the German trip, Paula monopolised Felix, as though he was her personal property. He was getting really fed up with her. All he wanted was to be left alone, get on with his job and return to England. Felix was not able to escape from her until they arrived in Hamburg. They were booked into a cheap and cheerful hotel. The Generator Hotel was next to the main railway station. Check-in went smoothly and people in the group went to their rooms to prepare for dinner.

It was damp and miserable outside, but Felix felt that he needed a walk, as they had a long night ahead of them. They were due to attend a dinner at the Rathaus with the councillors of Hamburg and other important people. Felix was looking forward to it and looking forward to meeting his old friend, Gunter. Felix had known Gunter for many years. He was one of those friends that you keep, as he knew too much. Felix loved old buildings that were steeped in history and Gunter was quite the historian. Old city hall was destroyed in 1842 by fire and it took nearly forty-four years to rebuild. It was a shame it would be dark as the group would not see the beauty of such a fine building from the outside.

Felix knew that there would be no expense spared on the meal and that the wine would flow freely. He wasn't sure what they would all do after the meal; there was nothing planned. He thought they might all end up in the hotel bar and drink it dry. Felix headed for the door and just as he was about to go out, he felt a tug on his sleeve. He looked down at the small hand gripping the material and the pink nail varnish covering the short, perfectly manicured nails. His eyes fell to meet a pair of big brown eyes looking up at him. They were almost pleading. "Can I come with you, please? I feel a bit sick after that long bus ride."

Felix's inner voice spoke to him. "Oh, no! Not her, not the twitterer! Tell her no." As he looked down at Olivia, he realised that he had not heard a complaint from her since they left Munich. He noticed her at times, when he was watching her friend Heather and trying to decide if he should make Heather his target. He found it hard to concentrate on anything but getting away from Paula most of the time. "Yes, come on then. We aren't in the best part of the city and I am not sure if these streets are for you. We can just walk down the street and back."

Olivia giggled as they went through the revolving door and down the steps. The air was crisp and clear, just as a November night should be. Felix smiled to himself as he felt an arm link through his. He could afford to be generous. Perhaps tonight might not be so bad after all. He hoped it would be a good one, the best one yet. Commuters filled the road. They were busy making their way home from work. Felix and Olivia walked slowly, in silence, stopping to look into shop windows that were dimly lit.

All at once, Olivia pulled him back and began to peer through a rather dirty pane of glass. "What on earth is that?" She was pointing at something to the front of the display.

Felix followed the finger and began to focus on the rabbit and chicken. "My goodness! No way, is that what I think it is?" Felix laughed.

"Yes, I think it is?"

"But that is impossible. How can a rabbit do a chicken? That is gross." Olivia began to laugh.

"Well, this is Hamburg, the city where anything goes." Nothing in Hamburg surprised Felix any more — he had seen it all.

Walking back up the other side of the street towards the hotel, Olivia asked Felix what was in the shops with no windows. She really couldn't be that naïve, could she? He told her they were sex shops, a bit like Ann Summers in England, but more for men. "Would you like to go in one?" A devilish grin came onto his face.

"Go on then, why not?"

Felix was quite surprised and pushed Olivia gently by the elbow towards a black door that had seen better days. They entered a long corridor with books and sexual implements on one side and curtained booths on the other. The man behind the counter gave them a strange look, as they were not looking like his usual customers. "I hate bloody tourists! They come to look and never buy," he muttered to himself.

Olivia noticed the booths and asked Felix what they were for. He smiled and decided to have some fun. "What do you think they are for?" He knew she would never guess. He was right.

"Changing booths? I really don't know." Olivia was making her way towards one, and before she could lift the curtain to look inside, Felix managed to pull her back.

"They are pumping pits." Felix's statement took her by surprise and she looked rather embarrassed. "Yes, you know, for men to…" Felix made a gesture with his hand.

"No way! You are joking? Oh my, that is disgusting. Can't they do it at home?" Olivia busied herself with looking at the underwear. "Felix, do you think many people buy this rubber stuff?"

Olivia was holding up a pair of red latex briefs as the man who was behind the counter scowled. "Stupid woman!"

Felix pointed to a sign hanging above the rail. "You don't speak German, do you? This says do not touch unless trying on."

Olivia sneered, and as she went to return the briefs to the rail, she knocked a display of vibrators onto the floor behind her. The shopkeeper was not amused and he began to shout at her. "Raus, dumme frau, raus, dumme frau." He was waving his hands about and getting quite irate. Felix stood and waited to see what would happen next.

"What is he saying, Felix?"

Felix couldn't resist and told her the truth. "He is saying 'get out, stupid woman'."

"Oh, is he indeed!" Olivia raised herself to full height, which was almost five foot two, and walked across to the shop counter. The red-faced shopkeeper stopped shouting as she leaned across the condoms towards him. "This won't do your blood pressure any good, you fat bastard, so fuck off." She turned on her heel and left the shop. Felix followed and they walked back to the hotel the way they came, in silence. Neither of them knew what to say after Olivia's little outburst.

When they reached the lift in the hotel foyer, she turned to Felix. "Well, thank you, Felix; that was a right adventure, was it not?"

The lift arrived just as Felix heard his name being called by the girl at the reception desk. "I best see what she wants. Will you be OK?"

"I am a big girl, you know. I will find my way, thank you." As the lift door began to close, Olivia winked at him.

The Germans did Felix proud that night. The shnitzels, sauerkraut, pumpernickel and frankfurters went down well with a good German beer, followed by an even better Riesling. The group were now on their sixth bottle of wine. Felix was becoming restless. He was tiring of the entertainment. It was the fat woman in the long silk beige dress and ill-fitting wig that finished it off for him: the impersonation of Marlene Dietrich was appalling and her rendition of 'Falling in Love Again' in a broken English accent was beyond belief. As Felix looked round the table, he noticed the 'Into the Sun' people laughing and enjoying themselves. People laugh at anything when they are drunk.

Felix began to study each person in the group, trying to gauge who was the most inebriated. The men didn't appear too bad, but the women; the women were looking more than a bit drunk. Were they on the edge of stupor? Perhaps they needed some fresh air. Felix was not a good judge of who might or might not be drunk, so perhaps they were just happy? His eyes met Olivia's across the table and she winked at him. He looked away without smiling back. He wished she wouldn't wink, but he wasn't too sure why. He was worried about what was going on inside him when those brown eyes met his. He really did not want to mess with this woman who, after the display in the shop earlier, showed him that she could be rather fierce and was a bit of a fire-cracker.

Felix discreetly watched Olivia throughout the evening; he could see that she stood out in the crowd and seemed to 'hold court'. He felt drawn towards her as she seemed to be fun. Was it the hair, the eyes, or was it the loud voice that even a deaf man might hear? Some of the women set their stall out that evening and Felix felt he could have taken any one of them. Heather wore a blue silk dress that stuck to her body in all the right places. He could feel the heat coming from her every time she looked at him. Paula looked amazing in a pair of black trousers and a short-sleeved red top that would tease any man. Her nipples were clearly defined under the thin fabric. It was a shame about her face. Louise was looking rather matronly in a black skirt and white blouse. Then there was Olivia, who wore a short, baggy, knitted black V-necked dress with green piping, black tights with knee-high stiletto boots. Olivia's hair was piled high on her head, with unruly strands falling about her face. She looked stunning in a slovenly schoolgirl type of way.

Felix turned to speak to Kevin. "Shall we get out of here? Shall we leave the ladies and get the metro down to the Reeperbahn?"

Kevin looked at Pablo and whispered. Pablo smiled and nodded. They all agreed to slip away singly and meet in the foyer. They would not take Garth with them as he was perhaps too young. He could stay with the women. One at a time they left the table to gather in the assigned meeting place. Felix was the last one out. The ladies were deep in conversation and had not noticed the slow exodus. The men hoped to slip away before they were missed.

Once in the foyer, the men retrieved their coats from the cloakroom and made for the door, only to be stopped in their tracks by a loud shout behind them. "Hey, where do you think you are going?"

The men turned together to see Olivia standing in the middle of the floor with her hands on her hips, with the rest of the women standing behind her. They looked rather comical, as though they were going to burst into a song and dance from *West Side Story*. Kevin and Pablo looked guiltily at Felix, who was now standing opposite Olivia. Was this to be a 'face-off'? Felix coughed. "Well, you see, it's like this: as we are in Hamburg, we thought it might be a good idea to go down the Reeperbahn. You all looked as though you were having a good time."

Olivia studied the men before her. She looked at each in turn, leaving a minute of theatrical silence. The sarcasm in her face was obvious. "And at what stage were you going to tell us?"

Felix looked at the other men for support. "Well, er…we didn't want to disturb you. It's not really the sort of place for women. You would not want to come with us."

Olivia put her head back and laughed. "You mean that you wouldn't want us to come with you! How would you know that if you never asked us? I knew where you were sneaking off to. I think we might have a better time down the Reeperbahn with you."

Kevin stuttered, "Look, Olivia, it might not be the right place why don't you stay here for a while and then all go back to the hotel."

"Kev, don't they have women down there, then?"

Kevin looked down at his feet. "Well, yes, I suppose they do."

Olivia turned to the women behind her. "Right, enough said. Are we going or are we staying?" The women looked amazed by what had transpired. They knew that Olivia was up front and says it like it is, but to go up against someone as powerful as Felix, that was another matter. Even Paula would not dare to confront him in the way Olivia just did. Olivia certainly either had guts or was very stupid. She turned to them.

"Get your coats." They quickly got their coats and proceeded to follow the men through the door.

They all boarded the metro and rode across the city. Felix was finding it hard to hide his annoyance at Olivia. He had a problem with forthright, bossy women and he was now putting Olivia into the same category as Paula. Paula was not quite so bad, but Olivia was a bossy, demanding she-devil. It appeared that Olivia had now taken over. "Well, let her." Felix consciously stopped a sulk and looked at Kevin giving him a wet smile. He realised that he had spoken out loud. She can make a mess of the evening, they can all go back to the hotel disappointed and then he would come out again, alone. Felix didn't really understand why he was being so petulant. Perhaps it was because he was looking forward to a man's night out, which could include sex with someone he might pick up. That would be rather difficult with women in the group. He didn't like it when women took over, it was something to do with Linda and the way she tried to rule his life. He sat quietly with the men, a frown clouding his face.

Olivia had not spoken much since they left the hotel and was sitting across the aisle of the train, looking out of the window, when she suddenly turned and grinned at the group. She looked round and saw an old couple sitting close by; she grinned at them, too. However annoyed Felix was with her, he had to laugh, and the rest followed suit. Olivia's grin revealed a pair of vampire fangs. Felix wondered when she had put them into her mouth. The old couple were startled and hurriedly moved down the train to sit somewhere else. Everybody laughed even louder.

It was a scene to behold as Olivia got out of her seat and began to dance about. No doubt about it, she certainly knew how to break the ice. They were all laughing now, and this encouraged Olivia to ape some more. She moved closer to them all. "We are out at night near Transylvania, it is soon to be the witching hour and the vampires will be about. Do not worry, my friends, I will protect you." She crossed two fingers in the way they did in the Hammer House of Horror films to ward off evil and then her voice changed. "We need to get in the mood if we are off to see some sex."

Felix turned to Kevin. "What have we let ourselves in for now? The woman is totally crazy!"

Before Kevin could answer, Olivia lifted the front of her dress to show an amazing pair of thighs that were wearing black suspenders and stockings. She turned round to reveal pert cheeks framed by black lace. Her workmates carried on laughing; they obviously knew her well and she probably got up to all sorts of antics in the office. Felix turned away and looked out of the window as he felt something stir inside him. What kind of an enigma was this woman? What might she do next? There were many facets to her colourful personality and she was like a rainbow. He was realising that his first impressions were wrong. He needed to enter into the spirit of things. Felix began to sing a Rolling Stones song, which was his favourite. The earlier drinking was now getting the better of him.

Felix could not decide if he liked Olivia or not. He knew he was becoming rather infatuated by her and wondered if he should stop grooming Heather and start smiling more at Olivia. Felix knew Heather would be a push-over, probably quite boring in bed and perhaps would not be worth the effort after all. Olivia, on the other hand, might be very interesting to take to bed. She was showing that she could have a good time, even though she might possibly be hard work, infuriating and a little dangerous. Felix could not work her out at all; one minute she was a woman and the next a child. He also began to realise that she was far more intelligent than he thought her to be. He also wondered if she could keep a secret. He could add to his secrets this night if all went well. He had to be very careful as he knew that most women were gossips and his little forays into women's knickers could ruin his career and reputation.

Felix began to watch Heather and Olivia out of the corner of his eye. He studied them as they chatted and laughed. The decision was made. He would chase the rainbow! If he didn't catch the rainbow, at least he would enjoy himself trying.

As they left the metro station, Paula commented, "Thank goodness we are off there. I didn't like that at all." She moved closer to Felix and linked his arm with an air of ownership he did not like. She pushed her breast into his side. Oh, no! Surely, she was not drunk, too? Felix really couldn't be doing with her on an evening he felt was already ruined.

It was a short walk to the Reeperbahn and conversation surrounded the antics of Olivia in the metro and the look on the old couple's faces as they moved seats. Heather caught up with Olivia, who was marching out in front of them. "Olivia, I can't believe you just did that!"

Kevin caught them up. "I can, and it was really funny."

Olivia put the vampire teeth back in her mouth. "Well, we might soon be seeing some neck sucking and who knows what else?"

Paula turned to Felix. "She is so stupid! I can't stand her."

Felix was rather surprised by the remark. "Oh, I don't know." He unhooked himself from Paula's grasp. "She seems to brighten the group up." Felix moved across the street to join the others, who were now looking at a window display. They walked on and turned a corner into the Reeperbahn.

At the top of the street, the group stopped to discuss what they were going to do. Some wanted to do some shopping and others to see a live sex show before returning to the hotel. They agreed to walk down the street and see what was what. Felix took the lead and as they began their journey into the unknown, Felix wished that he was somewhere else. Walking down the Reeperbahn with this motley crew was not part of his plan. He should have taken them back to the hotel and left them there. A feeling of apprehension fell over the group as they stayed in the middle of the street and slowly made their way to an adventure they would never forget. As the 'tour guide' Felix began to explain that the street was made up of strip joints, shops and erotic theatres. They could see men standing outside dimly lit doorways, bouncers standing beside brightly lit windows advertising the delights inside. Most posters and displays said the same thing: 'Three shows and one beer for twenty-five deutsche marks.'

Half way down the street, they stopped. Olivia was becoming impatient. "What are we going to do, then? Go in one or go back?" Felix stood back as a conversation began between them all.

The rain began to come down, harder than before, and these stupid people were discussing whether to go see a sex show or not, getting wetter and wetter. Olivia had the only umbrella and she was getting colder and colder as she danced about with more than a frustrated look on her face. It appeared that they were looking to her to make a decision for them. Felix could not fully hear what was being said, but he did hear part. Olivia was becoming more than impatient. "For fuck's sake, this is mental! Wait here." She turned on her heel and stormed towards the nearest door, where she began to talk to one of the older men wearing a black mohair overcoat. All the men at the doors of the venues were wearing the same coat. It was like a uniform.

Felix asked Kevin what was happening. "Some don't want to go in. Rachel and Heather do, it's the other women. It does seem rather expensive!"

Felix nodded in Olivia's direction. "What's she doing, then?"

Kevin laughed. "She is trying to see if she can get us in cheaper as there are a few of us."

"Oh, is she? She won't be able to do that: fixed price is fixed price. The woman is a complete lunatic."

Felix spoke to the others and then turned to where he last saw Olivia with the man. They were no longer there. He asked Kevin where Olivia and the man went. Kevin shrugged his shoulders, saying, "The man just grabbed her and pulled her inside; she told us to wait here."

Heather was concerned. "Shouldn't we do something? I am getting worried now."

Pablo spoke up. "I think she will be OK; she is a tough cookie."

Felix's question was answered. "We best just wait here for her, then."

After about ten minutes, Olivia came out of the building, turned to shake the man's hand and made her way back to the group. She appeared dazed and in shock. They waited in anticipation while she composed herself. "Bloody hell! That was an eye opener."

They all crowded round her and Rachel asked what they all wanted to know. "Why, what happened? Come on, tell us then."

Felix could see that Olivia loved the attention. "Well, it's like this. I think we should go in this one; it is still twenty-five, but he has agreed to give us an extra beer."

The group began to discuss again what they should do. Felix could see that Olivia was becoming irritated with them all, as the rain came down heavier than before. She looked lovely in the lamp-light, with her determined expression and the small frown that now ran across her forehead. Felix knew he made the right decision about who he was to groom for a night of passion. He loved a challenge. Before the night was over, the rainbow would be his. He believed he wouldn't even have to chase it.

A wet Olivia began to shout. "Right, I have had enough now." She walked over to Felix and began to pull him towards the door. She looked back at the group, the 'we can't make our minds up' people. "Do what the fuck you want — we are going in here." Olivia nodded at Felix. That was just what they all needed and they began to run across the street to join Felix and Olivia as they entered the building. It was black as black could be. Once they were inside, the group picked their way through crowded tables and narrow aisles as an escort showed them a table near the stage.

They were crammed onto a horseshoe bench, very close to each other. Waiting for their beers, Felix looked at Olivia, who was sitting to his left. Her eyes were sparkling in the lights shining off the stage. For the first time, he noticed how beautiful they were. Felix was curious. "How did you do that? What happened?"

Olivia gave a nervous laugh. "God knows. I almost died when he dragged me in here and all I could see was two people having sex on the stage. It was all so surreal. I thought of that song... can't remember it now, it's from a film or show... what was it?" Olivia smiled and closed her eyes, trying to remember. "I know." She laughed. "It was *Sweet Charity*, and the song was 'If They Could See Me Now'. I don't think anybody would believe it. My friends in the village would not believe this. I know I am drunk or I would not have been able to argue with the man. You know, he wasn't very nice at all." She linked her arm under Felix's and snuggled closer. He felt comfortable and smiled at her, asking if she was still drunk. "Not as much, sort of; not sober, and the night is yet young. I can get drunk again."

She winked. He wished that she would not wink at him. He felt she was teasing him and he had to be careful that he did not get the wrong message.

The stripper on stage finished her set and left as the second beers appeared and the curtain rose to a classroom setting. A tall, blonde woman entered through a door at the back of the set. She was dressed in a school uniform, a short gym slip and black hold-ups. Pigtails were adorned by big red ribbons. The woman strutted about and then sat on

121

the desk, crossing her legs provocatively. The men sitting by the stage at the front were certainly enjoying themselves. Music began to play and a man appeared. He was wearing a long shirt, hat, shoes and socks and no trousers, his dangly bits on full display. Olivia stiffened. "Why, he has no trousers on. Oh, my god! Is that his thingy?"

Felix smiled. Sometimes Olivia was so sweet. She had such a way with words. "How does he get it hard, then?"

There was complete silence in the auditorium as the man played with his 'thingy' in an effort to get an erection. It seemed to go on forever. Suddenly, without warning, the voice next to Felix screeched, "Take your bloody hat off, and it might stand up."

Felix was horrified. What on earth possessed her to do that? What did Olivia think she was doing? Out of nowhere, a large person appeared. It was hard to determine if it was a man or a woman. "You will be quiet now!" a voice boomed at them in a broken German accent. "You will be quiet or I throw you out."

Olivia took a swig from her bottle and coughed. "Sorry." Olivia shrank into Felix and he wondered if that was a breast, he could feel rubbing his arm. He began to wonder what Olivia's breasts were like. Were her nipples big or small, brown or pale pink? Perhaps he might get to see them later.

There was nothing better than watching sex to make a person want sex. Maybe Olivia might want sex when they got back to the hotel? Felix was brought out of his daydream by Olivia, who was tugging at his sleeve. Felix looked up at the stage and saw that the man had achieved an erection and was very busy shafting the blonde, who was now laid spread-eagled across the desk. Without warning, the man picked the girl up and, continuing to push himself up her. He carried her across the stage and down the steps on the right. She had her legs wrapped tightly round his waist as they made their way towards the table that was occupied by the 'Into the Sun' people. The man looked down at them, indicating that they needed to clear the table. Everybody grabbed their bottles of beer and clutched them to their chests while the man laid the blonde on the table and continued the show. Felix looked at the faces around the table. They were a picture to behold and he tried not to laugh. Rebecca and Garth, the youngest, were grinning from ear to ear. Kevin and a few of the ladies were a puce colour. Olivia did not move, and Felix could hear her anxious breathing. The two people were having sex, practically on the group's knees.

The blonde slowly turned her head and smiled at Felix. She had two teeth missing at the front. Olivia squirmed. "Gross, this is bloody gross." After what seemed forever, the man returned to the stage, still with the blonde on his erect member, and he continued to bang her on the desk, as before. The display ended and the sex partners walked off the stage without acknowledging the audience.

A stripper came on, standing right in front of the men sitting at the edge of the stage. As they looked up, they would have seen her next week's washing: This was a comment made by Olivia before she turned her attention to the group making them all laugh; she really was funny.

In hushed tones, the group began to talk about what had just happened. Felix turned to Olivia. "Are you all right, Olivia?"

Olivia did not look at him. "Not really. All the drink is coming through and I need the toilet." Felix told her the toilets were down the stairs on the left. "I daren't go on my own."

"Come on, then, I will come with you."

Once downstairs, as Felix waited for Olivia, he began to think about her. He could not quite figure her out. She was not like any of the other women he'd known. There was something about her. One minute she was the comedienne, making them all laugh: she was the complete and out-of-control drunk; she was the bossy organiser; and now she was the frightened child who dare not go to the toilet alone? Felix was a little bothered about the outcome of the night, and if he was to have her, he was not sure how to play the rest of the evening. Olivia bounced about between her sub-personalities like a bee searching for pollen in a field of flowers.

Felix once read a book by John Rowan. Linda bought it when she was in one of her 'I need to discover myself' moments. The book was called *Subpersonalities*. Felix read it one Saturday afternoon after finding it under some magazines in the lounge. He remembered it was something to do with the people inside us. It was all different facets of our personality that showed as different people at different times. Some people have a few and some have many, and each sub-personality comes into play at certain times, depending on the situation the person is in. Felix found this knowledge advantageous when chatting to a woman, as he could then change to suit and meet the woman half way, which in turn helped him woo her into bed. Unfortunately for him, Olivia changed so quickly it was hard to keep up with her, to even pre-empt what she might do or say next. She certainly was a challenge, but he would not be beaten and the night was yet young.

As Olivia came through the toilet door, Felix noticed how attractive she looked in the dimness. He hadn't really looked at her properly before. He noticed her legs on the metro, very nice indeed! He noticed her eyes sparkling when they were upstairs in the club and the beautiful smile that spoke of wickedness and hidden secrets. He realised that he was warming to her and actually was beginning to like her, despite their earlier encounters. Olivia was now peering into the half-light, looking for him. 'Yes,' he thought, 'she is a certain kind of pretty bordering on beautiful.' As she turned, Olivia saw him and smiled. It spread across her face and turned into a wicked grin. It was a beautiful smile. Olivia smiled a lot. She grinned a lot, too, and Felix began to feel he ought to get to know her a little better. He took hold of her hand and they walked, silently, up the steps together to watch the last two shows.

Felix was bored. Once you had seen one couple having sex, the rest just did the same in different costumes. He was busy thinking about Olivia and what might be between them later. She was sitting quietly beside him, she appeared withdrawn and he began to wonder what she was thinking; he smiled and wondered what might lie ahead. Or was he thinking who he might be lying with later?

Without warning, Olivia summoned one of the large bouncers who was standing behind them, and ordered a double vodka. "Would you like another drink, Felix?"

Felix was being rather sheepish. He nodded. "I'll have a beer, thank you." Courageously, he asked Olivia what she had been thinking about as he noticed she was quiet. "You looked a bit sad." He squeezed her hand and they smiled at each other.

"Was I? I was thinking about nothing, nothing at all." Olivia surprised him when the drinks came, as she raised her glass and downed the clear liquid in one. She then turned to the rest of the group and began to chat animatedly with them, ignoring Felix completely. He became invisible until it was time for them to leave. He didn't mind, as it was turning out to be a better evening than expected, and he watched the group and those around him until the lights went down for the next showing.

As they were leaving the building, Felix pulled Olivia back. "Are you sure you are OK?"

Olivia stopped, looked him straight in the eye and tilted her head. "They are beginning to bore me and get on my nerves." She nodded to the group who were now in front of them. "They are all so stiff and want to go back to the hotel to bed, for God's sake!" Olivia scowled and her eyes narrowed. "It's our once chance to have a ball in Hamburg." Felix asked her what she would like to do. He caught the look of distaste under the street light. "Lose this lot; they are beginning to do my head in and the night is yet young." The vodka did its trick and Olivia was now drunk once more. Felix saw an opportunity to get Olivia alone. It was something he had hoped for all evening.

On reaching the end of the street, Felix turned to the others. "Well, looks like the rain is over; some of you might want to walk back, as we won't all get in one taxi. We will see you tomorrow." Felix looked over at Olivia, who nodded her approval. He got hold of her hand and they began to walk across the street. The group huddled together, no doubt to have another major discussion about what to do, and Felix hailed a taxi. They both laughed as he quickly pushed Olivia inside, hoping to escape whilst the others were still bickering, only to find Garth trying to get in behind them. Felix held up his hand. "No, Garth, you go with the others, as we might not go straight back anyway."

Garth was startled by Felix's comment, he stood back and let go of the taxi door handle as it sped off into the night. Olivia laughed. "Aren't we going back, then? They will all talk about us."

Felix looked at her. "Are you bothered?"

Olivia laughed. Felix was beginning to love that laugh. "No, I am not bothered at all. Where are we going, then?" Olivia grinned up at him and snuggled closer.

"Let's go back to the hotel and have a nightcap, get to know each other better. It's very cold out here and we couldn't do that with Garth in tow, could we?"

As they began to chat, Felix realised that Olivia was rather clever and well educated. She had an animated face and never stopped smiling. They discussed many things, and it was good having someone intelligent to chat to. In fact, she was quite delightful. It was comfortable being with her and she was easy to talk to. Olivia made him feel as though they had known each other years and not just two minutes. She was a good listener, too. In this case, first impressions were very wrong and not to be trusted. Felix was wrong, as he sometimes was. He wasn't a great thinker and took things at face value. He probably let many a good girl pass him by, due to his first impressions and his first impressions of Olivia had not been that good.

Olivia told Felix about her bedroom at the hotel. She said it was the strangest bedroom she had ever been in. The bathroom was a mini-cabin with steps leading up to the door. It was quite bizarre. Olivia went on to say she did not feel comfortable in her bedroom as it was so big and was more than happy that they were only staying one night. "You really need to see it to believe it."

Felix stopped himself from speaking out loud. "If I play my cards right, I just might."

The taxi pulled up outside the main doors of the hotel and after paying the driver, Felix asked Olivia if she would like to walk down the street for a while. They could do with some fresh air after the smoke-filled night club. It bought Felix time while he tried to sort out his tactics. The commuter traffic was long gone and just a few pedestrians were strolling along the pavement. The flag stones were drying and stars were out and twinkling, the moon was high in the sky.

Olivia and Felix began to chat about television programmes that they enjoyed. She confessed she felt as though they had all appeared in a television drama that evening, as nothing seemed real to her. The evening was one she would never forget. She began to twitter. Felix didn't mind, as he hoped there was more to come that she might never forget. He just nodded in agreement with her. He was surprising himself with the feelings that were growing for Olivia and how interested he was in what she had to say. He was really beginning to like her a lot.

Usually, he didn't say much to a woman he was looking to bed. He just gave them the usual chat and compliments to make them feel special. He didn't feel that Olivia would fall for that. The other women were special for perhaps a moment in time and then discarded like old wrapping paper. He didn't feel there was much need to get to know them. They were merely an instrument that he played. There was no real need for the beginnings of a relationship as they were one-night stands and of no consequence.

For some reason, Lydia came into mind. She twittered, too. She was a stewardess for the airline he worked for when he first joined the aviation industry. He would see her in the airport and she was his first mile-high victim. Nothing went to plan on that flight.

Felix and Lydia were flirting for weeks.

"So, the next time we are in the air, shall we christen the small room?"

Lydia looked all coy, as though she didn't know what he meant. "Oh, I don't know, it will depend."

"We shall see, shall we, then? That didn't sound like a no to me."

On the next flight to Frankfurt, where Felix was due to do a PowerPoint presentation on the protocols of behaviour in flight, they started the ball rolling in the back toilet. It wasn't easy, and what should have been a quick romp turned into disaster as they were almost playing Twister up the wall. It all became very funny as Felix pushed Lydia up the sink and her firm bottom pushed against the tap, dislodged it and water began to trickle out. Felix stood up on the toilet to find a spanner in the overhead cupboard and banged his head on the light, which promptly went out. Lydia could not find her knickers and Felix got his belt caught on the door handle. Eventually, he managed to fix the tap and the light came back on.

A sharp knock on the door stopped them from continuing the clandestine goings on. "Is everything OK in there?"

"Yes, everything is fine." Lydia left the toilet first, to see a queue backed down the aisle. "I am so sorry, but this toilet is out of order. I have been trying to fix it. You may use the two at the front." It wasn't long before Felix sneaked out and returned to his seat.

Felix wondered why his thoughts travelled to that incident on the way to Frankfurt. He laughed out loud and after an enquiry from Olivia, Felix told her about his unfortunate experience with Lydia. He was enjoying the company of this woman on his arm, chattering away and keeping him amused.

When they returned to the hotel, Felix made his move. "Should I come and look at your room? If it is that bad, perhaps I can get it changed for you."

Olivia cocked her head to one side, before the wicked grin appeared on her face. "Well, you are the organiser of this trip, so maybe you should. I have some fruit, wine and cheese; that is, if you are hungry." She wasn't sure if she should have invited him to the room. She never gave it a second thought. "And if we were in a TV drama, I know what would happen next, and I am telling you right now, Felix, that is not going to happen. The obvious next stage to this evening is not going to happen." She put emphasis on the last few words as though she was trying to convince herself that there would be nothing untoward.

"I don't know what you mean!" Felix laughed. He knew what she was alluding to and said nothing in his defence. He turned and took her by the shoulders. "Well, perhaps it's best that I don't come, as I am finding myself becoming more and more attracted to you, and we are both consenting adults."

"Yes, we are, and I do not consent." Olivia tossed her head and began to walk towards the lift. She turned round with a frown on her face. "Well, it's up to you. If you would like to see a cabin in a bedroom, you know where I am. I shall not be going to bed straightaway as I am still rather tipsy. Or just call in on your way to breakfast."

Felix left Olivia in the foyer and returned to his room. He poured himself a drink and sat on the bed. Olivia certainly was a mystery of contradictions. He began to wonder if she were a game player, an ultimate prick teaser. Was she saying yes or no? He had met many of those in his time. They were the ones who led a man up the garden path and at the final crunch they said no, or even waited till you were near orgasm and then would change their mind. "No, get off." The man had to get off or he could be accused of rape. He had only come near to that once, with a woman called Carol. She came from Yorkshire and zoomed in on him at a fashion show that the airport authorities held in Manchester. He was very drunk that night, to the point of hardly being able to stand up. Carol sneaked into his room and climbed into his bed. Felix never had a problem with brewer's droop. In fact, he went the other way. Alcohol was his Viagra. He felt a hand on his crotch and believed it to be Kirsty, the young girl he chatted up earlier. He turned round and was upon her with vigour and nearly didn't hear the words: "Stop, you are hurting me." Felix hesitated and wondered if this was part of Kirsty's sex talk, before he pulled back and turned the light on. To his amazement, he saw the ugliest, orange coloured woman beneath him.

He jumped out of bed and asked her what she thought she was doing. Carol told him she had seen him giving her the nod and thought he wanted her. She was stood beside Kirsty at the time. "No, I was not giving you the nod. I hardly know you." He was choking on his words and very angry by now. "How dare you! How dare you come into my room! No. How dare you come into my bed uninvited! I am not that desperate. Now fuck off and leave me alone."

Carol dressed and left very quickly. Felix made a mental note to be more careful in the future. He never saw her again.

Felix's thoughts returned to Olivia. Had he broken down her defences? Would she now be malleable? Putty in his hands? He realised that she was a very strong woman who at times behaved like a crazed child. He felt that she was tenacious and knew her own mind. Olivia surprised him this evening with some of her behaviours, which definitely made her the rainbow he was always chasing. As Felix gulped down the rest of his drink, he began to think about Heather and if he should, perhaps, have paid her more attention. Maybe he would have been in her bed by now and not sitting alone. He knew Heather would have said yes to him, as he noticed her looking at Olivia and him several times during the evening, with a look of envy on her face.

Felix's thoughts passed to Paula, who he knew would have consented to anything with him. Paula kept her distance throughout the evening, but watched as he and Olivia were chatting and getting to know each other better. He did not like being watched and the scrutiny made him feel uneasy. Felix could not be sure why he and Olivia were of such interest to Paula, and a sixth sense told him that something just didn't add up. He wished he could read people's minds. Paula's would have been interesting to read this night. It took a special kind of man to know what a woman was thinking, as most of the time their brains were like a speeding racing car at Le Mans. They would turn a bend so quickly and it was hard to keep up with them.

He began to wonder where the rest of the group were and what they were doing. Had they come in yet? Were they alone in their beds? He was alone in his bed. Felix began to think about the night before in Hanover, in the restaurant where they had their evening meal. Felix sat across the table from Louise, who was paying lots of attention to him. As Louise spoke to him, her fingers stroked the stem of her wine glass. He knew this to be a form of suggestive body language and symbolised the woman stroking the penis. Louise was almost offering herself up to him like a dog's dinner and he felt very uncomfortable. Felix knew that it was the wine talking. He did not want Louise. Had it been anyone else, Felix might have enjoyed the body language. Louise was too desperate with no sex appeal, and sometimes she came across as a little needy. It would be like having sex with his mother. Felix liked the thrill of the chase and he did not feel that Louise would run far or very fast. She would probably spread her legs for him at the drop of a hat. Whilst Louise was trying to awaken his interest, Felix noticed Heather and Paula speaking intently to Olivia, whose head was bent and nodding in answer to whatever they were saying to her.

Now, in hindsight, as he lay on his bed in Hamburg, Felix began to wonder what they were talking about that night. It felt as though they were being conspiratorial that evening in Hanover. Maybe he was wrong and they were just having a girly chat? Maybe they were planning to spend more money in the shops? Every time they went out, they returned laden with bags. Women could be so confusing and he often wondered what went on inside their minds. Why did they have to shop such a lot? Felix soon forgot about Hanover when his inner voice spoke loudly to him, "You won't know if you don't go." "Oh, fuck! What have I got to lose?" As it happened, he didn't have to lose anything at all and there was only gain to be had.

CHAPTER FOURTEEN

Felix came to a decision. If he didn't go, he would never know. He showered quickly, sprayed some eau de toilette on his muscular body and patted his face with 'Mandate', a popular aftershave that was reasonably priced. He used a lot of aftershave and did not see the point in spending too much money on man perfumes when it all did the same job. A good smell sent out the right signals and he felt it was important to stay clean and smell gorgeous. He looked at himself in the mirror. "Felix, you still got it, man!"

Picking up the complimentary bottle of wine left in his room, Felix closed the door behind him. He took a deep breath and walked quickly to Olivia's room. He hovered outside in the corridor before knocking. He could not decide whether to knock on the door or not and the voice in his head was arguing with itself. "Go on, man, what have you got to lose? She can say yes or no. Yes, but maybe it's not the best idea I have ever had." Why did he feel so nervous? Why was he being so hesitant? This had happened many times before with many different women in many different places. The little voice in his head warned him, "Be careful with this one, she might be the one."

Felix tapped on the door, feeling the beads of sweat forming on his forehead. As the door opened, he heard the sound of 'Take My Breath Away' by Berlin. Very slowly, a tousled head of hair appeared. "You came, then." Olivia opened the door wider. She stood before him wearing an oversized T-shirt and a massive grin. The T-shirt was deep pink with capped sleeves. Felix saw a lovely person with a hint of crazy. He saw a girly woman who just needed to be made love to, or so he thought. Felix looked down at Olivia's bare feet. What lovely feet she had. Her nails were painted in the softest pink. The T-shirt left everything to the imagination and the navy-blue wording emblazoned across the front — 'I put a spell on you' — seemed an apt set of words.

"Is that right?"

"What?" Felix nodded at Olivia, who looked down at herself and laughed. "I have been called a witch before now. I can assure you that I am not."

Olivia's face was washed clean, showing a natural beauty in the half-light. Felix smiled. She was gorgeous without make-up. Most of the women he bedded were made up to the nines. They hid under layers of foundation and blusher, caked mascara and wrinkle-inducing eye shadow. Olivia looked surprised to see him. For some reason, Felix felt embarrassed and a big grin swept across his face as he held up the bottle of wine he was clutching in his hand. He felt a bit like a young schoolboy about to go on his first date. "Thought we might christen the cabin?"

"It is my bathroom. Why would I want to drink wine by the toilet?"

Suddenly, Felix felt very foolish and uncomfortable. Olivia looked at him, then she looked at the bottle and then back at him. She stared at him, expressionless, for what seemed an age. Just as Felix began to feel more awkward and wonder whether he should turn on his heel and walk away in order to save face, Olivia grinned as she invited him in. "Well, seeing as you have made an effort and also brought some wine, you'd better come in." He stepped inside and, true to her word, Felix found himself looking at a cabin at the far end of the very large room.

The lamp-light cast an eerie, warming glow around the painted walls. Olivia turned away and walked across to a small table with two chairs on either side. She sat down and crossed her legs as Felix watched her and could see the outline of what appeared to be a rather nice, pert bottom. He remembered he had half seen it when they were on the metro. "Oh, how I would like to feel those cheeks in my hands." His thoughts were running wild as he followed her and sat down on the other chair. The wildness in his mind continued. He would pull her towards him while planting wet kisses on her inviting lips. He just needed to get her to drink more and say 'Yes' to him.

Felix felt a stirring in his manhood, that important piece of flesh almost speaking to him. "Hey, I'm down here, don't forget me; never mind the lips."

Olivia went to get a glass out of the cabin. On her return, she held up an already-opened bottle of wine. "Shall we finish my bottle before we start on yours, then?" He noticed that it was Pinot Noir: the lady had taste. The bottle was half-full. Her glass was empty, with a small drop of red settled in the bottom.

So! She had been drinking before he arrived. Felix began to wonder if Olivia was a secret drinker. Olivia noticed Felix looking at the bottle. "It is my favourite wine. Did you know it is one of the hardest grapes to grow, as it is so susceptible to disease?" This was not what Felix was expecting from her, a lesson in grapes. He didn't care about grapes. He did care about the strength of wine and what it did to the woman he was with at the time. Felix detected the odd slur of a word and he wondered if Olivia was drunk. Was she ripe for the picking? Did he have to give her love words to get her into bed? What would it be like? It was beyond his imagination, as Olivia was not like any other woman he had ever met. She appeared to be her own person and very unpredictable. Most women were very predictable and a pushover. Olivia was not going to be a pushover.

She sat down after pouring Felix a drink and with a smile asked him if he was offended by her attire. "I can get dressed if we are going to sit here for long."

Felix pretended to think for a moment, cocking his head to one side. "No, it is fine, unless you are feeling the cold." He was preoccupied and was thinking how to remove the one thing between him and her body. He did not want her to be putting any more clothes back on.

They both sat silently drinking the wine. It was a comfortable silence and then they both spoke together. "Go on, then, tell me about yourself." They began to laugh and the ice was broken. Olivia told Felix all about her family, her hopes and her dreams. She loved her job and had only been with 'Into the Sun' for four months. She told him of her trip to Norway and the attention she got from a younger man in a nightclub, who thought she was much younger than she was. At this point, Felix began to wonder just how old she might be. It was obvious she was younger than he was. He would not have liked to guess her age. Olivia laughed as she said the young man asked her to sleep with him. She thought his request was sweet, but declined. All the while she kept sipping on her wine and pushed the glass towards Felix for a refill.

She carried on, "English men don't ask you to sleep with them. They make assumptions after a pie and a pint. They think if you are being nice to them you are saying it's all right to bed me. That trip to Norway was an eye-opener. The men were so polite, and do you know the Norwegians speak better English than we do?"

Felix had visited Norway a few times. He loved the fjords, the glaciers and the starkness of the place. "When I went to Norway, I think it was shut."

"What do you mean?"

"The roads were empty and a lot of the hotels were closed. I suppose I didn't plan the holiday properly."

"Oh, right. Well, me and Bjorn we had a kiss outside the hotel. There was no passion. It was more like a first kiss. Well, it was a first kiss. The second and third were like the first. Innocent."

Felix wasn't really interested in her kiss with the Norwegian. He was more interested in the kiss they would have not too far in the future. As Olivia went on with her story, she told him that all her colleagues came out on the balcony of the hotel and began clapping. She said it was extremely embarrassing. She said that she felt sad the next day when she left Alesund on the ferry and would probably never forget the young man in denim or his name. When they returned to England, her workmates began to tease her, asking what she would do if the young man turned up on her doorstep. She said her husband would kill them both. Her conscience got the better of her and she told Felix that she managed to track the young man down and sent him a poem.

She asked him if he wanted to hear it. If it was a route to the bed, he would listen to anything. Olivia stood up, took a gulp from her glass and struck a pose, before reciting:

"'I lied to you, it made me blue. I should have told the truth that day. Now in hindsight I have to say. Kisses sweet, desires unfilled. When I left, some tears were spilled. I came home to a husband, left a good memory in a different land, which I need to bury in the sand. Now I say sorry on my knees. I ask that you forgive me, please.'"

There was a wistful look on Olivia's face as she gazed down into her glass with a look of embarrassment. Felix asked if she might have slept with the Norwegian. Olivia scowled. "I don't sleep around. I drink and do some very silly things sometimes, that is all."

He refilled her glass in the hope that she might do some silly things with him later. He still might get lucky. Sometimes when a woman became wistful and a bit sad, she might also become vulnerable and need comfort. Felix knew many different ways to comfort a woman, and it always ended the same way: her legs wrapped around him as he exercised his knees.

Olivia asked Felix if perhaps he might like some coffee. He declined and accepted another glass of wine as he went into a panic. If she had coffee she might sober up, and he didn't want that to happen. A problem was arising for him as he began to slur his words and he realised that he, too, was perhaps getting a little drunk. He could always perform when drunk, but sometimes forgot the experience and this was one experience he didn't want to miss. That was if it ever got off the ground.

He began to tell his story. He was a good storyteller and rarely told the truth to anyone about his life. This woman before him seemed different. There was no doubt in his mind that he wanted to bed her and then he would leave, not wanting to carry the relationship further. He had enough complications in his life without adding another. There was something compelling about Olivia that made him let his guard down. He talked without hesitation. It all came tumbling out as he rolled quickly down the slopes of his life. Felix spoke of his sad marriage to a woman who seemed to like alcohol and money more than she liked him. Felix wasn't sure if he should tell Olivia about his mistress. But he did. He could not believe what he was doing, the words rolling out as he opened his soul to a woman he hardly knew. He had never, ever told anyone about the real state of his life. Felix had taken off his mask and let Olivia see the real person he was. This was very disconcerting. He stopped to take a drink of the potent wine, before opening the second bottle.

Olivia was watching him closely as Felix remembered part of a long poem by Charles C Finn. It was about masks and the different persona we present and how we hide behind masks. The words came to him as they sat in silent contemplation. He began to recite the poem to her as a reminder that we might not always be what we show to others. Here he was, half-drunk, sitting next to a cabin in a very strange bedroom in Germany, with a woman who, for some reason, made him feel comfortable enough to have taken his mask off and throw it away. He wondered what this pretty, honest and extremely sexy person was thinking?

Olivia was watching him over the top of her wine glass. She did not have to work at being sexy. She had no clue as to how sexy she was. She was a little naive perhaps? It all came naturally to her. She portrayed an innocence and humour that could melt the hardest soul. Felix sat back and they smiled at each other. The large T-shirt was hiding a body he so wanted to see. It was only hinted at by the cold nipples sticking through the material. He closed his eyes and remembered how her breasts were pushing into his side when they were in the erotic theatre earlier. Was he going to be a lucky man tonight? His mounting erection began to speak: "Hopefully, tonight you might pick the flower."

The next two hours passed quickly. During that time there was serious discussion and laughter. Part of the discussion was what might happen after they finished the last bottle of wine. It all became rather bizarre as they discussed whether or not they should have sex. It was all so natural as they bantered over the finer points of sleeping together when hardly knowing each other. That was not a problem for Felix, but appeared to be one for Olivia. A deep conversation took place about whether they should 'fuck' before the morning. "Well, you can't call it making love, can you? You make love with someone you love. What we are talking about is lust; the body needs a release. For that reason, it is not going to happen. I would not go with anyone just for the sheer hell of it."

"If that is how you feel, that is fine by me, Olivia. We can just be friends?" Felix was extremely tactful, believing that he might possibly wear her resistance down. He would tread carefully. He just had to wait.

Olivia kept changing the subject and scuttling down other avenues of thought, until she leant across the table onto her elbows and began to tell Felix about her encounter with a clairvoyant six weeks earlier. He could not keep his eyes off Olivia's face as she began her story. Her face was the most expressive and animated he had ever seen on a person. "I went to see a friend of mine, Alan Roberts. He is a clairvoyant and reads tarot cards. I met him years ago at a clairvoyant party. They were very popular once upon a time — took over from Tupperware or Avon, I think. I also went to him for some regression therapy. Do you know what that is? It is when you go back to past lives before this one. Awesome! It was all very interesting. I have always been interested in those types of things. There must be something else, Felix. We can't just end, or what is it all for? What do you believe in, Felix?"

"I am not sure, to be honest. There could be something else, but no one has actually come back to tell us. A lot of our pilots have seen strange things in the sky. I have a colleague who believes that we are an alien experiment. He pleads a good case for the theory, too. I think that we should not dwell too deeply on these matters as we are here and it is the here and now that we should be concerned with."

"Anyway, to cut a long story short… I hate that phrase; don't know why I said it. It is the most annoying phrase when someone says it. Alan told me this was going to happen."

Felix interrupted her, "What, that you would cut a long story short?"

Olivia laughed and oiled her vocal cords some more. "No! Alan told me the number six was important; he felt six weeks or maybe six months. He said I would sleep with someone else, not my husband. I found it all quite upsetting and got a bit cross. I told him he had the morals of a gutter rat and I was happily married. He stuck to his guns and asked would I like to take a bet out with him?" Felix sat quietly, listening to her, as she began to look rather troubled. "I told him no way would I ever, ever, sleep with another man. I forgot about it till just now; until we began to discuss the pros and cons of doing what you so obviously want to do." He was taken aback by what she said. Was she not that drunk, then? She seemed more than tipsy, but still in control. Could she read his mind?

Olivia looked away. "Some people do what psychics say in order to prove them right. People then say I was told this would happen and it has. Well, not this lady, she always does the opposite. So for that reason, Felix, there is no way you and I will be getting it on together, just to prove Alan Roberts was right."

Olivia went to the cabinet and brought back a bottle of Schnapps. Where had she got that from? "I complained about the cabin, you know, and they gave me this. I suppose if I drink it all I will not notice how eerie this room is." She took a swig from the bottle and handed it to him. He put it to his lips and gulped the warm liquid down. Felix was fascinated by the woman before him. He felt that age-old stirring in his groin once more. He wanted her so much. He wanted to savour every piece of her body and he had no idea how he was going to do that now. She put the glass down on the table and leant on her elbows, her head resting on her hands. She was slurring now. "No way is that going to happen, EVER! Keep the thoughts in your dreams, Felix. There will be no sex tonight, or EVER, with you or any other man."

Felix left the table to make a drink at the sideboard, where there was a small travel kettle, some mugs and the usual selection of drinks one found in most hotel rooms. Returning, he sat down and placed a mug of steaming coffee in front of her. "Olivia, here, drink this; you are sounding pretty drunk just now." It was his turn to speak and he gave his reply to her previous speech, now she was off her soapbox. "I respect you for what you have said and understand where you are coming from. It was all very interesting. Let it go and don't let it spoil what, up to now, has been an entertaining and educational evening. Yes, I admit that I fancy you — and what man wouldn't want to bed you? I am surprised by how much I am attracted to you, as you are not the usual type of female I go for. There is something about you that I can't quite put my finger on, and I would so like to make love to you."

"I would not disappoint you, either." Olivia smiled and looked down at her feet as he went on.

"There is something special about you, sweet and endearing, which I find enchanting." Felix looked at his watch. "Look, it is now three thirty and we have an early start; we both need to get some sleep, we have a long day tomorrow, today! So how about I stay here now and we won't get under the covers but just lie on top, as mates, and get some kip?" He was struggling on his quest, believing all to be lost and keeping the thought that there might be other nights when he could try and break Olivia's defences down, so he gave up. He took a last drink of his coffee and went over to the bed. "Do you mind?" Olivia was staring at him intently. "Don't worry, Olivia, I won't touch you... We shall just be mates. Come on, love, you look whacked." Felix lay down on the bed and swept his arm across the empty space beside him. "It's time to sleep."

Olivia returned the mugs to the sideboard before coming over to the bed and lying down next to Felix. A waft of her perfume hit his senses. He couldn't help but think that this was such a waste. He turned to kiss

Olivia good night, giving her a quick peck on the forehead. He put his arm round her and pulled her close. Olivia snuggled into him and kissed his cheek. "Thank you, Felix, you are a gentleman after all."

As disappointment began to set in, he realised that he had lost this one and had to let her go. As they began to doze together, the most amazing thing happened. Suddenly, without warning, Olivia jumped off the bed, taking the oversized T-shirt by the hem and in one swoop she pulled it over her head and threw it to the far corner of the room. A mass of pink flew through the air. "Fuck you, Alan Roberts. I'll do what I want, when I want, with whom I want — and this is what I want."

Olivia threw herself onto the bed and landed next to Felix, whose eyes were nearly popping out of their sockets. This was definitely a time when Christmas had arrived early. He began to laugh. He did not think he had ever seen such a lovely body. Olivia was definitely a woman to hold, a woman to kiss and make love to. This was a body to respect. This body was built to be caressed, stroked and kissed all over. Felix began to do just that. He pulled Olivia to him and kissed her forehead. He looked at those lips that were drawing him onto her mouth. As their eyes met, a thousand violins began to play inside his head. As their lips met, the violins got louder. It was such a pleasure feeling those lips on his, so soft and warm and compliant. She was delicious. She was tasty and malleable. His tongue entered slowly, making its way round the inside of her mouth. Felix felt Olivia's tongue rise to meet his and they danced the dance of tongue and of two people needing each other, slowly, sensually.

Olivia shuddered as he thrust his tongue in and out, exploring every part of her mouth. He tickled her lips that were so soft, moist and tasted exquisite. He tasted the nectar of sensuality on his mouth and that which was between his legs began to rise. Felix moved his hands up to cup Olivia's breasts. She had hidden them well. He was surprised that they were so big, so beautiful. They were firm and magnificent. He stopped kissing her and pushed her back as he looked into her eyes. "Olivia, are you sure?"

She nodded, her eyes widening in anticipation. He knew she was drunk and she was saying yes. He didn't care. His lips spoke to her neck with small nibbling kisses and then slowly moved down to a large brown mammilla. As he took it into his mouth, he felt a great comfort and began to suck, taking as much of her breast into his mouth as he could. His hand gently squeezed and kneaded the soft, perfectly formed orb.

"More." Olivia asked for more. Felix's hand left her breast, moving down to her belly. It was slightly rounded, a sign of her gift to humanity. She had children but no stretch marks. It added to her sex appeal.

Felix liked a woman with curves, although he rarely got one. Air stewardesses were like stick insects and not very nice to the touch. He did not like stroking bones covered in paper-thin skin. This was so different, so new to him. Felix continued to suck on the mammilla that nearly matched the hardness between his legs. He slowly stroked her belly, before moving his hand lower to explore further. He moved his head and found her mouth, beginning to kiss her as his hand forced its way between her legs. Olivia gasped and sighed, affirming the situation. To his surprise, Olivia was already wet, and as he began to rub her button of love, he had to control the mounting passion in his greedy erection. He so wanted to enter her now, but knew that if he waited, it would make a difference to the ultimate moment when he planned to leave part of himself inside her. As he rubbed his hand backwards and forwards, he felt the swelling of her button responding to his touch. He rubbed harder and moved ever nearer to the tunnel of mystery that he was so excited about. Felix stopped kissing Olivia and watched for the expression on her face to change as he thrust his fingers inside her. He felt the juices trickle out and wet his hand.

Slowly, Felix began to move his fingers, in and out. Olivia's eyes widened as he hit the G spot with such force that she cried out. He felt no resistance as he put in a third finger whilst savouring the ecstatic look on her face. He knew he was bringing her to the point of no return, when he suddenly stopped what he was doing and raised his wet fingers to her lips. Olivia began to suck on the fingers that had invaded her privacy and left her throbbing down below, her eyes never leaving Felix's face. He was lost in the gaze that showed him her soul. He was lost in the big brown eyes that were pools of delight, there for him to drown in.

Not many people got to see Felix as Olivia was seeing him now. She was seeing him in all his glory, doing what he did best. He went down to lick the juice that tasted so nice and confirmed the willingness of her body. He wanted to repeat the experience. He wondered whether to leave her a while and then go for round two. Felix pushed Olivia away so that he could see all of her spread out before him on the bed. "God, you are so beautiful." He slowly looked her up and down. In a flash, he was on her again. He thrust himself inside her with such force that she screamed out. They began to move in unison, her hips dancing the love dance that kept her wet and moaning. Felix knew exactly what to do. He knew how to pleasure a woman. He'd had enough practice. This was ultimately the best ever.

Felix rolled to the side, never leaving her, never withdrawing, but moving into a position so that he could continue his penetration and also rub her clitoris at the same time. Olivia's orgasm hit him like a waterfall crashing down a steep cliff. She was out of this world and he continued to thrust and thrust, deeper and deeper. Felix held his orgasm and rolled her onto her belly. Automatically, Olivia came up onto her knees, her pert bottom high up in the air, leaving nothing to the imagination, the juices running down to meet him, the wetness sending him an invitation he could not refuse. Felix put his penis to her mouth of passion and with one thrust entered her quickly, firmly and brutally, with such force he knew he was at the point of no return. He felt his thighs hit the back of her legs and he slapped her buttocks hard with his free hand. Olivia screamed. "Fuck me, fuck me harder!" she began to moan. She was definitely more than drunk now. The sound of total sexual fulfilment echoed round the room.

Felix obliged; even the most genteel of ladies forgot themselves at times like this. He lost himself in her words and dripping love tunnel. A thousand fireworks popped in his head as he began to spasm and his manhood began to spit inside her with such fervour, there was no holding back now. Olivia gasped as her orgasm met his at the same time. Her juices were mingling with his sperm in that precious moment when two became one. Never in a million years would Felix have expected this from a woman like Olivia. She had proved herself and knew exactly what she was doing. She knew how to please a man. She certainly pleased him. There was a small question at the back of his mind. "Is she that drunk that she doesn't know what she is really doing?" The devil in him did not really care! It was out of this world. They were out of this world.

No words passed between them until Olivia sat up. "I think I am going to be sick." She rose from the bed and ran into the cabin. The moment following such passion was lost in the sound of her retching over the sink. Felix was fast asleep when a sorry-looking Olivia emerged from her episode in the bathroom. She went to the bed and stood looking at the rumpled sheets, before lying down beside him. She fell into an unconscious sleep that only drunks are familiar with.

Felix's watch buzzed at five. He rose, dressed and kissed Olivia on the forehead. She slept on in oblivion as he returned to his room to prepare for the day.

CHAPTER FIFTEEN

When Olivia woke, the space beside her was empty. Felix was gone. She was glad of that, as she tried to piece together the happenings of the night before. She couldn't remember it all and the bit she did remember was best forgotten.

It was a pure coincidence that Olivia and Felix happened to enter the dining room together that morning. Olivia found it disconcerting that they were the last ones in. Some of the group turned and smiled at them. They were cynical, knowing smiles. The sort of smile that says, 'We can guess what you've been up to!'

As they were getting their food, she felt compelled to speak. "Do you think they know?"

Felix ignored her. He was trying to distance himself now. Trying to build a bridge between them quickly, so as not to be too familiar and give the game away. He was very confused by his feelings for Olivia after their spectacular union.

"Felix." Olivia repeated his name between gritted teeth.

Without looking, he continued to load bacon onto his plate. "How should I know?" He left her feeling bewildered and promptly went and sat down. Paula looked up and glared at him across the room. Heather, who was sitting beside her, smiled. Olivia looked around the dining room. There was only one place left and Olivia had no choice but to sit down opposite Felix. She tucked into her breakfast as though she hadn't eaten for days. The passionate workout last night left her ravenous. Felix was astounded at the amount of food such a little person could put away.

As they drank their coffees, Felix pondered on last night's session. He had no conscience; sex was sex. He wondered why he was feeling something for this woman and he was now in dangerous territory, as he never got attached to the women he slept with. They were just bodies to him and served a purpose. He felt that he had somehow taken her away from the group. She was apart and alone. She was marked. Why should he care? Felix felt uncomfortable as people got up to leave their tables. He couldn't be that stupid. They weren't stupid either and knew what went on last night. Something did not feel right, and Felix did not know what it was. His gut instinct screamed at him as he noticed that each one ignored Olivia as they left. They knew something, but he wasn't sure what. Olivia was staring into her coffee, looking lost and lonely.

The rest of the day went well as they travelled across country to Michelstadt. This town was a historical masterpiece that went way back to medieval times and would be of interest to German history buffs. It was very beautiful and worth a visit. Olivia sat at the back of the bus. She was very quiet, usually the life and soul of the party, but not today. There was an atmosphere on the bus. There was no laughter, just an air of trepidation which lay stagnant over the group. They reached the Weinheim Hotel at five, giving them a few hours to relax before going to dinner at the tourist office.

Felix parked the minibus at the back of the hotel and headed for his room. He did not want to be with these people just now. The journey was becoming unbearable and he was glad to close the door on the world and sit alone with his thoughts. He poured himself a whisky and lay on the bed, running through the events of the previous night, reliving the moments with Olivia. He remembered every minute, every move, every moan and every whisper. As he felt her above and below him, the privacy between his legs moved in anticipation of what might happen now. It was amazing what thought could do. Felix finished his drink, went for a shower and did what men do when they need relief from a throbbing problem.

Clean, refreshed and spent, Felix pulled on a pair of cream slacks and a denim shirt, before splashing on some cologne and heading for the bar. He was happy and whistled as he strolled down the corridor to the next whisky. The traditional Bier Keller was dimly lit. Paula and Heather were sitting in a corner, heads bent and deep in conversation. It looked rather serious. Felix ordered a beer and walked across to them. "May I join you, ladies?" He was being polite. They looked up, rather startled. Was that embarrassment he saw run across their faces or just a 'No'? "I haven't interrupted anything, have I? If it is private, I can sit elsewhere."

Paula patted the seat beside her and smiled. "No problem — it was just girl talk." Both women looked very uncomfortable, as though found out for doing something wrong. They fell into an awkward silence which seemed to go on forever. Felix asked them if they were enjoying themselves and looking forward to going home in a few days. "Yes, it's great." Together they looked at each other and laughed. Felix looked at them, wondering what it was they were hiding. Something was not adding up here and he always trusted his instincts. His mind stopped worrying about the unknown when he heard Garth and Rebecca laughing as they entered the bar. Noisy as ever, they ran across to the table and sat down, bringing mirth to a muted corner of the room.

Rebecca began. "We went for a walk. It's a bit dead out there. I like the buildings, though, very nice."

Garth continued. "She wasn't looking at the buildings. She was looking for shops."

Rebecca hit Garth. "Shut up, clod." They soon removed the awkwardness and broke the ice that was thickening before they arrived.

Felix began to wonder where Olivia was; watching the doorway, he was disappointed by each new face that entered the room. He left the others to chatter and went to the bar to order another drink. He began a conversation with two Germans about the state of the world, the Deutsche Mark and world currency. He soon became bored. Felix looked at his watch. It was nearly time to leave. He said his goodbyes to his chatting companions and walked over to Heather. "Where is she?"

"Where is who?"

"Olivia, of course; who do you think I meant?"

Heather shrugged. "How should I know? We share a room. I am not her keeper; maybe she is getting ready."

Felix didn't like Heather's attitude. There was definitely something amiss. As they all gathered to go outside, nobody mentioned Olivia. Nobody seemed to care at all. They did not stop, nor did they turn round; they just carried on out of the door. Suddenly, he heard a voice. "Wait for me, please."

Felix turned to see Olivia running across reception. She was looking as beautiful as ever. As Felix waited for her, he decided the women must have squabbled over something: putting it down to the bitching that can go on when women are together twenty-four/seven. They took on roles that were less than complimentary as they became a pack, and one would be singled out as fair game or a scapegoat. They were quick to gang up on the different one who stood out amongst them. They could be such dreadful bullies. Was that it? Had they ganged up on Olivia for some reason? Well, she certainly stood out amongst them. Her vibrant personality kept the others in the shadows of their own nastiness.

"I thought you weren't coming; we will be late." Felix took her by the arm and ushered her out of the door into the street.

Kevin drove to the venue, leaving Felix space to mull over the thoughts in his head. Felix's theory of women, groups and bitches was confirming itself. Olivia was being singled out by the others for some reason. Were they all in it together? He didn't think Louise was part of what was going on, although he could be wrong. He decided that perhaps he might get Louise on her own later and see if she would give anything away. He was fascinated by women. He found them to be multi-faceted creatures. They were quite disturbing, particularly when in a pack.

Olivia sat next to Felix at dinner, but hardly spoke. Was he imagining it, or was there now a wall between them? He knew that he had been rather abrupt in the dining room that morning. He had to be — he was trying to save them from gossip. Maybe he should have been a little friendlier at breakfast? After all, he was a bit short with her. It did not stop him feeling the sadness that she was now carrying. Did she regret the night before? What was wrong with him? Why should he care? He got what he wanted — but maybe he got more than he bargained for. Felix knew he didn't regret one single moment. It was one of the best sexual encounters he ever had, and there were many over the years.

Felix's mind wandered to one of his favourite songs, 'Right Next Door (Because of Me)', by Robert Cray. Was the atmosphere because of him as he drew up another notch on his guitar? There was nothing to be gained in dwelling. He shook his head and tucked into his sauerkraut. After dinner, they all walked across the road to a night club. It took a while for Felix's eyes to adjust to the darkness as he peered inside, wondering what the night would bring. A table was reserved for them. It was covered in opened bottles of wine and beer ready to appease their thirst.

Sometimes, Felix loved his job: it was good to have free alcohol and made the nights fun. He thought if he could get Olivia drunk there might be a repeat performance that no doubt would be even better than the night before. Felix noticed that Olivia had placed herself in a corner away from him. She was sipping vodka and not speaking to anyone. She looked so miserable and sad. He did not get an opportunity to talk to her again, as Heather monopolised him and would not leave him alone. Felix danced with Heather most of the evening. He found her rather boring, but thought she might be worth a grope. He noticed that Olivia was now twirling round the floor with Kurt, the tourist officer. She was laughing and chattering away; her mood had lifted and she looked as though she was enjoying herself. Maybe Kurt might get lucky? That was a nasty thought and Felix knew that Olivia would not sleep around. He felt a pang of envy, wishing she was dancing with him instead. He turned his attention to Heather, who was quite tall and although not pretty had a certain attraction about her. She was Olivia's friend and he found it hard not to ask prying questions about his previous night's conquest. Heather was not forthcoming and spent her time blowing in Felix's ear, thinking this was a sexy thing to do. It was obvious that Heather could not hold her alcohol. She was very drunk by the end of the night.

It was time for the last dance when the DJ played 'Stay With Me Till Dawn'. The dulcet tones of Judy Tzuke flooded the room. Heather pulled Felix to her and put her cheek on his. As he looked over his shoulder, he caught Olivia's eye: she was still dancing with Kurt, now being held tightly in his arms as she gazed across the floor at Felix. She caught his eye and winked. She was such a minx! It seemed like she was in a better place than she had been earlier. Felix felt a stirring in his loins and it wasn't due to Heather pushing herself against him for all she was worth. His eyes were melting into those big brown pools that were looking at him from across the floor. Heather moved Felix round and the eyes were gone, the moment lost to a memory. He felt the feeling that was beginning to grow disappear in a moment of disappointment. Heather was getting silly and tried to nibble his ear. The last thing he wanted was this woman to come on to him right now. Felix's mind was elsewhere and he wished his body was, too.

The evening ended and Felix had a private word with Kurt. He thanked him for his hospitality and found it hard not to mention Olivia. Was he jealous? His earlier feelings that something was amiss were confirmed. Paula and Heather were standing with Louise. They were chattering and laughing. Olivia was standing alone at the door. Felix couldn't put an expression to the mask she was wearing. He moved to the side of the room and watched her. What was that expression? It came to him. It was a brave face. Why? Why was Olivia wearing a brave face? The rainbow he'd been chasing was fading. He just saw a sad person who had lost her colours. These were supposed to be her friends, her work colleagues, and they now appeared to be shunning her. Surely it couldn't be because she was enjoying herself and having a good time? It was true she did have the men buzzing round her like flies, but the women wouldn't be jealous, would they? Olivia was rather naïve and wasn't even aware when the 'open' flies hovered. She was just Olivia, and what you saw was what you got; he knew that. "Bloody women! They could be such evil bitches." He walked across the floor to Olivia. He took her arm. "Are you all right, love?"

"Not really." She shrugged and did not want to talk to Felix. "I'm a big girl and I will survive. I just want to go home."

Felix took Olivia outside. He felt the daggers hit his back as he left the building. Women could be so vicious, and the atmosphere followed them onto the minibus. He sat next to Paula, leaving Olivia to sit on her own at the back of the bus. Felix felt he had to get to the bottom of what was going on. There were three days left before they were to go home and there were many miles still to travel. Things needed to be dealt with before they got out of hand and the atmosphere got worse. He had never encountered such behaviours before, and he really had to sort things out.

Felix decided that he would speak to Louise first, as she didn't appear close to Paula and Heather and sometimes kept her distance from them. When they reached the Weinheim Hotel, Felix stopped Louise and asked her if she fancied a nightcap. Everybody went to their rooms and Louise sat down beside Felix in the bar. He asked her what she would like to drink. "Just a coffee, thank you," she said. Felix persuaded her to have a brandy with her coffee: maybe it would loosen her tongue and he might just find what he was looking for. He was not sure how he was going to broach the subject of his enquiry and began by asking Louise if she was enjoying herself and how she felt the evening went. He was hoping that she might let something slip. This would be difficult, as he had known her for a few years and knew she did not gossip.

Louise told Felix that she was having a good time but could not speak for the others. He would have to ask them. He pondered a while before asking Louise what her thoughts were on Olivia, as she was the newest member of staff at 'Into the Sun'. Louise told Felix that she liked Olivia. She was full of life, liked a laugh, didn't have a bad bone in her body and was very popular in the office. She was a comedienne and always kept them laughing with her antics. Sometimes she could be easily led, which made her a bit naïve.

Felix thought that was a strange thing to finish off with. "Why do you say that about being easily led?" Louise began to blush and looked away. "She doesn't seem too popular here just now, does she, Louise? I have noticed an atmosphere and wonder what that is about."

Louise smiled. "Don't ask!" She looked down into her brandy glass and began to blush. Was this embarrassment? Felix knew he was on the right track. Nonchalantly, he threw a question. "I bet it's girls' stuff, a squabble about nothing?" Felix persuaded Louise to have another brandy, discreetly whispering to the barman, "Make that a double."

Louise drank the brandy. She didn't want to be sitting next to this man. She didn't want to get involved. She did not want him asking these questions. Louise had always hoped that one day she and Felix might perhaps get together. He was always so polite and well-mannered, and there weren't many men about like him anymore. Felix's eyes never left her face. Louise began to wish she was somewhere else. Felix knew she knew something: he could see it in her expression which spoke a thousand words. She was definitely hiding something. "Louise, what is going on?" His assertive voice startled her.

She put her glass down. "I don't know."

Felix challenged her. "I think you do."

Louise rose quickly and turned to face him. "Look, Felix, it is none of my business and I don't want to get involved. I don't know much. I suggest you speak to Paula; she seems to be at the bottom of all this. She has never liked Olivia, feels threatened by her. Ask Paula, not me." Louise turned on her heel and walked out of the bar.

Felix ran after her and, without thinking, turned her round and kissed her full on the lips. It wasn't long before they were naked on Louise's bed. All her dreams were coming true! After a quick roll within the sheets, Felix left a sleeping Louise to dream on.

So, Paula had some part in all this. Now he had to think of a way to get her to talk. That might be harder than expected. Felix needed to know what was going on with Olivia as his feelings for her were growing and this needed sorting out. It didn't matter what he had just done with Louise. As he walked to his room, he began to hatch a plan.

The next time Felix saw Paula, he asked her if they could have lunch together. He said he was sorry for having neglected her and that he was conscious that as leader of the team he should have been consulting with her throughout the trip. Felix knew that he would have to feed Paula's ego if he was to get her to open up to him and solve the ever-growing mystery.

Paula gave him a goofy smile and said rather sarcastically that she was surprised that he would want to lunch with her when he seemed so busy with other members of the group. Felix was repulsed by her. She had a nasty streak, which showed in her face. She answered that she would love to have lunch with him and today would be as good a time as any. As they were not leaving till the evening, they all had some free time. Felix was not looking forward to being alone with Paula. He knew where she might want the lunch to lead, and even a brave man would be foolish to take her to his bed. He was still trying to put his misdemeanour with Louise out of his mind and wanted no further complications on this trip. Felix wasn't that brave, nor was he that foolish. Perhaps he could string Paula along, say nice things to her and find ways to get her to open up. He could do that quite easily. Paula liked a drink, and it wouldn't take much to get her drunk and talkative. He then might be able to extract the information he was seeking.

At eleven-thirty, Felix joined Paula in the foyer. He could see that she had made an effort to look sexy. It was not working. Her mousy hair was pinned up on her head and she wore a bright green mini-dress that didn't actually fit her. The red lipstick did not suit her either. Not the way to dress at lunchtime really.

Paula ran up to him, all giggles. She put her arm through his and pulled him towards the door. "Come on then, where are you taking us on our secret lunch? Let's get out of here before anyone sees us." She put emphasis on the *secret* and *us*. No, no, no! He would have to be very careful. Felix raised his eyebrows: how would he manage a whole lunchtime with her? This could end up becoming very complicated.

They walked down the road to a small restaurant by a stream and sat outside at a table covered in a red gingham cloth and rustic homemade crockery. Although it was the end of autumn, the sun still held its heat and warmed the earth for a few hours, making it pleasant enough to sit outside. Felix ordered two shots of schnapps without asking Paula. When the drinks arrived, he lied about it being the custom for old friends to drink quite a few when they had not seen each other in a while. It wasn't really a lie, as that is what happens anyway. By the third drink, Felix could see that Paula's tongue was loosening, as she was beginning to babble. She was ripe for the picking. He chose his questions carefully as he began to slowly walk through her mind. She told him that everyone was enjoying the trip. Paula went on to say that she missed him and their conversations and was happy to have this opportunity to be alone with him and catch up. Paula's voice began to grate on Felix and he was quickly beginning to feel irritated. Perhaps it was because he wanted to be with Olivia. For a moment he wondered why he was doing this. He needed to solve the mystery of what was going on with Olivia. That was why!

Felix's mind began to wander as Paula droned on and on. He did not like her. He did not like her one bit. She was a crafty bitch, who misused her power as a manager and didn't have many friends. Kevin once told him that if she did not like someone, she made their life so hard at work that eventually they would leave. Was this what was happening to Olivia? Had Paula got some hold over her and was now going in for the kill? Since Hamburg, the atmosphere was getting worse and it was obvious something was very wrong, very wrong indeed. Felix was determined that he would find out before the end of the day. He watched Paula as she ate her meal. She did not have the finest of table manners and the way she ate was very off-putting. What a disgusting pig she really was. Felix would continue his act and humour her. He would do whatever it took to find answers to his questions. Well, almost! He might have to draw the line at sleeping with her, even though he had snorted with a few pigs in the past.

CHAPTER SIXTEEN

"Sir, sir, would you like another drink?"

The hostess put her hand lightly on Felix's shoulder and he was brought back into the present. "Er... yes, yes please." He smiled up at the young flight attendant, who was probably older than she looked. "I will have the same as before." Felix looked at the man seated beside him; he looked asleep, but he nudged him anyway. Adam opened his eyes. "Would you like another drink?"

"Yes, thanks, mate. Sorry, was just taking a nap." After a short polite chat with Adam, Felix learnt that Adam used to be a football referee and he had a boat on a river in Yorkshire. Felix finished his drink and closed his eyes, returning to Paula in Germany. His memory was becoming clearer all the while as to what happened all those years ago.

~

They were on their second bottle of wine when Felix asked the question. "So, what is going on, Paula? I have noticed an atmosphere and everybody seems to be ignoring Olivia; she doesn't seem to be part of the group."

"Nothing. Don't know what you are talking about." Her flushed face became redder. Felix poured her another drink. She knew, he knew, she knew. He needed to approach the subject from a different angle.

"Do you think Olivia is enjoying this trip, as your newest member of staff? I know you went to Norway and she told me she loved it. As my trips are important, I like to hear what people make of them."

Paula looked at him, trying to put on a sexy gaze, which wasn't quite working. "Why don't you ask her yourself, Felix? Let's not talk about her, it's time to talk about us." Paula sighed, made another attempt at a sexy smile and raised her glass for more wine. Felix obliged. He felt that this would be his last attempt to find out what was going on. He had already approached some of the others with subtle hints. No one was willing to speak, and just kept referring him back to Paula, telling him he should be asking her, not them. Felix needed her to spill the beans before she became incoherent. He had to manipulate this ugly, awful bitch sitting across the table from him.

He decided to take a risk. "Can I tell you something, Paula? Can you keep it between us, please?"

Paula perked up. "Of course, you can, and I think I know what you are going to say."

Felix looked surprised. "You do?" Taking a deep breath, he began. "You know, Paula, there is someone who I think is lovely, a bubbly, nice person who is really pretty."

Paula smiled at him and began to touch her hair and wobble her head about. She knew where he was leading and said, "Oh, Felix, I like you, too."

Felix ignored the body language and continued without hearing her. "It is Olivia. I don't think I have ever met anyone like her. She is so intelligent and funny. I am really beginning to like her."

Paula took a minute to process what was said and straightened her back, before leaning across the table, a malicious look slowly clouding her distorted face. A few moments passed. "You have slept with her, haven't you, Felix?"

This was totally unexpected. "No, of course I haven't. Why would you think such a thing?" Felix nearly choked as he took another drink of wine. Paula sat back in her chair and stared at him. He could see she was struggling with something. The silence continued and became more than uncomfortable. Felix ordered a brandy. He needed another drink. He needed to think quickly. He did not like lying, but it appeared there was no option in this instance. The last thing he wanted Paula to find out was what happened that night in Hamburg.

Paula smiled, more to herself than at him. "Well, either you are lying or she is lying then." Was Paula playing games with him now?

"What do you mean by that?"

"I am not going to tell you; why should I? I know what I know and one of you is lying." Paula repeated her question. "Did you sleep with her, Felix? She is married, you know. I don't understand. I thought that this trip maybe at last you and I would come together. I thought when we went down the Reeperbahn that this would be it for us, and then you disappeared."

Oh, no, here she went again. Oh, Lord! He had to stop her once and for all. No way would he ever sleep with her. It would never happen. Felix leaned across the table and took Paula's hand in his. It was time to come clean. "Paula, love, you are a manager in a place where I do a lot of business for the airline. We have a good professional, working relationship. We cannot ever have any other kind of relationship. You must see that? Contrary to popular belief, I do not sleep with every woman who crosses my path." That was a lie. He slept with most of them. There weren't many that Felix did not make a play for. There were a few disappointments, but he found his position made him a fanny magnet. Women loved men with power, and Felix had some power. It was his mission in life to bed as many women as he could before his prostate let him down. Felix wanted to spare Paula's feelings as much as he could and to keep hidden what happened in Hamburg. He couldn't be completely heartless. "That night we went down the Reeperbahn, we all had far too much to drink. Olivia was so funny and she looked beautiful and vulnerable. The outcome of the night was inevitable. She fell asleep; as much as I wanted to make love to her, I didn't. I am growing very fond of her and trying to sort my feelings out." Felix was about to come clean and at the last minute just couldn't do it. He could not betray Olivia. He thought too much of her and knew that she, too, would never betray him.

Paula kept her head bent and through her teeth spat, "You are a lying fucking bastard, Felix. I know you slept with her. She told me, you stupid creep."

Shocked by the remark, he looked beyond the stream and over the fields into the distance. He was stunned by the venom that came his way. Why would Olivia tell Paula? He would have understood if she told Heather, but why this flushed-faced drunken bitch? It didn't make any sense. Felix gathered his feelings and then made a grave mistake. "Do I need to ask why she told you? Perhaps I should ask her?" Felix had many secrets and did not like people knowing his business. He began to wonder if he had misjudged Olivia. She didn't appear to be the sort of woman to tell people things. He was rather confused and not too sure if he believed what he heard. Paula was downing another glass of wine and Felix became a little concerned, as she was already quite drunk. He might never learn the truth.

To the contrary, Paula went into overdrive and was in full flow. She was hurt by Felix's previous revelation about his feelings for Olivia. He had pulled the rug from under her and taken away her dreams. One night would have been enough for her, but she knew now that would never happen. Paula had the power to destroy the ever-popular, oh-so-pretty Olivia: everybody's friend. She got out of her seat and went to the lavatory. It bought her some time to think. She had the power now. She was going to destroy Olivia — or would she destroy Felix instead? She hated them both so much now.

Paula returned from the ladies' room wearing a smile. "Felix, can I have an espresso, please? Are you sure you want me to tell you everything? You won't like it!" Her smile turned into a smirk. She was enjoying her moment and revelling in the power that was now hers. The hatred was obvious in her eyes. "Ignorance is supposed to be bliss, but if you want to know, then I will tell you."

Felix nodded. Yes, he wanted to know. He wanted to know why this drunken woman before him knew his business. He prided himself on the secrecy which was his love life, or was that the secrecy of his sex life?

Paula picked her words carefully. "She did it for a dare."

Her words stung Felix. He felt a nasty taste rising in his mouth. "What do you mean?" He could not hide the surprise in his voice.

Paula proceeded to tell Felix about a conversation that took place the day before they reached Hamburg. "You have a way with the ladies, don't you, Felix? I have loved you from a distance for years. Louise has, too. We have had many discussions about you in the office after your visits. Louise is very nice, but a bit stupid. She always hoped that you would show some interest in her. I hoped that one day you might take an interest in me. Louise told me that she was going to try to get together with you on this trip. Remember that night in the restaurant when you sat together a few days back? I noticed you were beginning to get cosy with her. I had to do something. No way was she going to have you." Felix did not move and tried not to smirk, as Louise had her wish the night before. She probably enjoyed herself more than he did. Paula looked into

Felix's eyes. She was enjoying this. She was going to destroy them both with a single swoop. "Olivia was easy. She played right into my hands. I knew she was a wildcard, but I had nothing to lose. I got her drunk and the rest is history. It didn't take long at all." Paula stopped and took a drink. She looked at Felix, who was looking across at the fields beyond the stream. For a moment he wondered if Paula was lying. "I told Olivia some white lies about you and that it was in Louise's best interests that she had you instead of her. It doesn't matter now what I said to her about you. Olivia knew her job depended on what she did next. Everybody has their price, Felix, you know that. I found her Achilles heel; it was easy. I dared her to sleep with you. I told her why she needed to get you before Louise did. At first, she said No, she was not a whore. She was wrong, as that is exactly what she is. You think she liked you? No, she did what she did as a dare and to keep her job. You're not as good as you think you are, Felix. In fact, I think perhaps I had a lucky escape."

Paula could not stop. The horror on Felix's face fed her power. "Did you know you have a nickname? It is 'airport chipolata', not even the size of a sausage. Is that funny! You are not smiling now, Felix, are you? You could have had me and I would never have told a soul." The expression on Felix's face showed that Paula had hit where it hurt with her lies. Part truth was that she had discussed Louise's crush on Felix with Olivia and she dared her to get him before Louise did. However, she was not prepared for Olivia's reply, which put Paula firmly in her place and was rather embarrassing. Felix's face told Paula that following her hunch about him and Olivia was right. He had given the game away. She now knew for sure that Felix and Olivia spent the night in Hamburg together. She'd guessed, but just needed confirmation, which she had received by the look on Felix's face. "Now you see, Felix, your little Miss Popular is nothing but a gossiping, cheating witch. I planned it all and you both fell into my trap." Paula sat back, and the smile that had become a smirk, now became a grin. That was a job well done. She crossed her fingers under the table, hoping that Felix did not now confront Olivia. She worried that she might have her plans scuppered by the truth.

Paula added one last nail to Olivia's coffin lid, knowing that she would now be buried forever by Felix. Paula still believed that if she played her cards right, she might spend one night with Felix before they returned to England. "She bragged about it to us, even told the guys. What about that, Felix?" Felix didn't know whether to laugh or cry. He was lost for words, something that rarely happened. Had he read Olivia wrong? So perhaps she wasn't as sweet as he thought. He must have got it very wrong. His flames of passion that were burning for Olivia were slowly being damped down by the venom in this vixen's words and new flames of anger were slowly igniting. He didn't really have a reason to disbelieve Paula. It all sounded so plausible. Surely, she wouldn't be that malicious, so it must be true. Paula was honest about her feelings for him and told him about Louise's feelings, too. He believed that.

Felix's rainbow was fading fast, the colours lost in the fog of his disturbed mind. He reaffirmed his old belief: never trust a woman! He'd trusted Olivia, had warmed to her. She hit a chord and played music in his heart. All the while she was doing it for a dare? He shook his head; how wrong he was about her. She was just another bitch bag like all the rest. Olivia was no different. How wrong could he have been? "Come on, Paula, let's get back; the others might wonder where we have got to." He took Paula by the arm and helped her up. She looked into his sad eyes.

"You know it's not too late for us, Felix. I would never lie to you; I have waited so long." She watched as a hard look replaced the sadness on Felix's face and it set in an expression, she could not find a word to describe. It was a fixed mask of stone. As she put her hand on his arm, she sealed her fate. "I'm not sorry that I told you. I had to. You deserve better. It was only for one night. You never know, she probably sleeps around anyway. I hope you haven't caught anything off the cow. I have known she was a man-eater all along."

Felix looked at her in horror. How could someone be so malicious to the point of evil? He needed to escape from this one. He needed to make sense of the drunken ramblings of this spurned woman. How much was truth and how much had she made up out of spite?

Back in his room, Felix sat by the window. He watched as a rainbow formed through the afternoon drizzle. A teardrop ran down his cheek. He looked away. Disappointment brought tears that were alien to him. He was a stranger to this feeling and did not welcome it. He swallowed hard. In just one night, Olivia got to him. She entered a sacred place he kept locked for many years. She walked into his private space and played with his feelings. Then she betrayed him. Felix could still not be sure as to the truth. He was not willing to give the benefit of the doubt.

He'd had enough. He closed the book which was Olivia. He closed the book on what might have evolved into a happy unknown future with her. This would never, ever happen again with anyone. Felix's sadness turned to anger. He had been used and abused by the woman he let into his heart. They say what goes around comes around. Felix was now feeling the way the women he had picked up and let down must have felt. It was not nice, not nice at all. Felix made a mistake with Olivia. He would not make a mistake again. He did not know what he would do next or how he would react the next time he saw her. That remained to be seen. He would keep out of her way and she could deal with the group on her own. It was funny how quickly a growing love could turn to a growing hate. He lay down on his bed, closed his eyes and tried to get some much-needed sleep, only to be haunted by Paula's terrible words and the images of Olivia beneath him, moaning and whispering his name.

CHAPTER SEVENTEEN

Olivia pressed the button above her head and waited patiently for the steward. She was feeling all but patient now. The steward came from the back of the plane. "Yes, love, what can I do for you?" Was she looking at the double of Sean from Coronation Street? This was a television series that Olivia had watched from the beginning when she was a little girl. It became the longest running soap on television in 2010 and was even in the *Guinness Book of Records*. Sean worked in the public house, the Rovers Return. Olivia had a quirky sense of humour that saw the steward's similarities. It was hard to hide a smile. Olivia asked his name. She always wanted to know who she was talking to. She knew people liked being asked their name. It showed the asker was interested. Had she not been strapped into her seat, she would have surely fallen off it when he answered, "Sean, what's yours?"

"I am Olivia and could I have a brandy, please? Err... no, make that a double, please."

On his return, Sean was curious. "Do I know you? I am sure I have seen you somewhere before."

Olivia told him no, this was her first trip to America. Sean pulled a quizzical smile. He wobbled his head and continued up the aisle to bring Olivia the sandwich she had ordered previously.

Olivia watched Sean's pert bottom moving from side to side as he walked the walk of a happy man who didn't care and was proud. He was genuine, and Olivia watched in admiration; she might put him in her next book. Olivia never had to make the characters up; she felt it was best to use reality and colour it with fantasy. She drew on her life experiences and those who crossed her path on her life journey to make the characters come alive and be real. She spent a lot of time people-watching and listening to other people's conversations. She was also good at asking questions and had a knack of getting people to say more than they wanted to.

A few minutes later, Shaun was back. "Are you sure we have never met before?"

Olivia laughed. "I think I would have remembered you, Sean." She thanked him for the sandwich. She didn't feel very hungry now. It would keep. Olivia's hands were shaking when she took the glass and looked at the golden liquid that would hopefully help calm her down. She took a large gulp to steady her nerves after what must have been one of the biggest shocks she ever had. What were the odds of her seeing two men from her past after twenty-some years while on a plane to America? It was most bizarre, as not only were they all on the same plane, but Adam and Felix were sitting next to each other. Olivia took her bag from under the seat and eventually found her phone. She began to tap out a message: "You will never believe who is on this plane with me, not in a million years, ever!"

A swift reply came back: "Who? Who is there with you?"

"Do you remember the choreographer from the fashion shows? Do you remember my encounter in Hamburg? I saw them both, coming back from the toilets. Adam and Felix! They are sitting next to each other." The message went. "What about that? I winked and walked on by." Olivia pressed 'send' once more. She imagined her friend Anne jumping up and down in the kitchen, typing a message back to her. Olivia finished her drink and ordered another one before she heard from Anne again.

"OMG! No! Are you sure it was them? What are you going to do? Are you going to tell them about the book? Don't speak to them. Remember what they did to you. The bastards! I had to help you heal and mop up your tears; don't forget that, will you? Bastards! Be strong. Shall I come out? I am here for you, xxx."

Olivia smiled. Anne was like her little sister. They had known each other many years and were always there for each other. They had many secrets and shared many adventures in the past, but she didn't need her friend right now. She had to do this on her own. Olivia felt that she could deal with the shock of seeing part of her past on the plane. She took another drink and wondered what to do? Anne's words came back to her: "Remember what those bastards did to you."

Olivia always believed that what happens to a person was somehow their choice and she was a great forgiver. Whilst she had not chosen to have her heart broken, somewhere in the complication of her mind she felt she needed the experience for her personal learning and growth. Being such a positive person, she felt that everything that happens in life can be turned into an advantage. Some people thought she was totally daft, more than a little eccentric and living in a parallel universe to everyone else. Others knew where she was coming from and understood her.

All Olivia knew was that she was as happy as she could be, most of the time. It hadn't always been so. A person has to make their own happiness and luck, create their own destiny and not rely on others. Olivia began to think about Felix. It wasn't as though they had an affair or anything. It was more than twenty years ago and the details of that trip were buried somewhere in the filing cabinets that stored information in the back of her mind. Now she had seen him so unexpectedly, she located the cabinet at the back of her subconscious and the drawer began to slowly open.

Olivia never understood why she slept with Felix. It was one of the most stupid things she had ever done in her life, and she'd done more than a few. She had not listened much to Paula's drunken ramblings that night in the restaurant, but he, Felix, listened to Paula later. Olivia's problem was always that she was gullible, naïve and liked a challenge. She loved her little adventures. That night, Olivia was led up the garden path and dropped in the pond before she realised what was happening. Thank goodness she no longer drank to excess. She knew it to be the root of much evil. She was older now and somewhat wiser. Not all the time, though, and she was aware there were still mistakes to be made. Mistakes were to be learnt from and a person had to ensure they didn't make the same one twice. Not always easy. As the drawer to Olivia's memories opened wider, the whole 'German experience' came out without invite and brought out the feelings from that trip, in the form of flashbacks.

~

The restaurant was cosy, rustic, dimly lit and very German. Food was ordered and happy chatter was in abundance. Olivia sat between Paula and Heather at the end of a long pine table covered in a crisp white tablecloth. The boys sat next to them and Louise sat opposite Felix at the far end. Olivia couldn't understand why Louise was not with the girls, but she seemed to be enjoying herself with Felix. Olivia had not really spoken to him since the airport, when he carried her bags and she had to run after him across the cream marble floor. Felix was a little older than her. He was bald and she thought his arrogance and demeanour made him appear rather pompous, to say the least. She wasn't sure if she liked him and wasn't sure if she would want to get to know him better. In fact, she didn't think of him at all.

Olivia had no time for those who were 'full of themselves'; who blew their own trumpet. She did not think blowing one's own trumpet was about confidence, but more an obnoxious personality that needed to be heard. This type of person was to be avoided. Olivia did not judge people, but noted her observations of them for future reference. She just avoided those who bothered her. Felix didn't even bother her. He was just the man who organised the trip. She found herself watching Felix and Louise and wondered if perhaps they might be making a connection.

By now, the girls were rather drunk, talking silly and really enjoying themselves. Out of the blue, Paula began. "Look at her, the simpering bitch; she wants him, you can tell." Paula nodded down the table towards Louise and Felix.

Good grief, what was that all about? Olivia was taken aback by the comment. This was not the way a manager should talk, even if out of work, was it? "How do you know that?"

Olivia was cut short by Paula's next tirade. "Watch them! Can't you see what she is doing?" As Paula went on, Heather and Olivia smiled at each other and turned to look to the end of the table.

Louise was smiling, her eyes never leaving Felix's face. He was telling her something, and it all looked very cosy and innocent. Heather piped up. "What is she doing? Chatting and smiling?"

"No, she's not. Watch her hands on that glass." They looked again. Olivia noticed that Louise's forefinger and thumb were slowly going up and down the stem of the wine glass, which was half full of red wine.

Heather seemed totally unaware of the implications of the action. "Yep, she's playing with her wine glass; so?"

Paula turned to Olivia. "Do you know what it means?"

"Yes, I do."

Paula pushed Olivia in her side. "Then tell the idiot, will you!" She nodded in Heather's direction. Luckily, Heather did not hear her and Olivia began to think that perhaps Paula was totally out of order and should have more decorum as the manager.

Olivia looked at Heather to see if the insult registered. Heather was too drunk to notice that Paula had just called her an idiot and was preoccupied with the two at the end of the table. Heather could not take her eyes off Felix. She turned to Paula and Olivia and made a statement. "You know I think I could do him. He looks pretty fit for his age. I wonder if he has any condoms with him."

Paula burst forth again with angry words. "For goodness sake, woman, he wouldn't look at you!"

Heather was slurring her words. "What do you know? I haven't seen him looking at you that much either!"

Olivia sat back and waited. She wondered where all this would end. She knew the stories about Paula and members of staff. Heather was now trying to back track. She turned to Paula. "Sorry, that was the wine talking, not me." People had to keep Paula sweet if they valued their jobs, and life could become very difficult back in the office. Paula was a classic bitch manager who ruled with an iron rod. There was another story about how she got to be manager. Not nice!

Olivia sighed and went on to patiently explain, "Doing that with the stem of a glass with your fingers means that you are stroking the man's penis. You want him. Work it out yourself, Heather. She is subconsciously tossing him off."

Heather sat back in her seat. "No! What? How do you know that? Did you read a book or something?" Heather began to laugh and only stopped to take a drink from the glass she was holding. She began the same action with her glass and this set her off laughing again. Suddenly, her glass tipped over, spilling the crimson liquid all over the crisp white table cover. Heather stared at the mess and said, "It is not that easy wanking a wine glass off, is it?" Olivia sat back and raised her eyes, whilst Paula continued to send daggers down the table towards Louise and Felix.

The guys were engrossed in a conversation about football. They weren't interested in the ladies after spending all day together and were enjoying their 'man' time. They were a small masculine group that got on very well together and were more interested in beer-drinking competitions than fine dining and decent conversation. This was fast turning into a Bier Keller night as the alcohol took over. As the night progressed, they were all getting more inebriated.

Paula grabbed Olivia's arm, her nails digging in tightly. "You have to stop this; it can't happen, she can't have him." The desperation in Paula's voice was a cause for concern and she was not going to stop. "She can't have him, you make sure of that; don't let her have him, please. You can do it, Olivia, please."

Olivia was shocked. "What on earth do you mean?" What was this about? This manager appeared possessed. Olivia shook her head. "What do you expect me to do?"

Paula's eyes narrowed conspiratorially. "We can't talk about it here. I think if Louise doesn't make her move tonight, she definitely will tomorrow in Hamburg. Step in between them; don't let it happen."

Olivia sobered up very quickly as she tried to make sense of what was happening. This was utter madness, and she wanted no part of it. She excused herself and went to the ladies. The room swayed before her and she realised that perhaps she needed a coffee. She didn't drink often and tonight she had been rash with the wine. She hoped that when she returned to the table, the subject may have changed. It was not to be. Olivia returned to find Paula waiting for her. Even though Paula said she could not talk at the table as it was private, she went on. Her grip tightened once more on Olivia's arm. "Those rumours you heard about me; they are true. Not rumours at all." Enough said! Olivia liked her job and did not want to get on the wrong side of Paula. Olivia decided that this was the drink talking and by the morning Paula would have forgotten all she said. Olivia would take the rest of the conversation with a pinch of salt.

How wrong Olivia was. The next morning, as they boarded the minibus, there was Paula at her side, whispering maliciously in her ear. "Don't forget tonight, I am counting on you. Your job depends on it. Get that cow away from him and do it soon!"

Olivia did all she could not to sleep with Felix the following night. She got drunk and forgot how impulsive and reckless she could be. The 'just do it' attitude got the better of her. All thoughts of Paula's threats were forgotten as her pink T-shirt flew across the room, and the rest was history. If only she could have seen what the aftermath of her actions was to bring, she might have behaved differently. Hindsight is such a good thing, but totally useless. She did not do what she did to appease Paula or to take Felix away from Louise. That was far from her mind. She acted out of sheer stupidity, and too much alcohol destroyed her judgement.

Felix's behaviour towards her changed after that night in Hamburg. The trip became a living hell. Things began to happen that Olivia could not understand. Olivia suddenly found herself in purgatory and the worst days of her life were beginning. The day after Hamburg, things became rather strained and the group almost shunned her. She tried to speak to Paula, who ignored her. Olivia stood alone from the crowd and watched her friend Heather chat to Paula. Heather ignored her, too. That night, when Olivia went back to her room, she found Heather and her belongings were gone. In a blind panic, Olivia went to Felix's room. She thought he might know where Heather was, and Olivia needed a friend. She could do with some friendly hugs and cuddles in the lonely place she now found herself in. Olivia knocked on Felix's door. The knock received a curt reply: "Come in."

Felix was writing in a notebook, a half-drunk bottle of Pinot Noir beside him on the table. He did not look up. "Yes, what do you want?" He turned cold eyes towards her.

Olivia stepped back. Was this the man who the night before held her in his arms, kissed her passionately and sent ripples of ecstasy through her body? Olivia spluttered like a little girl. "I can't find Heather and I am worried about her. Have you any idea where she might be, please?"

Felix looked her up and down with distaste. "She no longer wants to share with you and asked to be moved." Olivia's jaw fell open: she was lost for words. "She has had enough of you. She knows what you did. They all know what you have done." Panic set in and Olivia could feel her heart bouncing against her ribs. "She said that she can't cope with you any longer."

Olivia did not understand what he meant. What was going on? Why was Felix being like this? She was lost for words. How did Heather know what she did? Olivia told no one. It was a secret. It was something that was best forgotten and she certainly was not going to repeat the night with Felix. As always, Olivia tried to turn the situation into something positive. She walked towards Felix, putting her hand on his arm. "I am not sure what you are talking about, Felix. I thought we were friends, especially after last night."

She felt Felix stiffen under her touch as he placed his hands firmly on her shoulders and pushed her away. "No, I don't think we are. You need to leave now."

Olivia felt as though someone had thumped her in the gut. Why was he being so horrid? She thought he really liked her, especially after all the things they did in Hamburg. A large teardrop rolled down her cheek, before the floodgates opened. She stood in the middle of Felix's bedroom like a little girl lost and all alone. The sobbing was annoying Felix. "Why are you being like this, Felix? What have I done wrong?"

He did not answer and rose from the desk, taking her by the arm. He led her to the door and threw her out into the corridor, slamming the door shut.

Olivia lost her footing and fell on to the carpet just as a couple were walking by. They looked at her as they went past. They stepped over her and carried on walking. The woman turned back and helped Olivia up. "Don't let security see you. They do not like prostitutes to use their premises." Olivia was horrified. The woman thought she was a prostitute at work?

Olivia turned and banged on the door. "Please, Felix, what has happened? Please let me in. We need to talk." The tears now were in free flow and dropping onto the carpet. Olivia continued to beg until the door opened a little and Felix peered out at her.

She heard his corporate voice. "Olivia, just go. Go back to your room. I don't take kindly to others knowing my business. You should have kept your big mouth shut. You have alienated all your workmates and made me look rather stupid. I suggest you keep very quiet for the rest of this trip. You behaved like a whore and used me. You know what you have done, so just go away now. I have nothing left to say to you."

Felix slammed the door in her face, leaving Olivia to return to her room and cry for the rest of the night.

The next day, the 'Into the Sun' group reached their next destination of Bremen. They checked into the Butthman in Zentrum. Check-in did not go without incident when Heather refused to share a room with Olivia. This made things very awkward, as the hotel was fully booked and there were no rooms left. Louise stepped in and saved the day: she had a double room to herself. "It's OK, I don't mind sharing." She smiled at Olivia, who was looking down at her feet in embarrassment. "We get on well, don't we?" Louise walked over to her. She took Olivia's arm and led her to the lift. She spoke in a loud voice so that the others would hear her. "Come on, we will have a right laugh together." Olivia was surprised by Louise's kindness and followed her into the lift.

As they went up to the second floor, Olivia thought about things. "I did not sleep with Felix so that Louise could not have him. I did not do it because Paula wanted it. I did it because I didn't think. I can be my own worst enemy sometimes."

Once in the bedroom, Olivia sat down on the bed, spluttering, "Thank you so much. I can't believe that just happened. It was awful. What have I done? Is Heather in a room on her own now, then?"

Louise looked at her. "No, of course she's not! She is sharing with Pablo now."

"She is sharing with Pablo?"

Louise put the kettle on. "Is there a parrot in here?" she laughed. "Are you on the same trip as the rest of us? Haven't you noticed? I thought maybe she might end up with Felix, but she has always had a thing for Pablo. At work they go to lunch regularly. She really likes him."

Olivia hadn't noticed much regards the group as they travelled round the countryside — she was busy looking out at the scenery and the small villages they regularly passed. Since the night in Hamburg, she was rather preoccupied with her guilt and she wasn't going to say much about that to anyone. The humiliation of being thrown out of Felix's room began a downward spiral for Olivia, as all she wanted to do was return to England.

Olivia shrugged her shoulders. "That is up to her what she does. Good luck to her. It is none of my business. She never said a word to me all the time we were together." Olivia picked up her towel and went to shower. She needed to wash the day off and prepare for the torturous evening.

The last two days went quickly, thanks to Louise taking Olivia under her wing and never leaving her side. Louise told Olivia she knew all about Hamburg. Paula told them all. This surprised Olivia, who had not breathed a word to anybody. She hated Paula and realised that she was the one making trouble. Olivia said nothing and kept her own counsel, although she was tempted to reveal all to Louise due to her kindness. What she didn't know was that Louise was feeling rather guilty after what happened with her and Felix. She was scared that Paula might find out that she slept with him too and that would be the end of her job. Olivia now wanted to forget all that went on in Hamburg and everything else. She just wanted to go home. She needed to heal and move on.

Rebecca and Garth also took Olivia under their wing that night and a small foursome developed that laughed its way to the end of the trip.

The three days that followed were quite terrible. Felix stepped back from the group. He was frustrated, as he could not ask Olivia why she told Paula about them. He needed to keep distance between them. He wasn't proud of himself for throwing Olivia out of his room. He was angry, and people do things when they are angry. He still wasn't sure if Paula had told the whole truth, and it looked like he would never know if she lied or not. He was inclined to believe Paula, as he had known her longer and did not know Olivia at all. Felix was not feeling too good about his behaviour towards Olivia. He was not one for saying sorry, and in his book, what was done was done. If Paula was telling the truth, then Olivia deserved all that she got.

Felix turned his attention to Heather and danced with her on the evenings they went out. He made a move on her one night and was surprised to find she was using him as a decoy. Nobody was fooled, as they all knew she was sharing a bed with Pablo. Felix began to feel that he was being used yet again. He was beginning to hate the women in this group. In his anger towards Olivia, he would have bedded Heather and possibly the ugly Paula, too. Actually, no, he might have drawn the line there. What a mess it all was, and he seriously began to wonder if he should continue to do business with 'Into the Sun'. Felix's arrogance got the better of him. His ego was in tatters and rationality flew out of the window. He could not wait to go home. He would have to give serious thought as to whether these tour operator trips were to continue.

On reaching Manchester airport, Felix rushed out of the arrivals gate into the arms of his wife. He lied about how much he'd missed her. Linda was always there after one of his trips. He knew she was trying to catch him out. She might be a drunk, but she wasn't a stupid drunk. After a quick word with Kevin about when they would next be meeting, Felix left the airport without a backward glance.

Olivia was coming out with Louise and saw the back of Felix. She could not stop the tear that rolled down her face. He had said goodbye previously to everybody in the reclaim baggage hall. Not to her, though: she was completely ignored. Olivia was relieved to get back, somewhat humbled by the whole experience. She felt dirty and abused, took responsibility for what happened and decided that it would never happen again, she didn't like the feeling of being a trollop. It wasn't long before Olivia was no longer working at 'Into the Sun'. Paula saw to that and made her life so difficult. When a tragedy hit Olivia's family, Paula found it the ideal opportunity to have her sacked. Olivia never saw Felix or heard from him again until now.

Over twenty years had passed, and Olivia was older and wiser. The happenings in Germany were buried under the heading, 'Things best forgotten'. The question remained in her mind as to what actually happened for Felix to turn on her like he did. She often remembered the night in Hamburg when the words 'if they could see me now' came to mind, reminded her of the sex show, her negotiations with the doorman, and she would smile.

There were some happy times, and she often told the story about the erotic theatre. It made people laugh. She only shared the full story of what actually went on with Anne, her confidante and best friend.

~

Olivia did not notice she was crying. She put her hand up to her cheek and felt the wet drops rolling down onto her chin. She wiped her tears. She didn't want to think of Felix anymore and began to think about

Adam. She looked at the other passengers on the plane. She wondered what their stories would be like if they were to be written. Everybody has a story to tell. A lot of people had things they want to hide. Secrets they hope to take to the grave. Olivia was still in the process of writing her story and she knew nobody would believe it. She realised that writing her story might also set her up to be judged. It didn't matter, as now she was at peace with herself and fully in control of her destiny. She was on a new journey and about to embark on another adventure in America.

CHAPTER EIGHTEEN

Adam could not stop looking at the picture of Olivia in the magazine. He found familiar feelings stirring inside, especially after that wink. It was many years since he felt that shiver in the bottom of his groin. He tried to dismiss it with a big sigh. It didn't work. He was beginning to wonder if it was good luck or bad luck that Olivia was on the same flight. Down the years he found himself wondering what became of her. Now he knew. He wondered if she remembered him. Did she wink at Felix or both of them? He put his head back and closed his eyes.

~

Adam was back in the room with Olivia, after being called down from his office. He saw Olivia standing before him, wearing a beaming smile that she carried with her all the time. His heart missed a beat. He now knew how much he missed her. He loved her. He wanted to take her in his arms and give her the words that were bursting to come out, but he didn't. Instead, he sat down, putting the desk between them. Olivia sat opposite. As she looked around the wood-panelled room, Adam's eyes never left her face. "How have you been?"

"I'm good. I have been keeping busy."

Adam wanted to ask her to meet him, but was afraid of the answer.

It was autumn now and the sun still had the warmth of summer. The evenings were cool and carried the aroma of burning wood and leaves. This was Olivia's favourite time of the year and he wondered if perhaps she might go for a walk with him one evening. He was afraid to ask her. They began to chat about nothing much. Adam told her that the boat was now in dry dock and he was going over regularly to paint it. The conversation soon dried up and hung about in an air of embarrassing silence.

Out of the blue, Olivia began to reminisce. "We had some good times on that boat."

"Yes, we did, and I will never forget them. I will never forget the times spent on the river together."

"Me neither."

"I might go over on Thursday and do some painting." He wasn't sure if he was talking to himself. He wondered whether he could now throw out an invite, but he didn't.

Olivia spoke to the wall behind Adam. "I think I might go to university and get the piece of paper I need for a career. Children are getting older and no one seems to need me now. I have time on my hands and am getting rather bored with life."

Adam was wondering why Olivia came to see him; this was going nowhere fast. It was good to be in the same room with her, but the stilted conversation confirmed to him that it really was over. "Would you like a coffee?" He spoke conspiratorially, as though he was not supposed to ask her.

"No, thank you. It's fine. I had one before I came out. I can't stay. I was just passing."

They chatted a while longer and when Olivia rose to leave, Adam wanted to pull her into his arms and feel the softness of her hair on his face. He wanted to run his fingers through her crowning glory that always looked so inviting and made her look so sexy. Olivia stood, awkwardly, before him, like a little girl. She looked down at her black skirt and straightened the white frilly blouse she was wearing. Neither of them knew what they were supposed to do next. They were like two teenagers with no experience. The embarrassment was obvious. Olivia's hand shot out and Adam shook it.

"Well, er... thanks for popping in. It's been nice to see you. Perhaps we'll bump into each other somewhere?"

Olivia smiled. "Perhaps we will, but I doubt it." She walked towards the door.

Adam felt an anxiety which was alien to him and the panic of maybe not seeing Olivia again grew. Once she was out the door, she might be gone forever. Adam had to say something. "Olivia, would you like to come to the boat with me next week? I have to do some work there. We

173

could have lunch somewhere nice?" He felt very stupid now. Why would she? He'd hurt her. They were over.

Olivia stopped and stood still. The seconds mounted. Adam could not read her back and became even more anxious. She slowly turned; the smile was no longer there, instead there was a frown topping a serious look. Olivia looked into his eyes as she put her hand on the door handle. "Yes, that would be very nice, thank you." She turned on her heel and as she went through the door, called back, "Call me." Then she was gone.

Adam sat down, running his hand across his brow, lost in a turmoil of emotions that would not stay still long enough to identify them. He was all over the place, and a butterfly turned in his stomach. He sat down in the dark, cool room and stared at the picture of a boat on a stormy sea on the panelled wall. Why had she come? What was the reason? Was there a reason? He could not let go of this woman who awoke the sleeping feelings within. Adam felt the beat of his heart as he realised that once more his head would be silenced and he would listen only to his heart. In true man fashion, he did not consider the woman but only thought of his own needs. He was not a selfish man and knew how to treat a woman, knew the words they wanted to hear. Right now, he could only imagine what the future might hold. He wanted a future with Olivia. He had too many commitments, but maybe one day. One day he might find the bravery needed. Surely, he wouldn't always be the coward that he was now. Adam would carry the image of that beautiful face and that beaming smile with him until the next time he saw Olivia.

The day they went to the boat, the weather let them down. As they drove into Sam's boatyard, the heavens opened. Adam stopped the car and told Olivia how sorry he was that he could not control the weather. He had some work to do on the outside of the boat and wondered if she would mind being on her own inside for a couple of hours.

"No, I don't mind. I have my notebook and I can catch up on some writing."

Adam went off to get some tools from Sam's shed and Olivia climbed the ladder up the side of the boat and went down into the cabin. A few hours later, Adam climbed down into the cabin to find Olivia curled up on the bench, fast asleep. He saw the open book on the table as he passed by. The doodles around a page filled with words caught his eye and he sat down, picking the book up. Adam began to read…

STOLEN MOMENTS

Ours is not to be together.
Ours is to live our lives apart.
Living, loving with another,
You remain within my heart.
Stolen kisses in a moment,
Stole dreams and thoughts of you.
Wishing, hoping, never knowing,
Stolen moments for all life through.

He began to flick through the pages that were covered in Olivia's small, perfectly formed writing, until he spotted a title that made him smile and led him to read again.

SEA OF HOPE

What are we doing to one another?
We are neither happy nor sad.
Limbo dancing through this mess,
Trapped in a rhythm of going nowhere,
We are cruising on a stormy sea of hope.
Full of exasperation and sorrow.
Sink or swim.
Dive deep for the treasure.
Bouncing with the surf until
We drown.
Options are endless.
Relationships run aground
Always trapped in a rhythm of going nowhere.
We are trapped on a sea of hope.

Adam looked up to see an enormous pair of brown eyes staring at him. He was startled by the intense stare. "Hello, you! Hope you don't mind?" He held the notebook up for her to see.

As Olivia sat up, she began to blush. "No, it's fine."

"These are really good, you know. I don't understand some of them, but I do know they are good." He smiled as her face turned a deeper crimson. "There is one thing I will always remember about you. It will be you always having a pen in your hand, scribbling into a notebook. Perhaps you should write a book. Can you remember the night you wrote that pantomime and used all the people we know as characters? That was wicked and so very funny; not sure if they would have laughed, though!"

"Yes." She took the notebook out of Adam's hand and stuffed it into her bag. "Are you hungry, Adam? I am starving." Olivia stood up and straightened her clothes.

"Yes, I am starving, too. Just give me a minute to change and we shall go and find a steak."

The clouds were sailing away as they entered the restaurant. The sun was trying to creep through the gaps, showing pools of deep late-afternoon blue. Olivia and Adam sat opposite each other and after ordering a starter of prawn cocktail, Olivia had to satisfy her curiosity. "Can I ask you something, please? Something you said earlier is bothering me."

"Fire away." Adam sat back and took a drink of his beer. He was not prepared for the small speech that followed.

Olivia put her hands between her knees and looked down; the expression on her face showed that she was struggling to find the words that she needed to say. Slowly, she began. "At the boat you said you will always remember me with a notebook and pen in my hand." Adam nodded. "Well, I am beginning to wonder what we are actually doing and why I came to your office that day. Do we continue as before? Stop now?" Olivia sighed. "The longer we carry on, we increase the odds of us being caught. Where is all this going? Is it going anywhere? We have got so many good memories now and I am feeling a bit lost. Should we quit while we are ahead?"

Adam watched her intently, seeing a myriad of expressions and emotions fighting on her face. So she wanted to continue in a relationship with him. He thought for a while. The silence was deafening, and then he took Olivia's hand in his. "I don't know, I really don't know. What I do know is that I have been so miserable without you. I have missed you, and without you in my life there is no reason for it. You are my joy, my reason to be. Do you remember all those months ago in Leeds whilst we were doing the second fashion show?" Olivia nodded. "Well, nothing has changed since then. Well, yes it has. I love you more. I dream of you. I need your kisses for my survival. I want to be with you and hold you every morning. I want you to be the last thing I see at night. You know how hard things are for me, having a wife and Gerry. It would be so hard to split up with Mary. We have children together and a grandchild now. There is so much to take into account. How would she live? Could she manage without me? I know we haven't had a marriage for years. No sex, no future. She doesn't want to do anything with me anymore and I am so lonely. Gerry has just become a habit I can't get rid of, but know I must. I am scared that she might tell Mary and then I have lost everything. If I rock the apple cart, I shall be the bad man." Adam shook his head to clear the gathering tears in his eyes. "I am really stupid trying to keep everyone happy, I really am."

What he did not realise was that Olivia could have been his everything, but the habit of juggling was a hard one to break.

Olivia looked sternly at Adam and with force delivered back, "Stop right there. Where did all that come from? I am sorry I said anything now, forget it. We don't have long together as it is and our moments together are so precious. I cannot make decisions for you. The ball is in your court. I am just waiting here."

The prawns arrived and the conversation halted. There was more than a little discomfort between them now. People who have affairs have to be aware of the consequences. How does anyone know what a right decision is? Olivia remembered the words from a good friend when she told her about Adam. "What on earth are you doing, Olivia? All married men are bad news. They never leave their wives. They are complete bastards and lie all the time. I thought you would know better than risk all for such an idiot. They stay in unhappy marriages because they are too cowardly and do not want to rock their little world and start over with the woman they really should be with, the one who loves them. He is lying to his wife and his mistress and will be lying to you too." Olivia did not think of the long term: she tended to live each day at a time. She had never mentioned leaving home and wished that Adam was stronger;

but after that soapbox speech of his, she knew there might never be a future for them, no matter how deep the love.

By the end of the meal they were satisfied and happy again, the conversation before the prawns forgotten. "Would you like to go for a walk?" After Adam paid the bill, they sang their way to the woods. They walked for a while hand in hand, before sitting down in a small mossy hollow that curled round them and gave them the privacy to enjoy the passion that they so badly craved. It was hurried and not very satisfying. Adam loved to spend time on foreplay, but as the clock was against them, this did not happen and the foreplay was a quick introduction to what turned out to be an unsatisfying 'bonk'. It was a shame, as the setting was a romantic picture of greenery and calm.

When they arrived back to his car, Adam pulled Olivia towards him. With fervour, his tongue found hers in their final kiss. "So, are we to continue? What do you think?" Adam could not lose her again.

There it was, that wicked grin, running across her face, dancing in her eyes. "I suppose that's for me to know and you to find out. I will call you."

As Olivia sped off, she turned the music up and Adam heard Curtis Mayfield singing 'Love To, Keep You In, My Mind'. He was sad to see her go. It felt like the first time he said goodbye to her, all those months ago. Before Olivia turned the corner, her hand came out of the window and waved back at him.

Adam sat in his car for a while, trying to make sense of it all. As he turned the engine on, he realised that he really needed to sort himself out. He could not go on like this. He was going nowhere fast, and life was in a downward spin.

The call came on a Wednesday morning a few weeks later. A sultry voice whispered down the phone, "What are you doing right now?"

Adam was taken aback, as he was not expecting Olivia to call again, even though she said she would. "Not a lot. Why?"

"Have you thought of me, of us? I have missed you. You want to come over?"

Adam wondered what Olivia was thinking. "When?"

"How about you come round right now?"

Adam looked at his diary. He had to be in Leeds by two and decided he could call in for a cup of tea on his way. He could hear Olivia smiling as he said that yes, he would come. "I am waiting." The call ended.

Adam sat stunned for a moment. There had been total silence from her since they were at the boat and at times, he thought that maybe she had changed her mind about continuing to see him. He argued with himself more than once as to whether she would call or not. He thought he knew her well enough and that she would keep her word. She said she would call, and now she had. Olivia loved to play games and perhaps this was one of them?

Adam drove up to an imposing detached house. He knew instantly that Olivia lived there, as the garden had her mark all over it. It was a colourful array of flowers dancing in the sunlight. Perhaps there were even fairies hidden under the leaves.

Olivia had a childlike quality about her that made you believe in fairies and Santa Claus, and her face would light up when she walked through her imagination and shared her thoughts. She had the ability to take people to another world with her stories and forget the stressful life that was part of daily living. The imagination is a wonderful thing as it can take a person anywhere to enjoy fantasy and dreams. Only Olivia could make a garden like the one he was walking through now. It was a very warm day and Adam felt the beads of sweat popping up on his brow. He hated having to wear a full suit for work. He had standards to maintain and his professional look meant everything when clinching deals. That is what the advertising world was about. The look!

Adam was nervous as he knocked on the door. He waited a few minutes before the green gloss door with shiny brass fittings slowly opened and there before him was the vision of his dreams, her long golden hair flowing below her shoulders. Her small, perfect feet were bare on the tiled floor. He knew what was hidden under an oversized pink T-shirt covered in the navy words 'I put a spell on you'. Olivia locked the door behind them and he followed her into a classical designer lounge. The décor surprised him. It was not as he imagined. Olivia presented as some wild, free-thinking, dizzy hippy chic, and he expected colours and chaos. Instead, he was surrounded by cool peach, beige and sage green. Yes, she certainly had taste. It was a comfortable room.

Adam sank into the soft dark green leather sofa and sipped the tea that was placed before him. It was strange, sitting in Olivia's house. He felt like he was trespassing and should not be there. It felt almost criminal and exciting. Surrounded by her own things and in Olivia's environment, Adam saw another side to Olivia and the complexity of the enigma that was this amazing lady. He felt a pull on his heart strings. He wanted her so much.

Adam wanted a life with Olivia and could not imagine being without that crazy grin and those laughing eyes. Olivia sat down across the room from him. She smiled and sipped her coffee, those big brown eyes staring at him over the rim of the mug. He found it hard to keep his eyes off the top of her legs that were barely covered by the T-shirt. He could almost see the mystery that was hidden beneath and found it hard to concentrate on the small-talk that was happening between them. They discussed the weather, her house and garden, his boat and her next project. At times, conversation dried up and he would look around in semi-embarrassment. She showed him around the house and they ended up in the snug, where Adam saw a giant jukebox. "Does it work?"

"Yes, of course it does."

"May I put something on?"

"Please do."

'Standing in the Shadows of Love' by the Four Tops filled the small room. "One of my favourites."

Olivia noticed Adam's discomfort and began to tease him. "Do you like me in this T-shirt?" She wiggled and began to dance to the music. He wished she hadn't done that, as a familiar feeling began to run through his veins. "Does it make you want me, Adam?"

"You know I always want you, Olivia. I want to see more and more of you, but you know we both have so many commitments and such busy lives. Why did you ring me? Don't you think this is dangerous and rather silly?" Adam wasn't able to read the expression on her face as she slowly danced towards him. She was in control. This was her territory. As the song ended, the atmosphere became electric with anticipation.

Olivia pushed Adam down onto the sage green futon. He looked up into a pair of wicked eyes. She now moved down and sat astraddle on him. He could feel her mound directly over his crotch and she moved, just enough to awaken the sleeping demon within. Olivia took Adam's face in her hands and kissed him very slowly, her tongue searching to find its mate. Tongues now doing the dance of lust, he felt his bulge go hard, very hard. He ran his hands down Olivia's body, feeling the shape beneath that awful T-shirt. Olivia didn't seem at all bothered by the fact that they were in her house. She took hold of his hand and led him upstairs. He did not put up any resistance. Didn't even think it was wrong. She opened the guest bedroom door. "We like to look after our guests."

They entered a cosy looking room with flowered wallpaper and a king-size bed that looked as though it was dressed to be photographed for a designer magazine. Olivia began to kiss Adam and then proceeded to undress him, starting at his tie, slowly kissing each part of his body as she uncovered it. Then she pulled his underpants down and his member sprang out, leaving him vulnerable. Olivia touched it with her forefinger. "Mmmmm... Well, hello there." Olivia bent down and kissed the waiting phallus, before pushing Adam onto the bed.

The T-shirt was soon flying across the room to reveal the perfection that was she. He was waiting for her to lie down beside him. Olivia surprised him and knelt on the pillow next to him. As she bent down to kiss him, her hand slowly stroked his belly, moving ever nearer to his vulnerability. Adam sensed that Olivia was to lead this session of their togetherness and was eager to follow. She was totally in control and he liked it. He was seeing another side to Olivia. He saw the wicked smile and felt in awe of this woman who was like no other. He began to wonder if she was a witch, as she reached for his testicles and cupped them in her hand. Adam groaned as Olivia gently squeezed them, before beginning to play with the small opening at the end of his manhood. "Slide down the bed, please."

Adam was happy to comply. Olivia moved her right leg over his body so that she was hovering directly over his face, before slowly lowering herself onto his mouth. His mouth opened to receive her and his tongue shot into her, to be enveloped by the softness of her mystery that was already moist with the welcoming juice of her love.

Olivia began to move up and down on him, giving him space to explore every crevice between her legs whilst she purred with satisfaction. Without warning, Olivia began to move the wide-open crevice of anticipation down towards his throbbing penis, which was standing magnificently to attention, waiting for her. She sat down on him in one brutal move. Orgasm came instantly to them both at the same time. Adam felt the trickle of her juices down his manhood and onto his legs. A slow trickle of wet ran across his throbbing member. Olivia did not stop.

Adam lay back and enjoyed the way Olivia's body danced on him, keeping perfect rhythm. She became a woman possessed as her buttocks slammed against his thighs, again and again. They hit orgasm simultaneously once more. It was a mighty explosion of tension and even more tension. Her taps of love turned on fully as she came and came again. She screamed as they hit the ultimate heights that are rarely achieved. This was a moment to remember; it may never come again.

Olivia collapsed onto his chest and they both lay together in the aftermath of a passion so rare. Adam stroked her hair and revelled in the aftershock of what had just occurred. How could he have this woman permanently, without upsetting his whole world? He wanted her to be his and only his, forever.

They dressed hurriedly as Adam was already late for his appointment. At the door, he turned. "You know that in December I won't be able to see you, what with family and commitments; you know how busy I get?"

Olivia pecked him on the cheek and pushed him out of the door. As Adam turned to walk towards his car, he heard her call after him, "I love you. An early Merry Christmas and I hope that next year will be all you want it to be." He certainly hoped it would, and he knew he would have to make some big decisions.

As he drove across to Leeds, Adam thought about what had happened. He really was in a quandary. Whilst the sex was brilliant, he worried about the recklessness that he had just seen in Olivia. She was complicating his life and he felt out of control. No man wants to be out of control. It is all to do with power and control that is intrinsic in the make-up of some men. When he was refereeing on pitch at a football match, he was in control. When he was planning an advertising campaign, he was in control. When he was staging some choreography and choosing music, he was in control. When he was with Olivia, he was not in control, and now that did not sit well with him. He really had to decide what he wanted and if this was not going too far.

They met a few times in the autumn and the run-up to December. Their meetings did not go too well and both left for their respective homes rather dissatisfied and with too many questions to be asked. Adam said that he would ring her and keep in touch. He didn't. He was out at various functions during December and neglected Olivia. He also neglected Mary and Gerry. He was busy being admired by the new women coming his way and he found it easier to enjoy himself if he dismissed the three women in his life from his mind.

Adam had an ego that at times controlling. He found his self-esteem in a mirror and his reflection told him all that he felt he needed to know. To say he revelled in the adulation bestowed on him by the clamour for his attention was an understatement. He did not want to ring Olivia, not even to wish her Merry Christmas or Happy New Year. He was struggling to keep the balance in his already chaotic life. He knew she would understand. She was the most understanding, forgiving person he knew.

By the time it got to the day when presents were opened and some people were happy and others disappointed, he was exhausted. Gerry went to her sister's in a huff as Adam failed to buy her the ring she wanted, and Mary's constant fussing was driving him mad. He sat in the corner of the kitchen, watching the mayhem round the table. The noise was deafening, as his sisters chatted far too loudly and their men (who he had nothing in common with bar the fact that they were married to his sisters) were discussing golf, a game he loathed. As he sipped his whisky, his thoughts went to Olivia. He wondered what she was doing and toyed with the idea of ringing her home and hoping she picked up the phone.

He imagined her sitting round the table with her family, her parents and a host of friends. Olivia loved to entertain and cook. She loved feeding people and thrived on playing 'the hostess'. Adam missed Olivia so much, and in his lonely times imagined them in bed together, kissing and laughing, remembering her body next to his, on top of him, underneath him, near him. It made him long for the first of January and the New Year.

Olivia was a very funny person and a great observer of life. She had a dry sense of humour that others might have called bitching. She was no bitch. It came out more as dry sarcasm. Could that be called bitching? In the bedroom department, she knew what a man wanted. She knew what Adam wanted and she always delivered. Yes, he missed her. Adam's longing for Olivia did not dissipate. It took a back seat as he played the happy family man and doting lover of Gerry. He was a liar and a hypocrite. He often lied to himself about his behaviour. He never took responsibility for any of his actions. It would always be the woman's fault. Was it his fault he married Mary?

No. He felt that she tricked him into it. She told him she was pregnant and after the wedding she told him she miscarried. How devious women could become when they wanted something. He never truly believed that she had been pregnant in the first place and began to hate her crocodile tears. Mary cried for a month about the miscarriage. Adam was too busy building his career to offer much comfort. He told Mary to pull her socks up and get on with life. It didn't take long before she fell pregnant again and she managed to keep that one.

Was it his fault that Gerry was living in a one-bedroom flat waiting for the crumbs he threw her? No, she knew what she was getting herself into by having a married man. She had never been happily married and Adam was an easy option to escape a man much older than she was. She married an older man for money and it was too late when she realised, he had a massive lock on his wallet. It was nothing to do with Adam. She provided exciting moments when he was bored at work and one thing led to another. He just couldn't help himself and this was another time in his life that he lost control. He always felt that Gerry used him, and now there was no letting go.

As he sat now in the warmth of his kitchen, Adam watched Mary. How could he escape the ministrations of a wife who was becoming more displeasing to him as the days went by? He was having difficulty with his physical husbandly duties and was always happy to turn his back on the mother of his children and dream of those big brown eyes, those big breasts that he loved to caress, those nipples he could not wait to kiss again. He wasn't dreaming of Gerry.

"Adam, Adam! You are daydreaming again. For goodness sake, get up here and carve this turkey; we are all starving."

He returned from his daydream to the real world and apologised, before taking the carving knife and slowly slicing the bird that was in the middle of the table. He began to imagine that he was cutting through Mary's neck. He would get through this day and the days to follow by thinking of the sweet Olivia. He would also get through the day by becoming very, very drunk and eventually he had to be put to bed by his brother-in-law.

CHAPTER NINETEEN

Olivia and Adam met in early January. They arranged to meet at their usual venue, the George and Dragon, a small, discreet hostelry in the middle of the woods near the Leeds and Liverpool canal. If they didn't have time to go to the boat, they would walk along the canal, laughing, joking and always kissing.

Olivia was late, and Adam sat nervously with his pint of beer, rehearsing the question he wanted to ask her when she arrived. It was a serious question and for the last fifteen minutes Adam had recited it many different ways in order to get it right. He knew it had serious implications for their relationship and that Olivia's answer might change their lives forever.

The door to the room opened and a flurry of snow from outside accompanied a figure in a large red winter coat and fluffy hat. Olivia practically fell through the door as a gust of wind blew her in. She was white all over as the sleet from outside stuck to her blue woollen coat. She removed it and hung it on the pegs to her right, before walking towards the fire, rubbing her hands and placing the palms towards the flames. "Good Lord, the weather is getting worse out there. I don't think I can stay long or I won't be able to get home."

Adam ordered a vodka tonic and they made small-talk about the end of the year and the festivities they attended. They rarely talked about their families; the guilt kept that subject away. They began to discuss all that they had done together during the previous year. All went well until Adam raised a subject that had bothered him. "I think you were a bit too reckless inviting me to your house that time. I know you like to live dangerously, but I do think that you sometimes push the boundaries a bit too far."

Olivia was taken aback by his comments. "I didn't hear you complaining when I sat on your face?"

There was an awkward moment when they looked at each other as though they were squaring up for a fight. They began to laugh. They laughed like two small children with a guilty secret, heads coming down together and foreheads nearly touching. Adam took hold of her hand. "I missed you."

They had a big secret filled with little secrets. There were memories no one could take from them and they would stay with them forever. It felt good. A comfortable silence descended and they sat watching the flames of the brilliant fire as the logs spat their heat out onto the stone hearth. Adam took a deep breath. "I have a question for you. Would you consider leaving your children for me?"

"Why do you ask that?"

"I just wondered. That was all."

Olivia began to study Adam's face. She had a habit of doing that when she was getting serious. She was not only a good talker and a good listener, but also a very good reader of facial expressions. Olivia took a drink and studied the burning embers, before turning abruptly towards him. "Would you leave your children for me?"

Always the coward Adam didn't stop to think. He said, "No."

Olivia smiled. "Then there is your answer." She went to the jukebox and a record Adam had not heard for many years began to play: 'Never Give Up on a Good Thing', by George Benson.

"Olivia, did you put that on for a reason?"

"Why would you say that?"

The air between them turned and became chilly. "You want another drink?"

Olivia looked out of the window. She was starting to feel uncomfortable. "No, I best be off; the snow isn't stopping and I will have problems if I don't go now."

Adam went to pay his tab at the bar and when he turned round, the room was empty. Olivia did not wait to say goodbye. He ran outside, but was too late. Only the tracks of her tyres in the deep snow were left behind.

As Adam drove home, he wondered why it all went wrong. Why did he ask Olivia such a question? What had he expected her to say? What would he have done had she said yes? Had he wanted her to say yes?

This chat was meant to be a step closer to their future together, and somehow it had all gone wrong. What could he do to sort his muddled mind out? He was supposed to say 'Yes', he would leave all for her and start again. He was a wimp and he was still balancing his life on the edge of the precipice that it was always on.

He thought about the other two women in his life and began to compare them. The minuses were many for Mary and Gerry. The familiarity was so boring. Gerry sulked a lot if he could not meet her needs, and Mary was happy doing the shopping and being his mother. Mary had forgotten how to be his wife and he was no longer her husband but more like her brother, who she mothered and fussed. The intimacy departed long ago and they were now more like house companions, the gap between them ever widening.

Olivia was so different. She was wild, unpredictable and passionate. She was so much younger than her age. She was positive and outgoing, but also reckless. She cared too much and it wasn't often that she had her feet on the ground. Olivia was the future. She was life, she was sunshine and laughter. The other two were clouds and rain. Olivia was also very good in bed and liked to take the initiative. She loved to be in control and made love like a tantric master. The other two were not in her league and there was no comparison to be made. As he was getting older, Adam was also realising that life was not all about sex and that what he had with Olivia was a bonus. He loved Olivia, but he loved himself more and he knew that sooner or later he would have to hurt her and end it for good, but he didn't know how. His ego would come into play and spoil everything. He knew that.

Adam was worn out by the constant arguments in his head. That voice going on and on about maybe Olivia was the one and would he take the plunge into a new life with her? He did not want to be the bad guy, and if he left Mary he would be. This was becoming serious, and while he did not really want to think about the future, he felt that was probably why he asked the question. Adam hadn't known that Olivia would answer as she did and, in a tiny corner of his mind, he hoped that she would say 'No' he could have then said that there was no point in going on. She would have made that possible for him to end it all. He would not have had to make his mind up about anything then. He said

'No' first and now he was so confused. He wanted Olivia. He didn't want Olivia. There would be a high price to pay to be with her. He loved her with a passion and it was all becoming too much for him. He was playing with fire and it was time to put the fire out. Did any of it matter as she walked out into the snow and left him alone?

Time began to pass them by and they saw each other less and less as work commitments and family began to engulf them once more. There was little time for personal pleasure. Adam did what he always did when he was in a stressful situation and could not make a decision. He found a diversion which could push much-needed decisions he might have to make to the back of his mind. He would think about them tomorrow. Tomorrow never came for Adam.

The diversion this time took him to Olivia's friend Fiona. Fiona lived near to him and she was showing some interest. He was enjoying the attention. There was no harm in a little flirting, was there? Fiona and Adam's children went to the same swimming club. Once or twice he felt her eyes on him when he waited for them in the car park by the swimming pool. At first, he wondered if it was because she might know about his relationship with Olivia, but dismissed that as he had sworn Olivia to secrecy and told her she must never ever tell anyone about them. He knew that Olivia was a law unto herself and so maybe Fiona did know. Of course, she knew! Fiona always picked up the pieces when Olivia was in bits about things to do with Adam. Fiona covertly flirted with Adam. He had known enough women in his time to know what she was doing. He flirted back. There was no harm in it. Was there?

Adam was chairman of the village Gala committee and the first meeting was due the first week in May. New members would be elected onto the committee and they desperately needed some new people. Some fresh blood was the order of the day. He arrived early at the hall and put all the chairs out ready for the doors opening at seven. Most of the village turned up and wriggled about on the uncomfortable fold-down chairs donated by the Conservative Club. Adam was reading the agenda, not paying much attention to the audience. He looked up and saw Fiona staring at him. He smiled and winked at her. He wondered why she didn't smile back. It was because she wasn't alone. He saw her talking to

189

someone sitting next to her. He couldn't see who it was as she was hidden behind Joe Freeman, the bodybuilder from the gym down the street.

Adam made a mental note to speak to Fiona in the break. She might introduce him to her mystery friend, who might be worth a few hours of his time. There is was again, his over inflated ego. He just couldn't help himself. The new committee was elected and Fiona got her wish to be on it. This would be brilliant, as she would see more of Adam. She couldn't tell Olivia how she was feeling, as she knew how much Olivia loved him. Fiona had Olivia's full support when it came to being on the committee. Olivia felt women should stretch out and do various things to reach their potential. Fiona was not like Olivia at all, unless you counted their mutual feelings about Adam. Yet they were such good friends and got on so well together.

As Adam came down the steps of the stage, he headed towards Fiona. She was standing alone. He looked round to see where her friend was and his eyes caught the door and saw the back of someone with long blonde hair leaving. He knew that back. "I'd better give her a ring tomorrow." Things hadn't been the same between them since the day of the question and both had good excuses for not calling each other. Olivia was busy fundraising again and he was busy organising the Gala. Both excuses were part-truths. They could have made time for each other. They were uncomfortable when they did speak on the phone and absence was not making the heart grow fonder; far from it. The distance between them widened as time passed and yet neither of them actually ended the connection between them.

One day, Adam was staring out of the window in his office when the phone rang, bringing him back to life. He answered with an abruptness used as part of his business voice. It softened when he realised who it was. His heart missed a beat and he could almost smell her perfume down the phone. They chatted about nothing and Adam asked Olivia if she would be at the Gala. This was something he was dreading. His worst nightmare if she turned up with Fiona. She said she wasn't sure, but would be in the area. He said that it would not be a good idea if she came, as Mary would be there.

Adam was also being openly pursued by Fiona now. He was enjoying every minute of it and the last thing he needed was Olivia to walk onto the field. Olivia asked him to call her later and if they could meet up before the procession for a drink. Adam thought that might be a good idea. This led to some telephone flirting which in turn began to stir the demon sleeping softly in his Tommy Hilfiger's. "I have missed you, but have been so busy," Adam lied.

"Yes, I know."

There was a lonely click as he put the phone down.

Gala day arrived and everything was running smoothly. Adam paid attention to what he was putting on and slapped on some Paco Raban; a gift from Gerry for his birthday. He forgot to buy her anything when it was hers and she went into one of her usual sulks. He made up for it later by buying her a bracelet during their lunch hour. Sometimes in their lunch hour they would wander round town and Gerry would pull him into this shop and that shop. It bored him. She bored him, too. A shopper he was not. But if it, appeased Gerry, it was a task well done.

In a second phone call, Adam arranged to meet Olivia in the Big Pirate at one o'clock. They were both going to bring a friend to make things less conspicuous, as everybody in the village knew him. Here they were again, living dangerously. As Adam came round the corner into the beer garden, he saw Olivia at a table with Anne. He recognised Anne from the fashion show. He remembered Anne's pert little bottom going up the steps before him. He saw she had put some weight on. She was still very attractive, but not for him.

Anne and Olivia were chatting to three men sitting opposite them at a picnic bench. It was obvious that they were all enjoying themselves by the noise and laughter coming from them. Adam realised that they were all flirting with each other and he felt a twinge of something alien to him; something akin to jealousy. His eyes rested on Olivia, feasting on her beige button-through dress. A long skirt with buttons opened showing more than enough of her tanned legs. He could imagine those legs wrapped around him. The bodice of the dress was pushing her globes of passion outwards, making them nearly overspill into public view. Beautiful strappy, flat sandals with orange gemstones adorned her feet. He could imagine kissing those beautiful feet. Her toenails were painted a soft tangerine to complement the sparkling stones that made her feet look like small works of art. It was uncharacteristically hot and Olivia was leaving little to the imagination. What Adam wouldn't give to be able to take her to the boat right now!

As Adam reached the table, Olivia looked up and their eyes met, speaking more than any words could. She smiled. "Hey, how are you doing?"

"Oh, God, is she drunk?" Adam spoke out loud.

Olivia patted the seat beside her. "Come here and sit beside me."

Adam nodded to the three men at the table. "Hi!" He knew them from the local football team. This could get awkward.

Then there was that wicked grin, followed by Olivia's words, "Adam did some fashion shows with me last year, didn't you? He is very good at what he does." Adam sat down and Olivia kissed him on the cheek, the musky smell of her perfume making its way into his senses, spreading a glow down between his legs.

Olivia rose to leave the table to go to the lavatory. She excused herself and went into the pub with Anne. They left the men talking about football. Adam watched the two friends as they walked across the grass and his longing for Olivia's body increased. She turned to catch him staring and then she winked. The mystical look that he was so used to now spread across her face. She was planning something and the butterflies in his stomach rose to amazing heights.

The men began to discuss the ladies in their absence. The conversation sank to gutter level. They were laughing as they wondered if the two girls might be up for a bit of a party and who would take which one and what they might be like in bed. Adam kept out of it until one of them turned to him. "So, which one would you like?" They were discussing Olivia and Anne as though they were pieces of meat, and Adam did not like it.

He laughed. "Neither, I am happily married to Mary." Adam could not fail to notice the look that passed between the three friends.

"Oh yes, of course you are."

Olivia and Anne returned carrying large glasses of white wine. Adam wondered what they were both whispering about. There was definitely a conspiracy afoot. Adam was ready for some excitement, as for the past few weeks work had been his only companion.

All talk of football exhausted, the three men left to go to the bar for more drink. They said goodbye to Adam and the girls. The tallest of the three turned round and spoke to Olivia. "If you ever fancy a night out, then let us know, nudge, nudge, wink, wink!" He sounded so crass and Adam waited for Olivia's reply; he knew her so well.

Suddenly, Olivia turned on them. "In your dreams, baby! Now fuck off." Adam looked down into his glass, trying not to laugh. Olivia sighed, "Thank goodness they've gone."

He raised his empty glass as he turned to see his friend Derek crossing the lawn. "You want a drink, mate?"

Before Derek could answer, Anne chipped in. "Right, shall we go back to mine, then? I have some champagne that needs drinking. It would be a shame to waste it, and it is such a beautiful afternoon."

Olivia took hold of Adam's hand under the table, squeezing it hard as she rubbed her leg against his. The provocation was too much for him as the blood began to pump into his love vessel. He hoped that this afternoon his ship would sail. They made a plan without speaking. Olivia and Anne left the two men and began to walk down to Anne's house. Adam and Derek were to follow in Derek's van.

"Well, those two, look like they're up for it; what do you think?" Derek didn't know that Olivia had been 'up for it' with Adam for over a year, and Adam wasn't about to tell him either. "I think that Olivia fancies you. I don't fancy her friend. If you want a stab at that Olivia, then don't mind me. I can wait and drink her friend's booze and who knows, a few more drinks and I might have a stab at her anyway. That Olivia looks as though she might be a goer and she's half drunk; it should be easy. Bet you won't even have to take her dress off."

Adam was becoming rather irritated by Derek. He really couldn't do with the way some men talked about women. Adam wasn't too sure about the conversation, and as they walked to Derek's van, he thought he'd better play the game and not give anything away. "Come on then, mate. I think someone might want a slice of this." Adam grabbed his crotch as he got in the van. As they drove down to Anne's, both men thought about what might happen next.

Anne was sitting in the garden when the men arrived. Adam looked for Olivia in the house. She was in the kitchen and he could not help himself. "Hi there, sexy! What you up to?" He grabbed her and pulled her to him, not before checking through the window to see that Derek was settled and talking to Anne.

Olivia sighed. "Oh my, it is far too hot to think today." She put her hand up to her neck and slowly lowered it to the top of her cleavage. She never took her eyes off Adam as she undid some more buttons at the front of her dress. He knew she knew what she was doing and it wasn't long before her knickers were off and they were rolling about on Anne's massive brass bed. The naughtiness of that afternoon gave Adam such an erection, he thought it might explode and he would end up with a burst penis. As they kissed, their tongues speaking to each other in a craze of tongue talk, Adam's hands ran around Olivia's body. They stroked her arms and legs. They squeezed her breasts until she gasped. A gasp brought on by erotic pain. His hands moved up her legs until his fingers found what he was looking for. The juiciness of her peach was asking to be eaten.

All time forgotten, they became sexual acrobats as arms and legs entwined and the force of his thrusting made her cry out in total pleasure. They fell off the bed onto the hard, wooden floor. One more thrust and it was over. They rolled over onto their backs and looked at the ceiling.

The aftermath of bliss was disturbed by Anne. She called "Hello, are you up there?"

They crawled about the floor trying to find the clothes previously thrown off in passion. Olivia called back, "Yes, we are up here. I was showing Adam your bathroom. Is that all right?"

Anne was smirking in the kitchen. "Yes, it's fine. I think Derek wants to go."

Adam was busy pulling his pants on, but what he didn't realise was he was pulling Olivia's knickers on. "Shall I go down first and it won't look so suspicious." Olivia nodded. He ran downstairs. Olivia ran down after him when she found his underpants and could not find her knickers, but it was too late. Before she reached the garden, Adam and his friend were gone.

Anne was sitting alone in the garden. "Did he like the bathroom, then?" She was grinning like a Cheshire cat.

194

Olivia placed the underpants on the table. "Yes, he did; he thought it was marvellous." Anne laughed, "Oh, he left those behind?" Olivia put the Tommy Hilfiger's in her handbag before saying, "He has gone off wearing my knickers."

CHAPTER TWENTY

Felix took a drink and turned towards Adam. "Do you know I think that I do know that woman?"

Adam was somewhere else, walking in his own thoughts. "Which woman?"

"The pretty one that just walked by and winked. I think she recognised me and that's why she winked. It has been years since I last saw her." Felix pointed to the magazine in Adam's lap. "That's her in the magazine."

Adam looked down at the picture of Olivia. "Oh yes, she is a writer now. How do you know her?"

"It's such a long time ago now. We were on a works trip to Germany. There was a group of us. About twenty years ago, if my memory serves me well. Never thought I would ever see her again. She looks like she has done well for herself. I wonder if I should go speak to her; she might not remember me. There again, she winked, so she must do."

Adam began to feel the heat rising in his face. He didn't often blush. He was blushing now. When he and Olivia became lovers, she told him all about Felix and the German trip. He remembered how much she cried. He remembered those tears running down her face as she recalled the night Felix threw her out of his bedroom. Felix called her a whore and the rest of the group were awful towards her as they travelled around Germany. What a bastard! Not nice, not nice at all! Adam would never treat a woman in such a way. He was a deserter and usually just disappeared without a word. Adam toyed with the idea of telling Felix what he knew. He looked out of the window, over the clouds towards the bright sun. He asked himself what would be achieved by his revelation. Nothing would be achieved at all. "Are you going to speak to her? It can't do any harm."

Felix pondered for a moment before nodding his head. "Yes, I think I will. I have waited a long time for this and have some grovelling to do."

As Felix rose from his seat, he looked back and saw the seat next to Olivia was vacant. He nodded to Adam. "Here goes then, see you soon." Felix slowly picked his way down the narrow aisle to confront his past. He wasn't sure what he was going to say or how to approach Olivia. He stopped just in front of her row as his stomach turned. Felix wasn't often nervous but he was now. He was just about to turn round and go back to his seat, when Olivia looked up and smiled. "Hello, Felix, it's been a long time. Would you like to sit with me for a while?"

He was taken aback by her friendliness. Was she expecting him? "Yes, please." His voice didn't sound like his voice at all. He sat down and took in the heady smell of her perfume. Then she surprised him by asking him if he would like a drink. "Yes, please." Felix needed a drink badly — not a glass but a bottle, as he was wondering if this had been a good idea after all. His palms became clammy. He hadn't felt like this for many years and suddenly felt totally out of control. Olivia was not behaving as he expected her to, and then he began to wonder what he had expected. There was a lot of catching up to do and he wondered what she knew. She had obviously remembered him, and so he knew the wink was for him and not the man sitting next to him.

Sean brought two glasses of champagne and flirted with Olivia. For a moment she ignored Felix and bantered with the flight attendant, who gave Felix an approving look, before turning and taking his gay self to the back of the plane. Olivia watched Sean walk away and readied herself for what was to come. Felix took a sip from his glass and stared forward, studying the back of the seat in front of him. He dared not look at Olivia as the shy feelings of a schoolboy began to take over. How was he going to start? What was he going to say to her after all these years?

Felix was a successful man nearly at the end of his sixties and was rarely short of words. That laugh, Olivia's laugh, had not changed at all and now he was scared to look at her. He could feel a stirring that he had not felt for many years. The longing and need within his body awoke. There was no need for chat-up lines in the looming conversation. There was a need for some crawling and to set things right. Who was he doing this for, himself or Olivia? It was probably a bit of both, as he had carried his bad behaviour with him for years and now, he had the chance to set things straight.

He summoned up the courage and began. "Olivia, can I talk to you, please?"

Olivia took a sip of her drink. "What about, Felix? I think the last time we spoke you said all you had to say to 'The Whore'."

'Ouch!' That stung. He deserved it.

Olivia fixed a smile on her face. She felt like a cat who was about to toy with a mouse; perhaps she ought to be merciful "Yes, that would be nice, Felix. I have no idea what you are going to say. If you feel you need to talk to me, I can listen." She turned in her seat, facing towards him. She had an idea what Felix wanted to talk about and raised her glass, tapping it on his. "Cheers." Olivia looked Felix in the eye as he began to try and justify his behaviour in Germany. She'd known it had to be about that: there was nothing else.

Olivia heard that a few months after she left 'Into the Sun', Felix came looking for her at the office. Her friend Jane, who worked in accounts, rang her to tell her. Olivia sensed Felix's hesitation. She began to help him. "I don't need a speech, just talk. I presume that is why you came to sit with me?"

Felix asked Olivia what happened after they all got back from Germany. She told him that life became increasingly difficult for her. Paula went out of her way to bully her and Olivia knew why that was. Olivia told Felix that she stood her ground and was not going to be ousted out by someone like Paula. Unfortunately, something happened in the family which forced Olivia to work part-time for a while. Paula did what she did best and began to tell lies to her boss. Olivia was asked to leave. They would not even let her work the week out — she had to pack her things and leave immediately.

Olivia stopped talking and looked down at her shaking hands. The feelings were bouncing back at her. She really did not want to do this. She did not want to remember. It was like digging up a dead body: very distasteful and rather smelly. She had spent so long not remembering, and she did not want to remember now. The flashback came anyway. "It happened about four weeks after we returned from the trip. I didn't know I had so many tears inside me. I had too many to cry. After the way you treated me and then losing my job just because my manager felt threatened by me, the inevitable happened. I broke down, Felix. I broke down!" Olivia looked at him, the blood gone from his face. Felix couldn't look at her as he was trying to hide his feelings. Olivia tried hard to stop her mounting anger. "Do you think I deserved that? Do you? What did I ever do that was so wrong for those things to happen? Tell me, do you know? It has remained a mystery to me all these years."

Felix took hold of Olivia's hand and looked into eyes that were full of tears. She snatched it away. Olivia's eyes looked like empty, bottomless pools of lost hope. "I am so, so sorry, Olivia; you don't know how sorry. If only I'd known. If only I had trusted in you. I should never have listened to the poisonous words of that jealous vixen. I fell right into her trap. How stupid was I?"

"I don't know. How stupid were you?"

Felix took a long drink. "I find it almost karmic that we are both on this plane together. I really want to set the record straight, but I can't turn back the clock and I might be able to put a wrong right." Felix took hold of her hand once more.

Olivia shook her head and pulled her hand away. "No, I don't suppose you can." She wanted him to stop talking and go away. A simple 'sorry' might do, or a simple act to turn the tables.

Olivia looked out of the window and took a moment to gather her thoughts and calm herself down. She took a large drink. "It's history now and no amount of answers to questions can put things right. It no longer matters to me. Time goes on and I am not sure if I want to hear any more, Felix."

A few moments of silence followed. "It matters to me, Olivia. Please let me speak. There is good reason we are on this plane together, don't you think?"

Olivia got up. She needed the ladies' room. "Sorry, Felix, I need to go to the ladies."

He moved to let her pass. "Shall I wait?"

"Please yourself!" Olivia threw the comment back at him as she walked up the plane, she didn't care one way or another. As she passed Adam, she turned round to look at him. Their eyes met and he smiled. It was a knowing smile. She did not smile back, but stared blankly at him.

Olivia closed the lavatory door with a bang and began to shake. She blamed herself for this. She should have left that wink alone. It got her into so much trouble in the past. She did not need to be reminded of a time in her life when her whole world collapsed after an awful time in Germany followed by the family tragedy which ended her life as she knew it. There was no pride in some of Olivia's past behaviours, only shame and memories of when Olivia was younger and had no idea what dignity meant. Olivia had a choice. She could go back and end the conversation or she could listen to what Felix had to say and maybe make him squirm a little. She splashed her face with cold water and patted her hair. She reapplied her lipstick and gave herself an encouraging wink.

Still unsure of what to do, she returned to her seat, hoping that perhaps Felix had gone back to sit next to Adam. No such luck, he was still there and he stood up to let her get by. "I took the liberty of ordering more drinks. I hope you don't mind?"

"No, that is fine, Felix." Olivia believed that using someone's name often in a conversation gave her control over a situation and it also showed respect. Olivia decided to tell Felix that she was not really interested in anything else he had to say, he never got the chance.

"I came back to see you at the office. Paula told me you left. She said she had no idea where you had gone. She said you did not like your job and it was the best thing that could have happened."

Olivia threw her head back, letting a cynical laugh escape. "What a surprise! She was very good at what she did." Olivia couldn't bear to hear that she devils name. It always touched her fury.

"I spoke to your friend. I think her name was Jane. She told me the truth about Germany. How Paula engineered the whole thing. How Paula did not want Louise to be with me, and how she kind of blackmailed you. I would never have gone with Louise anyway," he lied. "Jane told me you told Paula what to do with her plan, even though she threatened you with losing your job. What I don't understand, if that was the case, then why did you sleep with me anyway?"

"Good grief, Felix, what a question to ask after all these years!" Olivia thought for a moment. "I could say it was the drink. We drank rather a lot that night. Didn't we? I think that together with watching the sex show and getting along so well, you being so nice, it was just an inevitable ending to a good night out. I don't know, Felix, it just happened. I didn't think of consequences. I just did it. I can't give you an answer. I can tell you that it certainly wasn't because that awful person threatened me."

Felix took hold of Olivia's hand and squeezed it as he smiled at her. She smiled back at him as she pulled her hand away. "May I ask you a question now, please?"

"Yes, of course."

Olivia took a deep breath. "Why did you call me a whore? Why did you throw me out of your room when it was obvious that I was in such distress and needed you? I thought we were friends."

Felix shook his head. "It was bad, so bad. If I said 'Paula', would that answer your question?"

Olivia shook her head. "No. Not really."

"To begin with, she told me that she dared you to sleep with me and that you said yes, that you were up for a challenge. I didn't realise until it was too late that she trapped me into letting slip that we had spent the night together. She led me to believe that you broadcast everything we did that night. I think you know the rest. I was so angry, angry with myself, angry with you, thinking you had a big mouth and couldn't keep a secret. What we did was private between you and me. What hurt the most was that you were waking up feelings in me that I thought I would never have again. I even thought about seeing you again when we got back to England. I came to the office that day to ask you why you had done what you did, only to learn the truth from your friend, Jane. Paula had manipulated the both of us. She had no idea we slept together until I confirmed it. It was a stupid slip on my part and I should have known better. She lied about you and I believed her. What I cannot come to terms with is how I treated you that night. You gave me no reason to behave so badly. You were beautiful, funny and so lovely. I have lived to regret what I did. Can you forgive me?" Felix looked down at his knees as he remembered the night when he behaved like a turnip.

Olivia sat in silence, not moving. She was processing all that she heard. "Felix, I forgave you and I forgave myself a long time ago. I couldn't understand what happened. You made me feel like a whore and I sort of understood that, a little bit. I behaved like one. I believed you got what you wanted and perhaps it had not been that good, so why go there twice? Was it me that you actually wanted? I think that you just wanted sex and I was there conveniently drunk."

"Hang on a moment, Olivia. We had agreed not to have sex. I was falling asleep next to you. You took your T-shirt off and jumped on me."

Olivia thought for a moment, then a small giggle escaped. "Yes, you are right; but then we had such an awesome time. It was good. What followed wasn't good and it made what we did rather dirty. I felt used and abused. You were horrid to me and just left me hanging. I could not wait to get back home. You turned a wonderful night into something salacious."

Felix looked at Olivia. He brought his face close to hers and pressed his forehead against her forehead. His eyes never left hers. "We were both used and abused by Paula."

Olivia moved away from him. "I don't know. What I do know is that it was a massive learning curve for me. I learnt so much about myself and other people. I was the victim of bullying on that trip and when I returned home, I learnt that I am not a sheep, not a follower, but a leader. I developed a resilience that has stayed with me on my life's journey. It hasn't stopped me trusting people because I trust myself more now. Bad things have happened to me since, but I think what you did to me is the worst ever. You were forgiven, Felix, but never forgotten." Olivia changed the subject quickly. "So, are you still married?"

Felix told her why he was going to New York. He asked her how long she would be there and if perhaps they could meet up? Olivia asked him why they should meet. He had explained himself now and it was nice having a drink with him, for old time's sake. She ended their conversation. "Thank you, Felix, but I don't think we will be seeing each other again." He was dismissed as Olivia picked up her book and began to read. There was nothing more to say.

After an awkward pause, Felix got up. "Thank you for your time; it is much appreciated. Perhaps you might rethink and change your mind? Here is my card, just in case."

Olivia took the card from him and placed it in the back of her book as he returned to his seat. She was not able to see the words in front of her as tears were running down her face and she felt sick. She knew Felix thought he was doing the right thing and he wanted her to forgive him. Why couldn't people just let things lie in the past where they belonged? Did he think he could put things right? Well, at least she knew, and now there were no missing gaps in that chapter of her life. He hurt her beyond reason and he was now sitting next to the man who hurt her beyond reason too and who she had loved with such passion. She truly believed that she and Adam were meant to be together, but he broke her heart which took many years to heal. It also ruined her marriage. Olivia's thoughts would not stop.

Was she a whore all those years ago? After all, she had known Felix only a few days and then given her body to him. Maybe she was worse than a whore, as she gave herself for free? Olivia wiped her tears and took a big drink, emptying her glass. She sighed and returned to the pages of her book. The last chapter in Olivia's past was complete and now ended.

~

Adam was raised from his memories of the past by Felix sitting down heavily beside him. "You've been a while, mate. I guess she remembered you, then. Hope it went according to plan?"

"She hasn't changed much in twenty years; still as sexy as ever. The hair colour's different. Did I tell you her name was Olivia?"

"No, you didn't."

"I said what needed to be said and left her my card. I think she will be ringing me next week in the Big Apple. I wasn't that nice to her back in the day and I just had to fill in some gaps with her. I would really like to make it up to her and perhaps we might be able to continue where we left off before it all went sour." Felix's ego was nearly as big as Adams

Felix was obviously in denial, as Olivia had made it quite clear that they would not be seeing each other again. Adam tried to read the expression of his face, it wasn't a positive one. He wondered what really had just happened. He wanted to ask, but thought better of it. It was not his business, and men didn't usually talk about such things. Adam felt a twinge of jealousy. What was that all about? He knew Olivia well, as a sensitive soul who at times could be reckless and even dangerous. She gave off the aura that she was strong, and she was strong sometimes. She was also vulnerable when it came to relationships: she had her heart broken many times in her quest for love. She was an avid rainbow chaser. Adam wondered how many times Olivia's heart had been broken in the past twenty years after he, too, broke it for her. He wondered whether he should go and speak to her. He thought better of it, as he really wasn't sure what he would say.

Adam ordered a drink for himself and his neighbour. Felix looked as though he needed one. He sat back, wondering what to say to Felix next. He decided to let things be, as Felix might become suspicious of his questions. Adam looked back towards Olivia. He was not able to gauge the look on her face. She was busy reading a book. Perhaps he might catch her at the airport? He would think about it. Adam settled into a conversation with Felix about football and boats. Soon, thoughts of Olivia were erased from his mind. In his younger day, Adam was a football referee and he was still obsessed with the game. Felix supported Manchester City, and they were soon lost in 'man' talk.

~

Olivia was stunned. She sat in a daze, trying to make sense of what had just happened. She stared at the book in her hands. The words were swimming into one another as her anger, mixed with a little sorrow, got the better of her. After all these years, Felix is on the same plane with her and he says 'Sorry'? Why? Did it make him feel better? All Felix achieved was to send Olivia into a downward spiral to the dark places she had been to too many times in the past. A place where she hid all her regrets, even though she insisted on telling herself she never had any. Who was she fooling? Felix was one of her dark places.

Olivia asked Sean to bring her another drink: she needed to steady her nerves and stop her mind racing. Memories and pain were now popping up in abundance and she knew that she would have to take a look at them before they would go away again. They were beginning to crowd her mind and she would have to unravel each one in turn. This happened to her once before, years ago, and she nearly broke down as the feelings of despair and disappointment came with the pictures that floated through her conscience. Olivia had to make some acknowledgements back then that were not complimentary, nor pleasant. She had to walk in her shadow. She was in her shadow now. Carl Jung talked about the shadow, a lot. When she was training to be a psychotherapist, she read that the shadow is the other side of us, the dark side. It can hold all the things we deem to be wrong that we have done in our lives. The things that we choose to ignore, try not to remember and are not proud of! It can contain our blackest thoughts, the things we wish we had done differently, and most times we try to ignore it. Well, Olivia could not ignore the fact that she was on a plane going to America with two men who she placed in her shadow and who she had never expected to see again.

CHAPTER TWENTY-ONE

Olivia set her book aside and was soon lost in her turbulent past. She thought about Adam's all important, question in the pub that night when the snow came down. He said that he would not leave his children, so why had he asked her if she would leave hers? It was a big thing to leave children, and people do it for all sorts of reasons. When caught up in a 'love' thing, the decision can be very difficult. Some people can make the decision easily. This wasn't the case for Olivia, and she thought long and hard. Sometimes life was about choices, and choices can be so hard. A decision made can often be seen as a right one until long after, when it might turn out to be the wrong one.

Not long after that night Olivia was going to speak to Adam about his question and their future, she thought they could work something out. Instead he dumped her. She thought the world had ended and drove to Fiona's in floods of tears.

Later that night, when she was on her own in an empty house, it was easy to drink a bottle of whiskey. Olivia spent a lot of time on her own in that big empty house. Life had not turned out according to plan and she had to admit how lonely she really was. Perhaps that was why she had made bad decisions in the past and perhaps that was why she kept seeking love. That was no excuse for her dangerous, mental behaviours.

Olivia spent the next few days in bed. She told the family that she had the flu. They didn't believe her. Since when was flu accompanied by alcohol fumes? She fooled no one. The only fool was Olivia. She wallowed in the pity that surrounded Adam's words. She never wanted to get out of bed again. She felt like she was dying. She wanted the pain in her heart to stop. She couldn't stand a day without love. She made an agreement with herself to stop chasing rainbows.

This man that she thought loved her had knocked her off the top of her fantasy world. She was forced to return to the real world; and the real world, just now, was not a nice place to be. Adam's speech had come without warning. There were no signs, no lead up to it, and he'd showed himself to be the bastard that he was. Adam had abused her in a subtle, emotional way. He was soon to be history. Olivia couldn't stay in her pit of depression, as before long the family may become suspicious.

Olivia began to rebuild her life and wiped Adam from her mind. She wasn't one to hold on to things and the shame of her affair with him haunted her. She felt so bad about her big secret and would make it up to her family and be the person she ought to be, and not some adulterous floozy. She spent time with Fiona, who listened, nodded and smiled in the appropriate places, over many cups of tea. Olivia had not drunk alcohol since the night she looked into an empty bottle of Johnnie Walker's. Alcohol was a depressive, and she was depressed enough.

Even though she tried hard not to, Olivia's conversation would always turn to Adam. She had to convince herself that their relationship was over. Verbalising helped her to get it all out of her system. There can be much positivity in talking. It helped to talk with someone who knew Adam and his family, and Olivia trusted Fiona with her life. It was hard for Fiona as she had a secret of her own and she could not share it with Olivia. During one of Olivia's ravings, Fiona's mind wandered. "Who wouldn't love Adam?" He was good looking, successful and absolutely charming. One look from Adam could make a woman feel special. Most of the time, Fiona was only listening to Olivia with one ear, as her mind tended to wander into her own thoughts. Fiona would never divulge those thoughts to Olivia. Not that she would ever get a chance, as Olivia didn't stop for breath when she was on a rant.

Olivia was a good friend to have, and when Fiona said that she wanted to join the village Gala committee and didn't have the courage to go to the meeting, Olivia told Fiona that she would accompany her. She would not have to go alone. It was the least Olivia could do after all the support that she got from her friend. That evening, Olivia was excited as she felt that she was helping her friend take a step towards her potential. They entered the village hall and sat near the back. Olivia knew that Adam would be there, and when she saw him sitting on the stage, she placed herself behind a rather large man. She did not want to be seen. She hid from her hurt.

Just before the end of the meeting, when people were getting coffee, Olivia made her excuses and left. She did not want to bump into Adam, and Fiona was happy chatting to her new committee members. On her way home in the car, she went over the night's proceedings. She was happy for her friend. Olivia hadn't missed a thing and she saw the way Adam looked at Fiona. She knew that look so well. It was the same look she was given by Adam in the early days. The more she thought about it, the more she began to realise how much Fiona talked about Adam. She hadn't really noticed before because she talked so much about Adam, too. As she wondered why Fiona talked about Adam so much, Olivia made a mental note to mention this the next time she was with her friend. On most occasions Olivia listened to her instincts, but this time she didn't want to, as she might not like what she heard. She could not stop the whisperings in her gut and became rather annoyed. By the time she reached home, all thoughts of Adam and Fiona were dismissed as foolish, insecure thinking and forgotten.

A few weeks after that meeting, Olivia left work. As she walked across the car park, she saw Adam standing by her car. Panic set in as she got nearer to him. What did he want? The last thing she wanted was to speak with him. She was still nursing a broken heart. Adam looked as handsome as ever in his navy blazer, with his dark wavy hair blowing slightly in the breeze. She noticed he looked a little nervous and she resolved not to be taken in by any of his smooth words. To her, 'over' meant 'over' and she needed to move on. Adam did not take his eyes off her as she walked towards him. He gave her a self-conscious smile. "Can we talk, please?"

"I don't see that there is anything you and I have got to talk about." Olivia did not want this. She just wanted to go home after a long day at the office.

Adam's face changed to the little boy look she knew so well. It always crossed his face when he wanted something. "Please, Olivia, just a minute?"

No harm could be done in a minute. Olivia looked at her watch and then up at Adam. Her heart was racing and she felt that it might burst. She really did not want to hear what Adam had to say. Not after she witnessed the way he looked at Fiona at the meeting the previous night.

Olivia unlocked the car door and got in. Adam sat down beside her. "This is almost like old times." He sounded so nervous.

Olivia's hard face did not change. "It is nothing like old times. Now, how can I help you?" An awkward, few minutes passed in silence. Olivia began to tap her fingers on the steering wheel. Her sign of impatience made Adam realise she really did mean a minute.

"I am so, so sorry. I can't find the words. I made a big mistake and did a stupid thing that day when I said it was over. I can't get you out of my mind. I can't function properly. Olivia, it will never be over for me. You mean so much to me. My life was getting so complicated and I just panicked. There was so much pressure. Can you ever forgive me?" Adam turned to look at Olivia, who was staring out of her window. She was watching a pigeon flying past and he wondered if she had heard anything he said. He carried on. "It might be over for you, but it will never be over for me." He didn't realise that he was beginning to repeat himself. "You have my heart and soul." Olivia smiled. She thought about the Timi Yuro song, 'It'll Never Be Over, For Me'.

Adam ran out of words and sat there feeling more than a bit stupid. He could not tell what Olivia might be thinking, her face as cold as marble. In a low tone she began to speak, very quietly. "That day, that awful afternoon, I was about to tell you that, yes, I would leave my children for you."

Adam was shocked. "I didn't know that."

Olivia let out a small laugh. "Why would you? You said your piece and got out of the car. You practically ran back to your office." She sighed. "What exactly are you saying now, Adam? Are you saying that you are sorry, as I really do need to go and your minute is up?"

Adam put his hand on her arm. "Please don't. I need to talk to you properly. Just hear me out."

Olivia looked at her watch again. "OK, you have got another five, and then I really must go."

Adam began to speak with sincerity. "Since the first day I saw you my life changed. You gave me a window to really look at myself and what I was doing. I wasn't going anywhere at all. I have been so wrapped up in trying to keep everybody happy; I now know that I can't. In doing that I thought I was happy, and now I know that I am not. You brought laughter into my life. I just got into a mess and went into a panic. I don't think I can live if you are not in my life somewhere."

"Adam, you told me you loved me. People don't hurt the ones they love. You will live"

"I know, and perhaps I should have been more honest with you. I promise you that if you give me one more chance I will never, ever hurt you again."

"Adam, I really must go."

"Please, will you call me?"

"I don't know."

Olivia never admitted to Adam how things went from bad to worse after that awful afternoon in the car park. She'd never stopped thinking about him. She spent many a grieving afternoon looking out of her office window, hoping to catch a glimpse of him. Little did she know that he was doing the same as she was! Olivia kept her own counsel.

It took her one day to make up her mind and they began to see each other again. The passion was still there and it was even better than before. Very soon she was head over heels in love with Adam once more. When she felt strong enough, she broached the subject of Fiona. Adam shut her down. "What is wrong with you? I never had you down as the jealous type. Why are we wasting time talking about your friend? She is on the committee, that is all. Fiona is no way my type and I would not do that to you. My cheating days are over." It seemed a bit of an odd statement to make, as Adam was still cheating on his wife, Mary, and his mistress, Gerry. Adam finished his protestation. "I think we should be concentrating on us, don't you?"

A few weeks later, Olivia caught Fiona off her guard whilst they were drinking coffee in a bar in town. They had spent the morning shopping and now, with bags surrounding their feet, they were ordering lunch. Olivia had not told Fiona that things were back on with Adam. She didn't know why she didn't tell her. She just listened to her gut. They talked about anything and everything, until suddenly Olivia said something that was on her mind. "You fancy Adam, don't you?"

Fiona was taken off her guard. "Is that a statement or a question?"

Olivia felt her heart beginning to go a little faster. "Well, actually it was more of an observation."

By this time Fiona's face was puce and she looked as though she might faint. Her puce was followed by a hot shade of crimson. "That is an awful thing to say."

"Fiona, you go on and on about the committee meetings and talk about Adam more than is normal."

Fiona took a sip of her drink. "Do I? Well, you know I am really enjoying my time there and I do sometimes work with Adam. It's not like you are still with him, is it?"

The awkward moment passed and it wasn't until they were eating dessert that Fiona brought the subject up again. "I know how much Adam meant to you and I just would not do that to a friend. You two had a major connection that I don't think anyone could break."

Olivia began to feel that she should never have spoken. "I am sorry, Fiona, that wasn't nice of me. I just had this feeling that I couldn't quite put my finger on. I know you wouldn't do that." Fiona smiled. "You know, Fiona, it has been so hard for me. I really thought I loved the man. Did I tell you that he once asked me to leave home? I need to tell you something now and I am sorry that I did not tell you before." Olivia took a moment of composure. "We have been seeing each other again. For a few weeks now, and I think that soon he might be making a move. He might be making an announcement." Olivia watched to see what effect her words might be having on her friend.

Fiona's face was unreadable. "I am so happy for you."

Fiona wanted Olivia to shut up now, but Olivia continued. "I think we might be having a weekend away in the autumn before I start university. Just imagine me waking up next to him and having two whole days together! I am really excited. My favourite time for sex is in the morning, just at the time when you are half asleep and so relaxed. You know what I mean, don't you? Do you like it then?" Olivia was grinning and Fiona could not look at her. Olivia was in her wicked witch mode, and even though this was her friend, who was now looking more than uncomfortable, she was rather enjoying herself.

Fiona was slow to reply. She did not want Adam and Olivia to go away together. "Is it wise? Don't you think that perhaps he might dump you again? I wouldn't go if I were you." Fiona was in a mental mess. She spent so much time with Adam at the community centre and when she wasn't there, she couldn't get him out of her mind. Flirting every time, they met became a pattern of behaviour that they both enjoyed. The last time Fiona saw Adam, his lips touched hers in a 'bye' kiss. Fiona had felt a surge of blood rush round her body as the tip of his tongue touched her bottom lip. Olivia was right in her thinking. Fiona more than liked him. Fiona wanted him. She looked up and saw Olivia's eyes staring at her and felt uncomfortable under the gaze that appeared to be looking into her soul. Olivia had a habit of doing this. She was very good at reading people. She was reading Fiona now and Fiona was trying to shut her out. Could Olivia see what she was thinking?

Olivia couldn't stop and went on and on. She relentlessly kept barging into Fiona's mind with her chit-chat. Fiona had had enough. "Look, Olivia, there is, never has been, never will be anything going on with me and Adam. I shall come off the committee if you like and that will be that."

Olivia laughed. "Oh my God, who touched your fuse paper? What is this about? Have I hit a raw nerve somewhere? I am sorry, Fiona, but you have always wanted to know what we were up to. I did think there might be something going on between you, but I know that not to be the case now. Can't you take a wind-up?"

The two women picked up their bags and left the cafe. They hugged each other before returning to their cars, arranging to ring each other the following week. It never happened.

The summer passed very quickly and soon Olivia began to dream of her two days away with Adam. She hadn't seen much of him during the late summer months as Adam took his family on holiday and she was very busy also. They called each other now and then and even managed a few short trips to his boat. They only stayed long enough to catch up on some overdue passion.

The niggle in Olivia's mind never left her, and one evening on their way back from the boat she surprised Adam with another question. "Do you see much of Fiona these days?"

Adam responded and sounded annoyed. "Why should I? Why ask me that? No, and I thought we were never going to mention her again?"

Why was he being so defensive? "Sorry, Adam. I haven't heard from her for quite a while. I think I upset her the last time we met."

"Oh, why was that?"

"Well, I think she might be having an affair and I nearly rumbled her." Olivia wondered if they should not have had this conversation in the car as she could not watch Adam's face. She was driving. She always drove. A few minutes passed as they listened to the radio. A mile passed as Grover Washington Junior crooned 'Just The Two Of Us'.

The silence between them was broken by Adam. "It's funny that you should mention her! She has rung me a few times recently. She flirts with me, but she's not my type. I would not touch her with a barge pole. She sits next to me at the committee meetings. She isn't a patch on you."

Olivia accepted what Adam said and wondered if she was being a little touchy. She still had the 'niggle' and decided to ignore it. As she and Adam were getting close again, perhaps she was feeling a bit less confident with her decision. She screamed at her paranoia to go away. She knew if she continued that she would push Adam away. Men did not like jealous, prying women. She knew that she had to trust him. She must believe what he said, or what was the point of her being with him? They didn't speak much for the rest of the journey and Olivia was kicking herself. She should have kept her mouth shut.

A few weeks later, Olivia drove her other half to the airport. She now had a month of freedom to do what she wanted. She had the weekend to herself, as she could not ring Adam; she would have to wait till Monday for them to plan their wonderful weekend. Olivia blitzed the house and by Sunday night the place was spotless and her bag was packed for her first day at university. She was about to start her degree and there was no word to describe her excitement about that. The next day was a very full day of meeting new people and learning new things. She had no time to ring Adam and he didn't ring her either. Adam didn't ring on Tuesday or Wednesday. On Thursday, while she was in town getting her lunch, Olivia dialled Adam's works number. A woman answered and told Olivia that Adam was out and she needed to call back later. That was fine with her as she had some shopping to do.

After an hour in the travel agents checking up on weekend breaks, she went into Clayden's. This was an expensive shop that sold dresses and the most amazing lingerie. No way was she taking old underwear on her two days with Adam. She had waited too long for this and it all had to be perfect. She came up the steps of the shop laden with boxes, feeling a bit guilty about the amount of money she spent. As she reached the pavement, she didn't see the people to her right and bumped into them. Her boxes spilled out onto the floor and a pair of purple silk knickers and matching bra fell into the gutter. She fell to her knees and the couple she nearly knocked over bent down to help her. The man took her elbow and she looked up into familiar eyes. Adam was out with Gerry. Olivia wanted to die.

"Are you OK, miss?"

She felt so stupid and just stood there as Gerry handed her the underwear back that she had retrieved from the side of the road. Olivia could not speak. Gerry touched Adam's arm. "I think we best get back, Adam, we are going to be late. She will be all right." Gerry took Adam's hand and led him away. As Olivia watched them go, she didn't know whether to laugh or cry. Adam did not look back at her but Gerry did and smiled.

Olivia was back in the phone booth near the university. The same woman answered her call again. Olivia thought, "Who is this woman? Where is Adam?" It all seemed a bit strange. The woman asked her to wait. She was gone a while and Olivia began to panic as her money was running out and she had no change left.

"I am so sorry, but Mr Templeton will be in meetings all afternoon. May I take a message?"

Olivia was baffled, as Adam was always at his desk and always answered his calls. Where was he? "No, there is no message. I can call later, thank you." Olivia stepped out into the sunshine. She felt cold and lonely, until she realised that he might be working hard to clear space for their days away.

Olivia always had a plan, but this was not going to plan for some reason. She began to feel that Adam was avoiding her. She was going to be late for her lecture and ran up the hill to the main building, where she met some of her new colleagues. The rest of the afternoon was spent writing notes and trying to understand big words. No wonder lectures were boring when so many big words were used. At one point she held her hand up. The lecturer was not amused at being interrupted. He peered over his glasses at her.

"I am so sorry, but I don't understand your big words. Can't you speak in ordinary English, please?"

The silence that fell over the room was deafening, but she knew that she was speaking for many of the students sitting there who felt the same as she did, but dare not speak. Perhaps she should not have spoken either. The lecturer put his notes down and began to pace backwards and forwards. He suddenly stopped and addressed the whole room. "You have come here to learn, and when you graduate it will set you apart from others who will not be as scholarly as you. You will embark on professional careers that will require a special diction that allows you to master situations that others cannot. It was a good statement your fellow student made, but if she feels she is not able to change her thinking, she must question whether she should be here or not."

Olivia felt herself shrinking back into her chair. She leaned across to her neighbour. "I will never use big words to set me apart from others. What he just said was bollocks!"

On the way home, she began to think about her day, which hadn't gone too well. She began to make excuses for why Adam had not spoken to her when she called and for why he just walked off meekly with Gerry after he helped her up outside the shop. Why had Gerry turned round and smiled at her? Paranoia is like a snowball rolling down a hill. It starts off small and grows bigger as it gains momentum. Olivia laughed out loud. It all seemed so funny now. She sat, lonely, on the sofa that night with a bottle of wine, waiting for a call. The call never came. She was beginning to feel deflated and let down. She called his number once but put the phone down before it connected. Her positive side told her that Adam would be making things right for their trip and that she should leave him alone, he would call her when he could.

Three more days passed before Adam picked up the phone. The excitement of at last hearing his voice made Olivia babble. "Well, he has gone and I have been to the travel agents to get some weekend brochures." She did not mention the past few days or ask why he had not returned her calls. "So when can we go, where shall we go? I am so excited now." Olivia was clutching at straws and she tried to ignore the instincts that were now screaming at her. The silence on the other end of the line made her wonder if he was still there. "Adam, is everything all right? Are you all right?"

His voice sounded cold and clipped. "No, it is not, and I won't be spending a weekend with you and I don't know when I shall be free again. I am going now and I do not take kindly to being bothered at work." Before Olivia could answer, Adam put the phone down without a goodbye. The click confirmed the feelings in her gut.

Olivia stared at the receiver before replacing it. She was shocked and there was no comprehension as to what had just happened. The man who had just spoken to her was not at all like her Adam. She didn't know the man who had just spoken to her in that way.

She managed to sit through that afternoon's lecture, but her mind was elsewhere. Still stunned, she walked quickly to her car. She just wanted to be home. Had she been given the brush-off, or could he just not talk as there was someone there with him? The voice in her head growled at her. "Grow up, you silly bitch, you were given the brush-off. You are not that stupid, are you?" Olivia was glad to get home that night so that she could think. She sat by the phone, hoping that he would ring. She didn't have to think much before she felt an unaccustomed anger rising. "What a bastard! He has played me all along. How could he speak to me like that?" When she calmed down, she heard her good sometimes rather silly angel speak to her. "He is just busy with work stuff. He did not mean to hurt you. It will be fine. He will call you soon." Adam never called her again. Olivia never saw him again.

CHAPTER TWENTY-TWO

Olivia looked up to see Sean looking down at her. "Is everything all right?"

Olivia nodded, desperately trying to hold back tears. The flashback to when Adam dumped her was more than she could bear and she could not speak.

"Are you sure? You can tell me to mind my own business, but did that man who was talking to you upset you?"

Olivia nodded again. She looked over the seat in front and could see Adam and Felix with their heads bent in deep conversation. They were both laughing. Paranoia took over as she wondered what they might be laughing about.

"Would you like a drink?" Sean was worried about her. Olivia nodded. "Do you want the same as before?"

Olivia looked at him and nodded. "Yes, please, and I am sorry."

He laughed. "Hey, you have nothing to be sorry about. It seems to me it might be him who should be sorry!" Sean nodded across to where Felix was sitting and gently squeezed Olivia's hand.

Olivia had not seen Adam in twenty years, and now he was sitting a few rows in front of her with Felix, who was the biggest mistake she ever made. Adam would not know that she knew why he dumped her. It was four years after he put the phone down on her that she learned what it was all about, and the truth hurt. Now she was on her own after being divorced for many years. She couldn't stand a day without love, but she had to. She had thrown herself into her work and now a new chapter in her life was beginning.

~

Olivia was living on her own in her little cottage by the canal when one day her friend Molly rang her. "I have some gossip and it concerns you," her friend whispered conspiratorially down the phone.

Olivia was intrigued. "What's up, Molly?"

"Have you heard from Adam recently?"

Why on earth would Molly ask that? She knew it had been over for years! "Why would I? That bastard disappeared years ago. Talk about a snake!"

"I need to tell you something, and you need to listen. Perhaps it's not a good idea to come over this part of town for a while. I know that you like to shop over here when you visit Anne."

"Can I ring you back, Molly, I am just in the middle of something? I will be five minutes!" Olivia put the phone down and went to make herself a cup of tea. Whilst in the kitchen, she also had a shot of whiskey to steady her nerves. Whatever it was that Molly was going to tell her, she had the impression that it might be painful. It had taken her a long time to get over Adam, and her divorce was not what she'd wanted. She was still in shock as to how speedily her ex wound things up.

Settled in the window seat, Olivia dialled Molly's number. "Molly, is Adam dead?"

"Oh God no, he's not dead. He is very much alive. Adam and Mary have split up!"

Olivia felt a little annoyed with her friend. "Why are you telling me this?"

Molly went on to say that she didn't know the full story, but Mary's best friend had spoken to her. She told Molly that Mary knew about the affair between her and Adam. She felt that perhaps if Mary saw Olivia it might not be a good meeting. "I think you should lay low for a while."

Olivia could not believe it! Why would Adam tell Mary about their affair? It didn't make sense! The two friends continued to chat for a while, caught up with each other's lives and promised to meet up for a drink, knowing that they probably wouldn't.

Olivia was stunned. It was four years ago, four long years! Why had this all surfaced now? Olivia buried Adam years ago. She blamed him in part for the break-up of her marriage. She'd lived each day in the fear that her husband might find out about her affair. She could not live with the secret and stupidly she made a few waves at home and was asked to leave. Her husband was quite happy for her to go, as he was having an affair of his own.

The following day, Olivia drove over to Fiona's. She had not seen Fiona for a very long time. Curiosity got the better of her and she hadn't really fallen out with Fiona anyway. Life had taken over and Fiona was left by the wayside. Her old friend would know the whole story in detail, she was sure. Fiona was pleased to see Olivia and they chatted about life and about what they both had been doing for the past four years. Fiona finished her coffee and returned to the task of trimming the Christmas tree. Olivia cleared her throat. "I hear that Adam and Mary have split up. A little bird tells me that he told Mary about me."

It didn't take much for Fiona to gossip to her old friend, and Olivia sat back to listen. Fiona told Olivia that Mary told Adam that she was leaving him. She was having an affair with a man in the village she met at Yoga and she was moving in with him. Seemingly the affair had been going on for years. Adam went crazy. He was so angry with her that he told her about everything. He told Mary about every woman he had slept with. He set out to really hurt her and he did. She left him that night. Mary's upset turned to anger and she was on the warpath.

This was almost unbelievable. Why could Adam not have left her out of this? He was a betrayer as well as everything that she called him down the years. He was the reason her marriage ended. "So, where is he now, then? Has he moved in with Gerry?" Not that Olivia needed to know this.

"Who is Gerry?"

Adam must never tell Fiona about Gerry! Olivia shook her head. "Never mind, it's not important."

Fiona carried on with her decorations while Olivia lost herself in her thoughts. She was trying to come to terms with what she had just been told. Poor Mary! How awful for her, even though she, too, had been having an affair. Half the people that the snake slept with were Mary's friends.

"Do you want another cup of tea?" Fiona's voice broke the silence.

"Yes, please." Olivia's throat was dry with shock and she was rather numb, too.

Fiona returned from the kitchen. "For a moment I thought you'd come because you heard about me. I thought that is why you came."

Olivia took her cup from Fiona, who went back to the window and carried on trimming the tree. Olivia was startled by the words and came out of her thought cave. "What do you mean?" The silence became creepy. Then a veil of fog began to lift slowly. "Oh no, Fiona, you haven't had an affair, have you? You aren't cheating on Bob, are you? He is so lovely, and after what I went through! You know it really isn't worth it just for that moment's pleasure and then a lifetime of shame and heartache. Oh no!"

Fiona stopped what she was doing and looked down at the bauble in her hand. She stood very still and did not move.

Olivia stared at the frozen statue across the room and the veil lifted some more. She hoped that she was wrong. She hoped that she was very wrong indeed. Realisation began to stomp on her feelings. "Oh no, it was you? You went with Adam, didn't you? It was you! That is why he dumped me. How could you? You saw how much I loved him. How could you do that to a friend?" What a hypocritical comment to make when Olivia was a friend to Mary at the time she was sleeping with her husband. There was nothing to be proud of in that.

Fiona did not move. Olivia did not know whether to laugh or cry. She did not know what to do. It would not take much for her to cross the room and slap Fiona hard. She felt sick to her stomach. "I was right all those years ago when I asked you if you fancied him. You lied to me. I knew it." Olivia drank her tea before continuing. She had not finished. "When exactly was this?" She answered her own question. "I know it was when I went to university and we were planning to go away for the weekend. I know why we didn't go now. He was seeing you already. Wasn't he?" The thought of Adam and Fiona together became too much for Olivia and she began to shout. "Did you sleep with him? Did you? How could you do that to me? I was your friend!"

Fiona shouted back at Olivia, "And you were Mary's friend, weren't you? You were shagging her husband, name of Adam?"

Olivia sank back into her chair and held back the tears. She felt as though she had been hit across the face by a wet, slimy fish. "I paid for that. Don't you think it screwed me up? You were Mary's friend, too. Oh goodness, what a mess it all is. Was?" A very uncomfortable silence descended on them both as there seemed nothing left to say, until Olivia began again. She needed to know everything. "Did you sleep with him or just have a grope? Were you sleeping with him the same time I was and he was still sleeping with Mary and Gerry?"

"Olivia, will you tell me who this Gerry is?"

Olivia stood up and took her bag. She really didn't want to stay another minute longer. She wanted to go. "Well, did you sleep with Adam or not?"

Fiona looked across the room at her. "That I am not going to tell you, but I will tell you one thing. You came between us. Wherever we went, you were sort of there; your presence made it very difficult."

With her hand on the door handle, Olivia turned to look at Fiona, who had still not moved. "Wow! That is some consolation, then." Olivia had to get away from this woman, this Judas who had fallen into the snake pit. They had both been taken in and stupidly their friendship was no more. Before she left, she said, "Gerry is Adam's mistress. He has her ensconced in a flat down the road. I fooled myself and I was number three in his love triangle. I always thought that I was the one and he was too weak to make his move. I loved him so much and he ruined me and my life."

Fiona carried on trimming her tree.

Olivia drove home in a daze. She gabbled to herself all the way to her front door. "How could they do that to me? She was my friend and he was my lover. I would have left my life for him and I ended up without one because of him. I really loved him." She couldn't find words to express what she was feeling. The words of that last phone call to Adam were ringing in her ears as though it was only yesterday. She began to sob and badly needed a drink.

After a hot bath and half a bottle of gin, she felt calmer and began to play some music. It wasn't long before she was singing along to 'A Day Without Love' by the Love Affair.

She thought back to the days after Adam was so rude to her on the phone. He was so cold. How could someone turn like that? Turn he had, and Olivia was lost at the time. She listened to the words of the song again and thought back to when she would drive past the end of Adam's street just to catch a glimpse of him. She was like a stalking love-struck teenager. 'A day without love is a year of emptiness.' There were four years of emptiness and questions; now she had the answer. She had spent many nights lying awake trying to work out where it had all gone wrong. She now knew exactly why Adam did what he did. It was a lie. It was all a lie. It was just an illusion. Olivia made a toast just before her tears began to fall. She raised her glass. "Well, you bastard, I can last a day without love after all. I had to. You got your comeuppance. Well done, Mary. I salute you!"

CHAPTER TWENTY-THREE

Olivia did not notice when Sean left her a drink. She was glad of it now as she was thirsty after staggering about in her history. She never thought that the journey into her future would be crowded by the past. She could not believe that Adam and Felix were sitting just a few yards away from her and chatting like best buddies. She could not believe that she had been so foolish as to wink at them. How stupid was that?

The worst thing of all was when Felix came and tried to put his wrong, right. She loved watching his discomfort and the way he grovelled. Olivia wasn't a nasty person, but firmly believed that your misdemeanours catch up with you eventually. They had certainly caught up with Felix. She smiled. At least he had the decency to apologise after all these years, and that chapter was ended now. The smile turned into a laugh when she thought about the cheek of the man as he gave her his card, expecting her to have a drink with him. Why on earth would she want to drink with a bastard, the Jekyll and Hyde of the aviation world? In her past, Olivia spent many days chasing rainbows, only to see them disappear as quickly as they came. Now she was chasing her dreams which did not include any rainbows.

Olivia called Sean to bring her another drink. They were due to land soon and the bar would be closing. Her experience on the plane since taking off at Manchester hours ago was indeed surprising. Two ghosts from her past haunted her on the flight. They were the two men she had written her book about. It was just unbelievable. The uninvited memories hurt so much. Always thinking that she had resolved everything, she now realised that was not the case. Olivia remembered the lines of a song, 'But they just say I'm sorry and really shouldn't worry, there'll be another day.' There would be many other days, and sorry did not make things right — it just made them easier. The way Olivia coped with things she had done in the past was to file them away in her mind, lock the door and throw the key away. Now those two up the aisle had not only brought the keys to her, they had pulled out all the memories from behind the door — and she was not grateful for that. She knew that Felix had spoken to her to make himself feel better for what he did. It wasn't to do with her at all.

Olivia could forget about Germany now as Felix had answered all her forgotten questions. That episode in her life was nicely tied off and could be forgotten now. Not just quite yet as the memories did not stop her hurting. She hid her tears well and wallowed in regrets that were filled with sadness. She wallowed in the shame of her behaviours. She could not go back and undo all the things she had done in the past. Feelings too long repressed hit her in waves of despair. All she ever wanted was to be loved. She had made so many mistakes and still had not found a soul-mate. He never appeared. She pushed away the list of men that had come in and out of her life. Now was not the time.

The pilot announced that they were making their descent into JFK and Olivia calmed herself. As she looked at her photograph in the inflight magazine, she acknowledged that she had achieved her lifelong ambition to become a writer. She never thought she would find a publisher or receive an award. She had initially written a book for her friends and started a group on Face book, posting her writings regularly. It became her motivation to write as the readers kept asking for more. Beyond her wildest dreams, she now had an appointment with someone in Los Angeles to discuss a film. Wonders never ceased. No one ever knew what was round the corner and Olivia was turning corners rather quickly. She spent many days at her kitchen table, scribbling in notebooks and on pieces of paper. She woke many nights at the witching hour and wrote until she fell asleep. Her hard work and dedication were now paying off.

As the undercarriage of the plane came down, Olivia felt excitement for her future. She was already thinking about the sequel to her first novel. It was a slowly evolving work in progress. She would write about what happened next and about the highs, lows and the laughs that could be had and the positive things in life. She was thinking of calling it 'Elusive Butterfly', after the song by Bob Lind. Olivia's passion for music was almost obsessive and she loved mentioning songs in her writings — so why not name a book after one? She still wasn't sure, and she had plenty of time to think things out.

The touchdown was completed without a bump. Olivia rose from her seat, as she wanted to be away quickly with no more encounters from the past. She was eager to meet her future and determined to leave all behind her on the plane.

Adam and Felix were busy arranging to meet up. Little did Felix know that he had more in common with Adam than just football and boats! Both looked back to where Olivia was sat. Adam caught the back of her as she was leaving the plane. He returned to his conversation with Felix and began to wonder how he could get rid of him now as he needed to do something rather quickly. "Look, mate, I shall go now as I need to make a call." He pushed his way into the line moving towards the back exit of the plane. He called back to Felix. "Call me."

Felix caught up with Adam by the carousel. They watched the conveyor belt go round and round. Felix's case came out first and he bade Adam farewell. As he shook Adam's hand, he gave him a man hug. Felix liked Adam and believed that he had found a new friend. Perhaps one day Felix would tell Adam about Germany and the encounter on the plane. Perhaps Adam might tell Felix that he already knew. Felix still wasn't too sure about having spoken to Olivia. If he was honest with himself, his ego was a little bruised. He did not feel that he was forgiven, and that was the intention: to seek forgiveness and have a clear conscience. As Felix left the crowd, he turned and his eyes met Adam's. Felix shouted, "Call me!"

Adam was still waiting for his case. It must have been the last one to come out. At this rate the taxis would have all left for the city and he may have to wait. The next case out was very colourful. It caught his eye, reminding him of hippy days in the sixties. He looked around. "She must still be here then!"

The case went round and round, and no one picked it up. Adam looked around the emptying hall. Where was she? As his case had still not arrived, Adam took a stroll, finally stopping outside the lavatories. He wondered if Olivia might have gone into them. He didn't feel comfortable hanging round the door and walked over to the coffee shop. Two women were sitting at a table, chatting to each other. One of them laughed as she looked around at Adam. She looked him up and down, ready to do an appraisal. He smiled at her.

Suddenly, her friend jumped up. "I have to go. I see my case. It's been lovely catching up. See you soon." The woman ran across the floor and picked the hippy case off the carousel and left.

Adam sighed. It wasn't Olivia's case after all and he had missed her. — She must have gone. What was he doing? He could have spoken to her on the plane. Instead, he chose to wallow in memories that were playing havoc with his sanity. Disappointment and panic began to weave their way through his heart as he realised his loss. He quickly walked back to the carousel to see the last case come through the plastic curtain. It was his.

Customs was, a nightmare. American Customs always were. No one smiled and it was a mind-numbing experience. It was a relief to get through. Adam was feeling tired. He was not actually paying attention as to where he was going and when he realised it was the wrong way, he turned sharply and almost fell over the woman behind him. She accepted his apologies and, he made his way towards the exit. Passing some booths on his left, he began to look in each one. His heart missed a beat when he saw Olivia chattering away on the phone. Adam moved across the corridor and watched her. As she replaced the receiver, he ran across to her. "Well, Olivia, what a surprise!"

"No, it's not." She said rather bluntly. They hadn't spoken in over four years and she did not want to speak to him now. "You saw me on the plane and you have been looking for me. You have spent the last five minutes staring at me from over there." She pointed exactly to the place Adam had just vacated. Adam felt really stupid and did not know what to say. Olivia felt the tears prickling behind her eyes. She did not like this at all. "Were you looking for me?"

"Err... no!" Adam lied. "This cannot be a coincidence, though. Maybe it was meant to be. How have you been, Olivia?" Adam was babbling and they both knew it. He realised how dumb he sounded with the words that followed.

Olivia watched Adam try to unravel the mess his words were making. She was nearly enjoying the moment. Adam stopped and looked at the floor. He knew how much he had hurt her all those years ago. Fiona told him. He could never quite get it on with Fiona, as all the while Olivia's face floated before him. When they were together, all he did was talk about Olivia. Fiona began to tire of Adam at the same time he began to tire of her, so their parting was mutual. Both felt rather guilty about what they had done. As usual, Adam could not help but feed his ego and he just couldn't go a day without some kind of love.

Adam never took responsibility for his actions and always managed to blame the other person. His problem was that he could never say no. When Mary announced that she was leaving him, he had never felt such anger. No one left Adam. He left them. It was natural that he would hurt Mary in the way he did. All his secrets rushed out of his mouth and it was too late to take them back. Adam could not forgive himself for what he had done to Mary; she didn't deserve that. He could not forgive himself for betraying Olivia, either. The others did not matter to him. He was unsure of what to say next and did what he always did. Now he looked down at Olivia with puppy-dog eyes. He was always good at putting the face on that could melt the hardest heart. Not this time!

Olivia turned to walk away, her legs shaking. "Why should you care how I have been, Adam?" All she really wanted to do was put her arms round him, but that was not going to happen. As she turned back towards him, she smiled. "Adam, we don't really have anything left to say to each other, do we? I think you said it all when you told your wife about me." Olivia could not see any point in the conversation continuing. "I am sorry, I really must go. I haven't the time for this. Someone is waiting for me."

Olivia was still upset by the things that Felix had said to her and she did not want disturbing any more. She continued walking without a backward glance. She could hear Adam behind her, following like a lost dog. If only the ground would open up and take either him or her away!

"Please, Olivia, please stop!"

Against her better judgement, she stopped and looked at her watch. "OK, you have got five minutes, and then I must go."

Hadn't she said that once before to him, many moons ago? Adam didn't ask her who was waiting for her and assumed that it must be a man. He could see that she had aged well and no way would she be on her own. Adam had rehearsed all the words he was going to say to her after she winked on the plane. Now they seemed to be in hiding and he couldn't remember one of them. How could he put things right? How could he right the wrongs from years ago? Adam was never lost for words, but now he was. He began to fumble in his pocket. He produced a business card and handed it to Olivia. "I don't know how long you are here for, but it would be good if we could get together. I have so much I have to say to you and I won't be able to say it in five minutes."

Olivia took the card and looked at it, before turning away. Adam grabbed her hand. The electricity flowed between their fingers. Olivia sighed. She needed to get away from this man who was stirring up the sleeping feelings within. The feelings were screaming at her: "You haven't got over him, have you? Have you?"

With all the strength Olivia could muster, she pulled her hand away and began to walk, roughly pulling her case behind her. She did not look back. She left the airport with her past staring after her. She left him there, in arrivals. She forgot all about the two cards that she carried, one in her book and now one in her pocket.

Adam watched her go with a deep sadness in his soul. "You did it to yourself, mate. She won't call you, will she?" Olivia's attitude made it quite clear that the road was closed and there was no green light. He now realised what a mistake he made all those years ago. It was hopeless. He was such a fool to let his physical urges get the better of him; to blight a future with Olivia.

"She was the one, wasn't she?" the sarcastic voice in his head carried on for a while. Adam felt his tears, but they would remain inside. He wasn't a man to cry.

His phone rang. "Is that you, Mr Templeton?"

He didn't recognise the American voice. "Yes."

"My name is Terence. The office sent me to pick you up. I am waiting outside."

Adam walked out onto the pavement. The clouds were clearing and the sun was coming out after the rain. As he was greeted by his driver, he looked up and saw a rainbow. The cab followed the rainbow into the city.

"Do you mind if I put the radio on, sir? I like to listen to music when driving."

Adam watched as the rainbow slowly began to disappear. "Yes, that is fine." The rainbow was just an illusion made by tears from heaven, and Adam was just a fickle game player who'd lost the game. The driver turned the music up and as Adam sat back in his seat the tears began when the words of the song wafted round the car.

"A day without love is a year with emptiness... was our love just an illusion, I'll really never know... did you have to go... I can't stand a day without love."

To be continued.

PLAYLIST

A Day Without Love	Love Affair
Rhythm of the Night	De Barge
You Don't Have to Take Your Clothes Off	Jermaine Stewart
I Want You	Marvin Gaye
We've Got Tonite	Bob Seger
Love is Love	Culture Club
Unchain My Heart	Joe Cocker
Whose Making love to Your Old Lady	Johnnie Taylor
One Night in Bangkok	Murray Head
Together in Electric Dreams	Human League
The Music of Goodbye	Al Jarreau
Here We Go Loving Again	Dillard and Johnson
Loving on Borrowed Time	George Benson
Classy Lady	Noel Porter
Rainbow	Rolling Stones
Take My Breath Away	Berlin
Stay With Me Till Dawn	Judy Tzuke
Love to Keep You in My Mind	Curtis Mayfield
Standing in the Shadows of Love	The Four Tops
Never Give Up on a Good Thing.	George Benson
It'll Never Be Over For Me	Timi Yuro
Just the Two of Us	Grover Washington Jnr
Elusive Butterfly	Bob Lind